Carolina Breeze

Center Point
Large Print

Also by Denise Hunter and available from
Center Point Large Print:

Barefoot Summer
The Wishing Season
Married 'til Monday
Falling Like Snowflakes
The Goodbye Bride
Just a Kiss
Sweetbriar Cottage
Blue Ridge Sunrise
Honeysuckle Dreams
On Magnolia Lane
Summer by the Tides
Lake Season

**This Large Print Book carries the
Seal of Approval of N.A.V.H.**

Carolina Breeze

DENISE HUNTER

CENTER POINT LARGE PRINT
THORNDIKE, MAINE

This Center Point Large Print edition
is published in the year 2020 by arrangement with
Thomas Nelson.

The text of this Large Print edition is unabridged.
In other aspects, this book may vary
from the original edition.
Printed in the United States of America
on permanent paper.
Set in 16-point Times New Roman type.

ISBN: 978-1-64358-699-1

The Library of Congress has cataloged this record
under Library of Congress Control Number: 2020942081

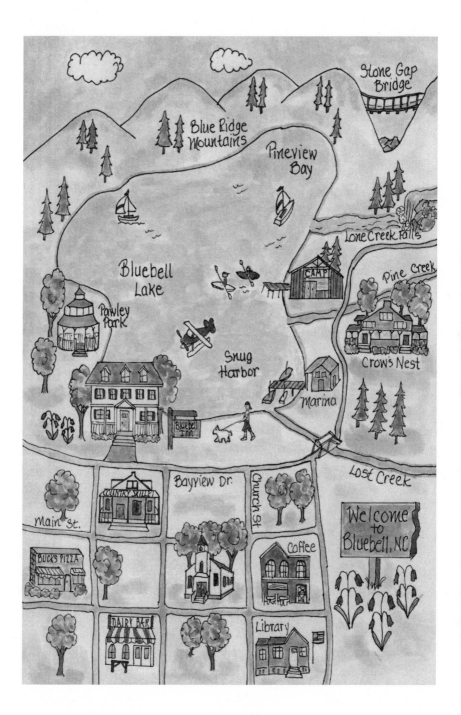

Carolina Breeze

one

Before she even opened her eyes Mia Emerson knew it was going to be the worst day of her life. But just like all other days, Saturday, May 30, would only last twenty-four hours. She could do this.

She forced her eyes open against the buttery sunlight filtering through her sheers. She'd get up, shower, dress in her disguise. Then she'd run down to the Busy Bean and linger over the newspaper as she did nearly every Saturday morning.

She pushed back the covers and sat up, her eyes catching on the dress she'd dropped to the floor before crawling into bed. The memory of the night before washed over her like a bad dream, making her stomach twist hard.

It had been almost midnight by the time the film had wrapped. The cast and crew of *Twelve Hours*, high on adrenaline, celebrated at one of LA's most popular nightspots. Mia was as excited as everyone else.

This was only her second leading role. *Into the Deep* had catapulted her to the top of the rising stars lists. And now, having been cast opposite Jax Jordan in his latest action film, her career had never looked so promising. It was a little after two when Mia decided to call it a night. By then the others were tipsy or downright drunk. She said good night and made her way outside to hail a cab. If the night had ended there, she'd have nothing on her mind but the next day's dreaded date. But it hadn't.

Her phone buzzed an incoming call. The screen lit up with her best friend Brooke's face. They'd been besties since they were seven, when Mia's mom had hired Brooke's mom, Lettie, to be their housekeeper.

Mia answered. "Making sure I haven't thrown myself over a cliff yet?"

"Don't be silly. There's not a cliff for miles. Did I wake you?"

"Very nearly. I didn't get in until almost three." She pushed away the instant flashback of Jax approaching her outside the building.

"The shoot wrapped then?"

"It's in the hole."

"What are your plans today? Let's meet up, do something fun."

"Take my mind off things, you mean?"

"We'll start with the Busy Bean because I'm just a good friend like that. Then we can be tourists for a day. We can do the Walk of Fame, take a stroll along Venice Beach, and whatever else you want to do. Plus, I made reservations for tonight. We're getting gussied up and going to Musso and Frank."

"Aw, you're so sweet. But I know you're swamped with work."

Brooke handled props, a job that required a detail-oriented individual, and her next film started Monday.

"No worries, I'm all ready for it."

"Why can't you be human like the rest of us? A little procrastination never hurt anyone, you know."

"I'm not taking no for an answer. Jump in the shower, and I'll meet you at the coffee shop in an hour."

The aroma of roasted beans perked Mia up as she entered the bustling shop situated just outside her Beverly Hills neighborhood. It was tucked away and not named Starbucks, making it more popular with locals than tourists.

Caffeine. She needed caffeine. And possibly a time machine.

She was a little early, so she stepped into line. It was almost eleven o'clock. What would she have been doing right now if Wesley hadn't called things off? Getting manicures with her bridesmaids at Le Luxe? Writing Wes a wedding day note, to be delivered by his best man? She would've written that she loved him more than life itself. That he was everything she could've imagined in a life partner.

She would've been wrong. So wrong. She'd

thought he was just what she needed. But she'd been wrong about that too.

She blinked against the tears and moved forward with the line. How did this still have the power to wilt her knees? It had been almost four months. She ducked her head, tugged the brim of her ball cap down.

Brooke was right. She needed to stay busy today. She checked her watch. Thirteen hours left: an eternity.

The person in front of her stepped aside. Her turn.

Mia's eyes were probably bloodshot, but she pasted a big smile on her face and greeted the barista. "Good morning, Bree."

As Bree's gaze fell on Mia her smile fell away, eyes going flat. "What can I get you?" she asked in a businesslike tone.

Mia blinked. Bree must be having a bad day. "Um, I'll have my usual. And a large hot cinnamon spice tea, please."

Bree punched it in. "$10.42," she said without making eye contact.

Mia handed over her rewards card and tried again. "It's gorgeous outside. Busy day?"

"You could say that."

Mia tucked a few bills into the tip jar.

After swiping her card Bree handed it back wordlessly and grabbed two cups, writing the orders on them.

The stranger behind her cleared her throat, and Mia moved down the counter.

Had she done something to offend Bree? Yesterday they'd chatted a quick minute, but Mia couldn't remember about what. All the baristas were friendly. One of the reasons the Bean was her favorite shop.

Maybe Bree's son had had a meltdown when she left him at day care again. Or maybe her mother's dementia was getting worse. Mia said a quick prayer for the barista and moved down the line.

The espresso machine whirred loudly. Greta operated it with quick, efficient movements, her dark ponytail swinging behind her.

"Good morning, Greta," Mia said after the machine went silent.

Greta's gaze shot to Mia, and her face went hard. "Morning," she finally said in a tight voice.

What in the world was going on? Mia glanced around at the other two busy baristas. Normally they all greeted her no matter how busy they were.

Greta set her drinks on the counter and went on to her next order.

"Thank you," Mia said.

But Greta didn't respond or even make eye contact.

Mia collected the drinks, a vague feeling of shame washing over her. She must've done something, but she couldn't imagine what.

The shop was crowded, and she suddenly felt a little claustrophobic. She slipped past the line and out the door to the gated patio. It was a mild and sunny day, and heaven knew she could use a little sunshine.

What had gotten into her friendly neighborhood baristas? Maybe someone had gotten fired. She tried to remember if they'd been friendly with the other customers, but she hadn't been paying attention. Or maybe it had something to do with her canceled wedding. But that news had broken months ago.

As she settled at a table for two near the sidewalk, her phone buzzed with a call. She pulled it from her pocket. Brooke.

"Don't tell me you're running late," Mia said. "Because I'm pretty sure that's never happened."

"Where are you?"

Mia frowned at the intensity in her friend's tone. "At the coffee shop where I'm supposed to be. Where are you?"

"Um, listen . . . change of plans. I'm picking you up. I'm just around the corner."

"Ooo-kay . . . What's going on, Brooke?"

"I'll tell you when I get there. I can see the shop now. Come out to the curb."

Mia stood, hooking her purse on her shoulder. "You're being very cryptic." She spotted Brooke's white Toyota. "I see you. Be right there."

Mia disconnected, grabbed their drinks, and made her way to the curb. She had a terrible feeling this day was actually going to get worse than she'd imagined.

two

Mia set the drinks in the cup holders as Brooke pulled out into traffic. A car behind them honked.

"What's going on?" Dread had leaked into Mia's bloodstream, causing a rush of adrenaline. She scanned her friend's face, but other than tightness at the corners of her eyes she looked normal. "What's happened? Are you all right?"

"I'm fine. It's not me."

"Not your mom." Mia had hired Lettie after her own mother had passed and had seen her moments ago on the way out the door.

"No, she's fine." Brooke had the steering wheel in a death grip. "Mia . . . tell me what happened last night. At the wrap party."

Oh, the wrap party. Someone must've seen what Jax did and told Brooke. She had a lot of friends in the business.

Mia sighed. "I was going to tell you over coffee. Jax had too much to drink. I went outside to get a ride home, and he followed me. He came out of nowhere and laid one on me. I feel just awful, Brooke. I told you I sensed something while we were filming, but he never made a move on me before."

"So . . . it wasn't mutual?"

Mia gaped at Brooke. "Of course it wasn't mutual. He's a married man. I'd never do that."

"Sorry. Sorry, I do know that." She tossed Mia a sheepish look. "But he is Jax Jordan. And he does have that dimpled grin. And that sexy cleft in his chin."

"Don't forget the perpetual five o'clock shadow. But he's *married*. Anyway, who told you? I didn't think anyone saw."

Brooke gave her a look that made her tremble from the inside out. "Oh, Mia. I don't know how to tell you this."

"Tell me what? You're scaring me."

Brooke turned onto Mia's street and began the winding uphill drive. She slid Mia a sympathetic look. "Someone snapped a picture, honey, and it's on a celeb page."

Mia sucked in a breath. But the kiss had lasted all of one second before she'd pushed him away. It couldn't be that bad.

Brooke handed Mia her phone, already opened to the *Hollywood Reporter* website. The headline screamed, "MIA STEALS EMMA'S MAN!" Below it were pictures, the largest of them a profile view of a seemingly steamy kiss. She and Jax weren't recognizable in that shot, but the photographer had gotten a picture right before that kiss in the instant Jax had taken her face in his hands, when she'd been too shocked to move.

"This isn't . . ."

There were other pictures too. One of them embracing earlier that same evening when the mood had been celebratory. "I hugged everyone!"

Another photo of them walking side by side, laughing together as they left the set one evening.

"This makes it look like—"

"You know how these rags are. They don't care about the truth. Only selling their so-called stories."

"Maybe I can, I don't know, get my lawyer on it. Pay someone off, do something to head this off . . ."

"I hope it's not too late, hon. You know how quickly these things spread."

Even before Brooke finished speaking, Mia was opening another page. Her stomach sank as she saw the story was front-page news there as well. The same pictures. The same story . . . a little more tastefully told. They didn't outright accuse her of stealing Jax from Emma. But those pictures . . .

She closed the page and checked social media. "It's trending on Twitter."

She thought of Jax's wife seeing this, and her gut twisted hard. Emma was pregnant with their first child. "Poor Emma. I have to call and explain."

Brooke gave her a look. "Explain what? That her husband came on to you, and you rejected him?"

"Well, I can't have her thinking we're having some tawdry affair."

"Leave that to Jax. He can handle himself."

Despite his bit of flirting on set, Mia liked Jax. He worked hard, and in spite of his celebrity he didn't act like he was above everyone else.

But Mia wasn't naïve. Jax wasn't about to tell his wife he'd come on to another woman.

She looked at the pictures. They told a story—a story that wasn't true, but people would believe what they wanted. And Emma wouldn't want to believe this was Jax's fault.

Neither would anyone else. Emma was America's sweetheart, following in the footsteps of women like Meg Ryan, Julia Roberts, and Reese Witherspoon. Mia was only an up-and-comer.

"They're making me out to be a home wrecker, and nobody's going to believe I'm innocent." Her eyes dropped to the pictures. "This is going to ruin my whole career, Brooke. Everything I've worked for."

"Don't get ahead of yourself. You know how these stories can be. As soon as something bigger comes along, people will forget. This might not amount to much."

"I hope you're right. I should call Nolan."

She pulled up her agent's contact and tapped on his number. He'd been expecting her call and did what he was best at, talked her off the cliff.

19

Told her to stay off social media. She expressed her concerns about losing her next role in *Lesser Days*. Fiona was the role of her dreams, the one she'd been waiting for, and the studio had a reputation for a high standard of integrity. The contract she'd signed had a morality clause.

Like Brooke, Nolan assured her this would pass. That addressing the gossip would only fan the flames. Better they hope for another scandal to come along and steal the headlines.

When she got off the phone she told Brooke what he'd said.

"You know what?" Brooke said after a brief silence. "You have a break in your schedule right now. You could skip town for a little while."

"That makes it look like I'm guilty."

"Maybe you're right." She slid Mia a look. "At least filming is done, and you won't have to see Jax anymore."

"We'll still have all the publicity when the movie releases."

"Awkward. Hopefully this'll blow over by then."

Brooke slowed as she came around the final corner before Mia's rambling ranch. But as they rounded the bend they saw the cluster of vans parked on the street in front of the driveway. News vans.

"Get down," Brooke said.

Mia dove for her ankles, her heart drumming

against her thighs as Brooke gave the car gas. "Did they see me?"

"I don't think so."

Great. A media circus in her front yard. How long would they stay? How was she going to make herself go home? She'd been photographed many times, but not like this. Not as the center of a scandal.

"Is anyone following?" Mia said into her knees a full minute later.

"I don't think so. They don't know my car. That's illegal anyway, isn't it?"

"Doesn't mean they won't do it." They weren't allowed to shoot on private property with telephoto lenses either, but that hadn't stopped them from publishing an unflattering picture of Gwyneth Paltrow emerging from her pool last week.

Brooke made a couple more turns, heading back down the hill. "I think it's safe to come up now."

Mia cautiously sat upright. They were in a quiet part of the neighborhood, at least a mile from the scene at her house. What was she going to do? Where was she going to go? If she went home she'd be trapped there unless she wanted the hassle of the reporters every time she came and went.

"I'm going to have to go away and hide out for a while," she said resolutely. She'd have to juggle some things on her calendar. Benefits, luncheons, appearances. Her standing appointment with her "little sister" Ana Maria from the Big Brothers Big Sisters program. Missing this one grated most of all.

"Maybe that'd be for the best," Brooke said. "You could stay with my mom."

Mia imagined the paparazzi surrounding Lettie's house in the quiet little subdivision of LA. "I'm the last thing she needs. Until all this dies down."

"What about . . ." Brooke gave her head a hard shake. "No, never mind. That's a stupid idea."

"What?"

"Nothing really. I wasn't thinking."

"Brooke."

"All right, but when I tell you, you'll think it's a dumb idea too. I was just remembering the confirmation you got—your honeymoon trip in North Carolina . . . See, I told you it was a stupid idea."

Wesley had booked them at an inn on Bluebell Lake, and it had been nonrefundable. Mia hadn't realized he hadn't canceled the reservation until she'd gotten an email a couple days ago.

Maybe this was a sign from God. "Well, at least that would be someplace quiet. Not to mention already paid for."

"Sweetie . . . it was supposed to be your honeymoon."

"And now it could be a little vacation—on Wesley's dime."

Brooke gave her a look.

"It was your idea."

"It was a terrible idea."

Wesley had pushed for Lake Cuomo in Italy for their honeymoon, but Mia had wanted to go to the town where her mother had grown up. Katherine had left home at eighteen to pursue her Hollywood dreams, changing her name and cutting ties with her family.

Mia's father had left when she was five and, especially after her mother died, Mia craved those familial roots everyone else seemed to have. Maybe her grandparents were gone, but she'd always wanted to visit Bluebell, where they'd lived until they passed away. Imagine her surprise when she found out that the inn they'd owned was still there.

When the topic of the honeymoon had risen between Wes and her, she'd pushed the issue. And since Mia had graciously conceded to Wes's mother in almost every aspect of the wedding plans, Wesley let her have her way.

Bluebell Lake was tucked away in a quiet little town in the Blue Ridge Mountains, the perfect spot for a honeymoon. And the perfect place to disappear to. How would it feel to go to the place where she and Wes were supposed to honeymoon? Not good, she was sure. But at this point she really didn't have the luxury of avoiding pain and regret.

"I'll need a flight," Mia said.

"Mia."

"Do you have a better idea?"

"What about your clothes and things?"

"I'd rather buy new than go back home and become bait for those vultures."

"I could send my mom to get them."

"I'm not having Lettie deal with all that."

The idea was making more and more sense. Maybe going on her honeymoon alone was a strange idea, but she couldn't shake the feeling that it was also the right idea. There was something about the dot on the map that had always felt like home.

"It's settled then," Mia said with more bravado than she felt. "I'm going to North Carolina."

three

L evi Bennett stowed the lawn mower in the shed and locked up. The sun was setting across the lake, swathing the sky in hues of pink. The last light of the day lit his way up the sloped lawn toward the inn. The property looked nice, the grass spring green, the flowers lining the walkway in full bloom. Overhead the trees swayed gently in the breeze, and the sweet scent of lilacs wafted by.

Memorial Day weekend—the official start of lake season—was always a busy one, but this one had been off the charts. He could hardly believe his baby sister Grace had graduated high school yesterday. It had been bittersweet without their parents. Levi had felt the need to make everything perfect for her, but try as he might, he could never fill their parents' shoes.

He'd had that same frustration since they'd died a year and a half ago: trying, and failing, to be everything Grace and Molly needed. He was the oldest, after all. The "man of the house."

He slipped in the back door, his stomach growling. The lawn had taken the better part of the afternoon, and he hadn't eaten since breakfast. The inn was quiet, the last of their guests having checked out this morning, and the scent of lemon cleaner filled his nostrils. He found his sisters in the dining room, huddled over the pizza he'd ordered thirty minutes ago.

"Hope you saved some for me," he said.

Grace's long blond hair hung over her shoulder in damp strands. She plated a slice of pizza, the cheese stretching temptingly. "Better hurry."

Levi grabbed a chair and tore off a slice, giving silent thanks as he bit into the heavenly mound of meat and cheese.

"What a weekend, huh?" Molly brushed her dark ponytail over her shoulder. "Full house and a graduation to boot. We survived."

"It's not over yet." Levi was thinking of the honeymooners arriving tonight and staying a week.

"Who rents out an entire inn just for themselves?" Grace asked.

"Rich people," Molly said.

"You would know." Grace gave Molly a droll look.

Molly's boyfriend, Adam Bradford, was a hotshot author. He'd recently moved from New York to Bluebell just to be near Molly.

"You'd think they'd just rent one of the McMansions if they wanted privacy," Grace said.

"Houses don't come with live-in help," Levi said. "That's what I wanted to talk to you guys about. They're paying a lot of money for this week, and I'm sure they have rich friends they can recommend us to. So let's be on top of all the details, all right?"

Grace rolled her eyes. "Aren't we always?"

"Relax," Molly said. "The honeymoon suite is perfection itself."

"And we've been cleaning downstairs all afternoon. Didn't you notice the gleaming floors?"

"It looks very nice. What about the other rooms?"

"We'll clean them tomorrow," Molly said with a shrug. "It's just the two of them; they won't need all seven rooms."

"True." He was less than pleased with that answer. But maybe he was overthinking it. He had a tendency to do that sometimes, as his sisters were quick to point out.

"Is the Fusion cleaned out?" Molly asked.

Levi finished chewing. "What does that matter?"

Molly gave him a sheepish look. "Did I forget to tell you? I may have offered the couple your chauffeur services."

"My what?"

"They requested a driver." Molly shrugged. "What did you want me to say? They're paying a premium."

Great. Just great. He had a list of things to do this week. And driving around a couple of rich lovebirds wasn't on it. "Is there anything else you might've forgotten to mention?"

"Breakfast in bed? But I already notified Miss Della. She's on board."

"No blue M&M's or imported water?" Levi asked.

Molly's eyes gleamed over a slice of pizza. "Now, now, that's no way to talk about our guests."

"You'd be a much better tour guide," he said to Molly. "Why don't you do it?"

"Are you going to clean the rooms and do laundry?"

He pressed his lips together. She knew he'd rather wear a tutu in the Fourth of July parade.

"Besides, I promised Adam I'd help research his next story. I'll be at the library every spare moment this week."

Levi turned to Grace, looking at her beseechingly.

"Consider it done." She smiled sweetly. "I'd be happy to help out."

"You would?"

"Of course. It's the least I can do."

Wait a minute. What was she— "Oh no, you don't. You promised you'd finish your college apps this week, and that's exactly what you're going to do."

She'd procrastinated the whole school year, reminding him that her preferred colleges had late application deadlines.

Grace gave him an innocent smile, wide blue eyes blinking. "Have fun chauffeuring."

"Relax," Molly said. "It won't be that bad."

"Yeah," Grace said. "They're honeymooners. They probably won't even leave their room."

Levi shot her a look. Maybe she was nineteen now, but he didn't want to think his baby sister knew much about honeymoons or the things that went on during them.

"What?" She flipped her damp hair over her shoulders. "You know I'm right."

Their entry alarm dinged, no doubt announcing their guests' arrival.

"Speak of the devil," Grace whispered.

Levi wiped off his hands and pushed back. "I'll get it." Might as well get used to being at the couple's beck and call.

Mia stepped into the inn and pushed the door shut behind her, cool air brushing over her skin. The foyer smelled pleasantly of lemons, and the plush rug cushioned her steps. Other than the scrape of a chair from another room the inn was silent.

She scanned the small lobby, her eyes going to the grand staircase opposite the door. She wondered if her grandparents had been the ones to restore the railings. Their mahogany tones gleamed under the light from the antique chandelier.

The inn was located on the edge of town. It had been almost dark out as the driver had navigated the windy shoreline, but Mia could see the moonlight gleaming off the water and the silhouette of mountains around the lake. It was hard to imagine that her mother's childhood had been anything other than idyllic.

Mia's gaze swept to the right where a living room was situated, a set of French doors beyond it. To the left a darkened hallway extended past the check-in desk.

"Hello?" she called.

Her heavy purse tugged at her shoulder. It was filled with toiletries she'd purchased at the airport. It had been a long day, and she had a raging headache. There was no easy way to get from LA to Bluebell. There'd been a layover in Dallas with Charlotte the final destination. She'd taken a long Uber to reach the inn, and had she mentioned her head was killing her?

She took off the ball cap she'd been wearing all day, dragged the ponytail holder from her hair, and massaged her scalp. *Ahhhh.* Much better. Now she just needed a soft bed and eight hours of sleep. Maybe more.

At least she'd managed to avoid attention as she traveled. She looked different without makeup, and most fans didn't expect to see her schlepping through the airport in yoga pants and tennis shoes.

She gave a weary sigh, stepping closer to the desk and scanning it for a bell. She was ready to put this long day behind her. Two long days.

"Mrs. Hughes?"

Mia flinched. A man strode across the living room in slim-fit khakis and a black polo bearing the inn's logo. He was several inches taller than her five-foot-ten frame. He was also not hard on the eyes, with dark hair and tanned skin setting off his clear blue eyes. He put her in mind of Liam Hemsworth.

He offered a smile and a hand. "Welcome to the Bluebell Inn. I'm Levi, one of the owners."

"You can call me Mia."

"Nice to meet you, Mia. How was your trip?"

"It was fine, thank you."

Fine. A knot tightened in her gut—something about having been called the name that was supposed to have been hers. She'd spent the past two days avoiding people and in frantic discussions with her agent. She hadn't had time to process the wedding that had never happened, but coming here brought equal parts relief and dread.

She swallowed against the lump at the back of her throat. *And now is not the time for that, Mia.*

Levi was clicking and clacking at the computer. "If I could just have a credit card for incidentals. Your stay is already paid for, of course."

She slid her Visa across the desk, hoping he wouldn't recognize her name.

"Perfect." *Click, click, clack.* "Our honeymoon suite is tucked away upstairs in the corner of the inn, so it should be nice and quiet for you."

"Great." Mia signed the paperwork he slid across the counter.

"Here are two keys. As soon as Mr. Hughes comes in, I'll show you around, then take you up to your room."

"Oh . . ." This was where she was supposed to tell him it was just her. That there was no groom, no husband, no wedding. But she was afraid that darn sting behind her eyes was holding back a flood of tears and saying those words would release the dam.

"Would you mind if you and I just went on up? It's been a very long day."

Levi blinked. "Of course. Whatever you'd like."

He led the way up the stairs, making small talk and giving further information on the inn and the area, little of which registered. The room was, indeed, tucked away in the corner. For that she was grateful.

"Here we are, room one. If there's anything you need, feel free to call down."

"Thank you."

As he walked away Mia slid the key into the lock and turned the old glass doorknob. The inn had oodles of character, and she'd be glad to appreciate every last detail—tomorrow. For now, the bed beckoned. She flipped the switch, lighting two bedside lamps.

Her eyes fell on a vase burgeoning with red roses, then on a bottle of champagne chilling on a rolling stand. Only then did they finally settle on the luxurious king-size bed, strewn with hundreds of red rose petals.

Her stomach clenched hard as she imagined, just for a moment, the way this moment was supposed to have played out. Wesley carrying her over the threshold. She was in his arms, laughing at his silliness and swooning over the romantic setup. He would set her on her feet and pull her close, whispering words of love in her ear.

She reached for her phone, the urge to Google him again strong. What was he doing today? Was he sad at the thought of their canceled wedding? But the last time she'd looked him up she'd seen a picture of him and some European model at a premier.

It was the last part that gave her the strength to resist temptation. That and the fact that Wesley had never loved her at all. He didn't deserve her longing, and he didn't deserve a starring role in her daydreams.

Her gaze returned to the romantic touches, to the big bed she'd be practically swimming in all alone.

She didn't want to sleep here tonight. She just wanted a regular old room. But she didn't have the nerve to go back downstairs and face the handsome innkeeper. To admit she was here, on her honeymoon, all alone.

Her gaze slid to the bedside phone. She could

simply call down. Surely they had another vacant room. Something smaller, something less . . . this.

Before she could stop herself, she picked up the phone and dialed. It only rang once before it was answered.

"Front desk," the familiar male voice said. "How may I help you?"

"Um, hello, this is Mia in room one. I was wondering if you might have another room available."

There was a brief pause. "Is there something wrong with your accommodations?"

"No, no, it's wonderful, I just . . . Perhaps another one would be more . . ." She couldn't find the word to complete the sentence.

"I'm so sorry, but our other rooms aren't available at the moment. Is there something specific I could do to make your room more comfortable?"

"No, no. That's all right. It's fine. I'm sorry to have bothered you." She hung up and covered her heated face. The room was beautiful, scrupulously clean, and full of Southern charm. The canopied bed was high, the duvet thick and luxurious-looking. He must think she was a spoiled brat.

She was going to have to explain the situation tomorrow. Maybe by then she'd be well rested enough to maintain her composure.

four

Levi wandered back into the dining room, his mind on their new guest. The new Mrs. Hughes was a natural beauty with dark-blond hair that tumbled over her shoulders in long waves. It had been impossible to ignore the perfect planes of her face, her high cheekbones, or her almond-shaped green eyes.

His sisters were chatting over the pizza box as he dropped into the chair opposite Molly. There were three slices left, but he seemed to have lost his appetite.

"What's wrong?" Grace asked. "We left you plenty."

"Something's not right." Levi spoke in a low voice, even though their guest couldn't possibly hear them.

"With the guests, you mean?" Molly asked.

"Guest, singular. She checked in alone with no luggage . . . and no new husband in tow."

Grace's forehead crinkled. "That is weird."

"I'd assumed her husband was parking the car and bringing in the luggage. But he never came in. And anyway, if they hired me to be their driver for the week, they wouldn't have a car with them at all."

"Are you sure she's our honeymooner?" Molly

asked. "I hope you didn't just accidentally let out their room to a guest off the street after they rented the whole place."

"Of course not. The name on her credit card was Mia something—her maiden name I'm sure. And to make things weirder she just called down and asked if we had another room."

"For her?" Grace asked.

"Yes, for her."

"That's our best room."

"Well, get the other rooms cleaned tomorrow," Levi said. "I'll offer her one of those tomorrow if she still wants to switch."

Molly bristled at his bossy tone.

They couldn't afford to lose the money this couple had paid. And they sure couldn't afford a bunch of negative publicity from a rich power couple.

"If the suite isn't good enough," Grace said, "she's not going to be satisfied with the other rooms anyway."

Levi shook his head. "Something strange is going on. Did you handle all the special requests?"

Molly gave him an affronted look. "Of course I did. The room is perfect. These aren't our first honeymooners."

"Maybe her groom got detained back home by an emergency or something and will be joining her later," Grace said.

"Or maybe he's coming later tonight," Molly said. "Maybe he just had to stop at the store for something."

"Well . . ." Levi said, still trying to shake the memory of the woman's vulnerable eyes. "It's really none of our business anyway."

"What about the breakfast in bed?" Molly asked.

"What about it?" Levi pushed back, thinking of the pile of bills he needed to sort through. "They paid for it, so we need to follow through."

Especially since the money the couple had paid for the stay was long gone.

five

A sound woke Mia. It took her a moment to realize where she was, and when she did her heart sank. Morning light filtered through the slit in the heavy drapes. The bucket of champagne and vase of roses were still in place, their floral fragrance perfuming the room. But the velvety red petals now lined the bottom of the bathroom waste bin.

The smell of cinnamon in the air made her stomach give a hearty growl. She hadn't eaten since breakfast yesterday.

A tap sounded on the door, and she realized that was the sound that had woken her. It seemed too early for housekeeping. She'd just ask them to return later.

She crawled from bed, grabbed the thick white robe from the armoire, and slipped it on. She caught a glimpse of herself as she passed the mirror. Her long thick hair was a snarled mess, and she had a pillow crease running across her cheek. Surprising, since she hadn't thought she'd lain still long enough for one to form.

She pulled the door open a crack.

A young girl, maybe college-aged, smiled back at her. Her blond hair was pulled back from her pretty face, and she was holding a tray of food.

"Yes?" Mia said.

"Good morning. I have your room service order."

The food looked good and smelled even better. "I—I didn't order room service."

"It's part of your package—breakfast in bed. Shall I bring it in and set it up for you?"

"Oh. I can take it from here. But thank you. It smells delicious."

The girl handed over the wooden tray, which was heavier than it looked. Two glasses of orange juice, covered in plastic wrap, threatened to slosh over the sides. Four golden muffins were nestled in a basket, and two bowls of granola and yogurt sat in the center, topped with fat blueberries.

Breakfast for two. Of course. What other little romantic surprises awaited her?

"You can just set the tray outside your room when you're finished. Or leave it and we'll remove it later when we clean your room."

"All right, thank you." Mia gave the girl a smile and closed the door, sighing deeply. Maybe this trip had been a terrible idea after all.

Levi perched on the stool behind the front desk. Usually mornings were busy, full of checkouts, assisting guests with their luggage, and providing directions to their next destinations. Sometimes he assisted them with boarding passes or made recommendations for airport accommodations. The personal service was all part of staying at an inn.

But since they had only one guest, the inn was silent this morning. Even the phone had been quiet.

He awakened the computer and checked his email. His personal credit card statement had arrived, but he didn't want to see the balance. The inn had run in the red all winter, and the business credit card had already been maxed out. He'd paid it down with the honeymooners' payment so the girls wouldn't know just how tight things were.

They didn't know his personal credit cards were maxed out too. It just about killed him to make only the minimum payment each month. He'd always been a cash-up-front kind of guy. But he'd be able to pay off his debt once the season got rolling. At least that's what he begged God for on a daily basis.

He saw an email from his former boss back in Denver. Curious, he opened the message.

Hello Levi,

I hope it's all right that I attained your current email address from Vince Gunnerson. You may have heard through him that Farber Construction's business has boomed since you left.

While growth is a positive factor, as you know, it also requires an expansion of staffing.

Your departure, while completely understandable, left a great deficit in the area of project management. We've never fully recovered from the loss in that area and are suffering even more now that the business is expanding.

I'm not sure how things are going for your family business. Hopefully they've settled in the year and a half since you've been gone. But as I told you when you left, you will always have a position at FC.

In fact, in light of our very busy upcoming season, the board has asked me to approach you. I think you'll find the offer attached very generous.

I hope you'll consider coming back to FC, Levi. There is abundant opportunity for career advancement.

Sincerely,
Thomas Wellborn

Levi couldn't stop himself from clicking on the attachment even though dread was already coursing through his veins. He scanned the document, swallowing hard at the bottom line.

They were offering not only a promotion but a healthy increase in his previous salary.

He stared at the figure, his stomach in knots. He couldn't accept it, no matter how tempting it was.

Ultimately, he needed to see his sisters settled— Molly living out her dream in Italy, Grace in college without a boatload of debt hanging over her head. And none of that could happen until they sold the inn.

But the inn was far from solvent. While they'd done all right last summer, the winter had been even slower than he'd anticipated. He soft-pedaled it to the girls in their monthly meetings, fudging numbers and focusing on the marketing plans he had for the upcoming lake season.

And yes, he hoped and prayed that marketing would translate to dollars. Especially since the charges for it had gone straight to his credit card. But mostly because he had to make this inn work. He couldn't stand the thought of failing his parents—it was eating away at his insides.

He rubbed the back of his neck where tension had gathered. The base of his skull beat with a headache. His eyes swept over the email again. Man, he missed his life in Denver. He missed his freedom, his excellent salary, and having a job he was good at. It won't be much longer, he promised himself.

The phone rang, jarring him from his thoughts.

He took the call and was encouraged. The man was looking to book a family reunion in October, which was off-season. It would be a nice influx of revenue. Unfortunately, he discovered as the man continued, the inn didn't have the space the large group required.

A while later he heard Grace coming down the steps. He closed out the offer and his email program.

Grace rounded the corner, widened her eyes at him, and jerked her head toward the living room.

Ooo-kay. Rolling his eyes behind her back, he followed her through the living room and into the dining room. Once they were inside she pushed the French doors shut, closing off the room, even though the whole inn was empty but for the siblings and Mia.

"I just took up their breakfast," Grace whispered.

"I know," he whispered back at her dramatically. "You passed me on your way up."

"I thought I'd do a little detective work, you know, try and figure out what was going on. So when she opened the door I looked past her, very casually, and the bed was empty—there was no one else in the room that I could see. Although he could've been in the bathroom, I guess. The door was almost closed, but I don't think the light was on."

"Get to the point, Grace," Levi said when

43

he should've just cut her off. He could see all this was leading somewhere, but their guest's personal life was none of their business.

"I'm trying. I didn't recognize her at first, without her makeup and everything, and the hallway is fairly dark, so it took me a minute. It was her voice that tipped me off."

Levi struggled for patience. His sister could drive him crazy sometimes. Both of them, actually. "Grace, I have things to do, so if you don't mind—"

"Our guest is *Mia Emerson*," she blurted.

"I know that . . . I checked her in, remember?"

Grace rolled her eyes. "*The* Mia Emerson, Levi—of *Into the Deep* fame."

"*Into the Deep*? The movie?" Well, that would explain her incredible good looks.

"Yes, the movie, Levi. Do you live under a rock? She's a superstar. She's on magazine covers, and she's going to be in the new Jax Jordan movie this fall. You *have* heard of Jax Jordan?"

"Of course I've heard of Jax Jordan," he scoffed. "He's been around forever."

"I can't believe Mia Emerson is staying right here, under our roof."

Levi narrowed his eyes at her. "Please tell me you didn't ask for her autograph."

"Of course not. I was a consummate professional. I didn't even let on that I recognized her. But do you know what this means, Levi? Do

44

you know how connected she is? If she tells all her friends about our inn, we could become the new getaway for the Hollywood elite. Can you imagine?"

He rocked back a little at that. He didn't care one whit for the Hollywood elite. But the inn sure could use an influx of influential people. A word or two on social media from a movie star or a mention in a magazine could make a huge difference.

"Is her new husband an actor too?" Levi asked. That would bode especially well.

"What do you think I am, a groupie?" She pulled out her phone. "Let me see what I can find online."

"You shouldn't be prying into our guest's personal life." Even he could hear his halfhearted tone.

"Hey there." Molly entered the dining room from the kitchen, still wearing an apron. "Miss Della had to leave early for a doctor's— What's going on? You have a funny look on your face."

Grace looked up from her phone. "Our new guest is Mia Emerson."

"What? The actress? Are you sure?"

"Positive. It took me a minute to recognize her because she was straight out of bed, but her voice gave her away. It's definitely her."

"Oh my gosh, that's amazing. Did her husband ever show up?"

45

"I don't think so. I didn't see him. I'm Googling 'Mia Emerson wedding.' I think she was engaged to some actor, but I can't remember who it—oh, here it is. She was engaged to Wesley Hughes." Grace continued reading and scrolling then sucked in a breath. "Oh no. They broke off the engagement."

"When?" Molly asked.

"Where are you even getting this information?" Levi asked. "Those tabloids are just a bunch of gossip."

"I know that," Grace said as if insulted. "This is a reputable site. They broke up months ago—the party line is, it was a mutual decision. But inside sources claim he broke up with her."

"Why would she come on her honeymoon alone?" Molly asked, a pained look in her amber eyes.

"It was nonrefundable, remember?" Levi said. Thank God. Otherwise the business credit card would still be maxed out.

"A drop in the bucket to someone like her." Molly leaned over Grace's shoulder and began reading.

Guilt pinched Levi hard. Here they were gathered around Grace's phone, prying into this poor woman's life, which was apparently spread across the internet like a picnic blanket.

"Enough." He snatched the phone from Grace's hand and closed out the browser.

"Hey!" Grace said, reaching for her phone.

He handed it back. "This is none of our business. And I believe you have some college applications to fill out today." He looked at Molly. "And don't you have some rooms to clean? I'd like to offer her one of them first thing."

Molly slapped a hand across her forehead. "Oh, jeez. The roses. The flower petals. The champagne."

Grace winced. "No wonder she wanted another room."

"I called her Mrs. Hughes." Levi flinched at the memory. Mia had looked so tired last night, and he obviously hadn't imagined the vulnerability in her eyes. The last thing she'd probably needed were reminders of the wedding that had never happened.

"What's with all the celebrities showing up?" Grace asked. "First Adam, now Mia."

"Maybe we're becoming the new trendy vacation spot," Molly said.

"All right, here's the plan," Levi said, putting on his business face. "We show no signs of recognition. We treat her as we would any other guest, anticipating her every desire, always smiling . . ." He nailed Molly with a look. "But never prying."

"What?" she asked, all innocence.

"No autographs or, heaven forbid, selfies."

This time the look went to Grace. "And no telling anyone she's here."

"Not even Sarah?" Grace said. "She wouldn't say anything."

"Not a soul. Discretion is part of being an innkeeper. You know that."

"I know," Grace said, pouting. "But what fun is it having her here if we can't tell anyone or even acknowledge it?"

"We're not here for fun. We're here to keep Mom and Dad's dream alive."

After drilling the two of them with a look, he returned to the front desk. Maybe he'd been a little heavy-handed. But they'd all sacrificed a lot to see their parents' dream come to fruition. Molly had given up that internship at an Italian resort, Grace had given every spare moment of her senior year, and Levi had put his life in Denver on hold.

And now he'd also be giving up a promotion and raise.

But all of that came second to taking care of his sisters. He had to do everything in his power to make sure the inn was the rousing success his parents had dreamed it could be. And as the business guru in this endeavor—not to mention the oldest child—it was all riding on his shoulders.

six

Mia set aside the half-empty breakfast tray. The orange muffins had been delicious, the granola delightfully chewy and flavorful. Her stomach was full and no doubt confused about the sudden influx of carbs. But a day or two of eating like a normal person wasn't going to wreck her figure—or her career.

No, a good old-fashioned scandal was going to do that for her. She whispered yet another prayerful plea that God would bring the truth to light, and soon. It had been a while since she'd really spent any time in prayer. She couldn't even remember the last time she'd opened her Bible outside of church. Now that filming was done she needed to get back to her regular habits—and keep them going.

But for now she was just glad to be tucked away someplace where no one would think to look for her. No one knew where she and Wes had been going for their honeymoon, much less that she might do something so crazy as to actually come here alone. Brooke, Lettie, and Nolan were the only ones who knew her whereabouts.

And while Mia wanted nothing more than to remain in her room all day, she desperately needed fresh clothes. Her spirits were low, even after chatting on the phone with Brooke, who'd made her promise to stay off the internet and especially off social media. #MiaStealsJax. Apparently the scandal had picked up steam, and the paparazzi were stalking Jax and Emma everywhere.

Chances of being recognized here were lower, but if she were, the paparazzi would turn this little town upside down. Wouldn't that be fun. She'd just have to make sure that didn't happen.

She prayed Nolan and Brooke were right, that a little time—and perhaps a fresh scandal—would smooth this mess right out.

Mia forced herself out of bed and into the shower, not bothering to wash her hair since she'd be wearing the ball cap again today. She winced as she put on yesterday's dirty clothes. At least there was only one person who'd seen her in them, and he probably wasn't working this morning.

She swept her hair into a ponytail and pulled on the ball cap, tugging the brim down to her well-groomed eyebrows. Her eyes looked tired and a little puffy after last night's crying jag, but no one was going to recognize her here like this. She slapped her cheeks to bring some color to them. She was blessed with a face that didn't necessarily need makeup, but she'd pick up some basics while she was out anyway.

It was almost noon by the time she left her room

and made her way down the hall to the staircase. The steps creaked as she went down, but it was a homey sound. The idea of her grandparents walking the same route day after day made her smile. Just being here in this house, this town, gave her a connection to the past she'd always sought.

Mia would walk to the stores—they were just down the street a block or two. Filming had been done indoors last week, and she felt starved for a bit of sunshine and fresh air. Besides, she was eager to scope out her family's town.

When she rounded the front desk, she stopped at the sight of Levi perched on a stool. He was wearing a white Bluebell Inn polo that set off his tan.

He straightened at the sight of her. "Good morning, Mrs.—I mean, Mia. I hope you slept well and enjoyed your breakfast."

"I did. Thank you." Mia stopped in front of the desk. There was something different in his countenance this morning, but she couldn't put her finger on it.

"Our other rooms are available now, if you'd like to take a look. They're a bit smaller, but we have a—"

She waved him off. "The suite is wonderful. Thank you, but I'll just stay put." He had to be wondering where her groom was, but thank God he was too professional to mention it.

"All right. Is there anything I can do to make your stay more comfortable?"

"Everything is perfect. I was just going to do some shopping. Is there someplace nearby you'd recommend for clothing?"

"There are a couple stores in town that sell outdoor apparel for hiking, climbing, and such, and other stores that stock touristy things like shirts and hats. Most of those have the Bluebell Lake logo on them though."

She bit her lip. "Oh. I was thinking more like regular clothes: jeans, tops, a sundress?"

He was already shaking his head. "You'd have to go to Asheville for that kind of shopping."

"No problem. That's what Uber is for, right? Thanks for your help." She pulled out her phone and turned toward the door.

"Um . . . I'm afraid we don't have that here."

She blinked. "You don't have Uber?"

"Well, we have Ernest Farnsworth, but he only drives on the weekends, when he's not working at the marina." He straightened from the stool. "But no worries, I can drive you. I'm actually at your service this week for all your traveling needs."

She noted his stiff smile. "Excuse me?"

"It's part of the package. I'd be happy to take you anywhere you need to go."

And still no questions about the mister. Well, maybe this would be a good opportunity to get that conversation out of the way.

"Well, thank you. I'd appreciate that, if you're sure it's not an imposition."

"Part of my job. Asheville's over the mountains, about forty minutes." He pulled a set of keys from his pocket and walked around her, opening the door for her. She put on her sunglasses as she followed him down the walkway. There was nobody about, but no point taking chances.

When he reached a silver Ford sedan, he opened the rear door for her. She paused only a second before stepping inside. Even when her driver drove her to the set she didn't sit in the back. Really, she only did that in a limo, and that was a rare occasion. The formality seemed unnatural here in the sticks.

He got into the driver's seat, started the car, and put down the windows. "I'll put these up in a minute, just letting out some of the stuffy air."

"It's all right. I like fresh air." She filled her lungs with a breath full of pine and the sweet scent of some flower. She'd have to get clothes appropriate for hiking. She was used to being busy and didn't want to leave too much time to wallow in her misery. Plus, the exercise would keep her fit. It would be refreshing to burn calories on trails rather than at the gym. She glanced at the ridge of mountains rising up over the still lake. Not to mention the grand views.

The lake was nestled in the mountains like a baby in a cradle. She scanned the panorama, wondering what her mother had thought of it. On the rare occasions Bluebell had come up, her mom had scoffed at it. But Mia thought the little lake town seemed like the ideal place to grow up.

Levi had no sooner gotten outside of town than he put up the windows and cranked up the air conditioning.

Mia shifted in her seat, feeling disconnected there in the back. The professional distance wouldn't help when she tried to explain why she was here alone. Maybe she should just let it go— he was obviously going to. But it would feel like an elephant in the room whenever she saw him, and she'd grown up with enough elephants to know they didn't belong indoors.

She cleared her throat and looked at the sliver of his face she could see in the rearview mirror— basically his very blue eyes and the dark slashes of his brows.

"So, um, listen," she began, her heart beating ridiculously hard, "you must be wondering why I'm here alone."

He kept his eyes on the road. "It's not really any of my business."

"Still . . . I'll be here a week, and I'd just rather have it out there if it's all the same to you. My fiancé and I broke off our engagement months ago, and I decided I needed to get away for a while. So here I am."

"I'm sorry to hear that."

"Thank you, but it was for the best." It had taken her some time and distance to believe that. When she mourned now it was only for what she'd thought they'd had, not what had actually been. An important distinction.

"Well, I hope you'll feel at home at the Bluebell Inn. If you need any suggestions for things to do, let me know. There's not much by way of nightlife even in the summer, but there's always Asheville."

Mia had no interest in "nightlife." And she didn't want to talk about herself anymore. "How long have you owned the inn?"

He navigated a curve as they started through the mountain pass. "It was actually my childhood home. My sisters and I inherited it almost two years ago when our parents passed."

"I'm sorry for your loss."

"Thank you. They'd dreamed of making it into an inn and running it in their retirement—it used to be an inn years ago. Are you cool enough? I can turn up the air."

"I'm fine, thank you." She wondered if he was always so attentive. He seemed like a nice guy. But in her experience good-looking men usually came with big egos. Heaven knew she'd worked with enough of them. But Levi seemed refreshingly unaware of his appeal.

"There are some nice boutiques in Asheville," Levi said. "Nothing like—well, I'm sure you'll find some clothes to your liking at one of them."

His eyes tightened at the corners, and she realized he'd been avoiding eye contact since she'd come downstairs this morning. She thought of the way he'd ushered her into the back seat like she was some kind of diva. The way he'd assumed she was interested in the area's nightlife and would prefer boutiques to a department store.

All of these facts added up to only one thing. He'd recognized her. Her breaths grew shallow at the thought.

She stared at him in the rearview mirror and decided to face it head on. "You know, don't you?"

"Excuse me?" Still no eye contact.

"You know who I am."

He cleared his throat. "Of course I do. I checked you in."

She didn't know if it was his reticence to admit the truth or the fact that she'd been recognized that frustrated her more. If he knew who she was he might also know of the brewing scandal. What must he think of her—a woman who'd been recently jilted and was now trying to steal another woman's husband?

Worse than that, what if he outed her to the media? Had she come all this way for nothing? Why had she presumed she'd be safe on the backside of nowhere?

She wiped her sweaty palms down her yoga pants. "I know you know, so you might as well admit it."

Finally he met her gaze in the mirror. Something in his eyes softened in the instant before they turned back to the road. "All right. Yes, I do know who you are."

She closed her eyes. "Great. Just great."

"I thought you'd feel more comfortable if you were incognito."

No wonder he'd been so accommodating. A social media post from a celebrity like her could tank his business. Or put it on the map.

People only gave to get. You'd think she'd have learned this lesson long ago. Maybe she wasn't in Hollywood anymore, but even people in quaint little towns had agendas of their own.

"You don't have to worry about a thing," Levi said. "Discretion is a part of my job."

So he said. She shook the negative thoughts from her head and tried to be conversational. "So, I guess you saw *Into the Deep*?"

"Um . . . only the original version."

"From 1974? How did you recognize me then?"

He paused long enough to let her know he was reluctant to answer.

Oh no. He knew about the scandal somehow. Why had she thought she could fly under the radar out here? She had to do something to keep him from selling her out.

"Look, I really don't want anyone to know I'm here. It's important that I just lie low for a few days—"

"I won't say anything."

"—so what'll it take to keep you quiet?"

His eyes met hers in the mirror, holding for a long beat. "Excuse me?"

Her face heated to the tips of her ears. "Sorry to be so crass, but I could tell by the way you hesitated that—"

"I hesitated because my sister is the one who recognized you."

"Your sister knows too?" She couldn't keep the frustration from her voice.

His eyes squeezed in a wince. "Both my sisters, actually. But they won't say anything. You have my word."

She barely held back the wry huff. His word. If she had a document with all the "words" people had taken back she'd need a file the size of a dump truck to house them all.

"You're our guest, and we take your needs seriously. You have nothing to worry about where we're concerned. I can't guarantee someone else won't recognize you though."

She supposed that would be his excuse when he leaked her whereabouts for a hefty finder's fee. "Actually, people usually don't recognize me when I'm wearing my disguise. Especially not when I'm so far from California."

"Well, that'll work in your favor then." He took them through a series of hairpin turns.

Mia stared out the window at the thick green woods, suddenly feeling even worse than she had this morning when she'd awakened. Should she cut her losses and leave now? But she really did want to explore Bluebell. She wanted to revel a little while in the town and imagine her ancestors living there. Imagine what life might've been like if she'd grown up there too.

Besides, where would she even go? She could be recognized anywhere. At least the innkeeper hadn't told anyone about the scandal.

Yet.

seven

Levi stowed Mia's shopping bags in the trunk. He'd been waiting in the car, windows down, for over an hour. Not long considering all the bags she'd emerged with.

"Did you get everything you need?" he asked, opening the rear door for her. "The boutiques aren't far from here."

"I'm shopped out. But would you mind stopping at Barnes and Noble before we head back?"

"Of course not." He got in the car, started it, and put the windows up. He turned the air conditioning to high and pulled from the parking space.

She'd been less friendly since he'd admitted he knew who she was. He guessed he couldn't blame her. Being famous was probably a pain in the butt. A huge invasion of privacy.

Still, he felt the need to be congenial. He didn't want her thinking poorly of the inn, after all. When she left he wanted her to recommend it to all her celebrity friends.

"I don't know if you had a chance to see it, but we have a fully stocked library at the inn. Feel free to borrow anything you'd like."

"Thank you."

"What do you like to read?" he asked.

"Memoirs mostly."

"I would've thought fiction since you're in movies."

"I like fiction too."

He started to mention that Molly's boyfriend was a famous author, but being a name-dropper probably wasn't the best way to disarm her.

"So, why Bluebell?" he asked. "It's not exactly on anyone's list of best summer spots."

She hesitated for just a moment. "Actually, my grandparents used to own the inn."

Levi's eyes sharpened on hers in the mirror. "The Bluebell Inn?"

"Yes. My mom grew up there."

"Was your grandfather Governor Jennings?"

"No, he was Paul Livingston."

Levi smiled. "Paul and Dorothy. They owned the inn from '63 till '86."

Mia perked up. "You know of them?"

"Of course. They're part of the inn's history. Wait. I was always under the impression the Livingstons didn't have children."

"My mom was an only child. She left home at eighteen, and she was estranged from her family. My grandparents died before I was born, but I've always wanted to visit Bluebell."

Estranged. Levi supposed that was why Dorothy had never mentioned her daughter in her journal. Too painful.

"Did you know your grandmother kept a journal? We have it in our library."

She briefly met his gaze in the mirror, a spark of interest in her eyes. "What? Are you serious?"

It made him feel a little heady to feed that hungry look in her eyes. "Dead serious. I'll pull it out for you."

"I'd love that."

A glance in the rearview mirror afforded him his first view of Mia's smile.

He stopped at the bookstore, and she returned moments later with a small bag. Once in the car she pulled off her ball cap and ran her fingers through her hair.

The drive home was quiet. Mia was on her phone, texting someone. There might as well have been a glass partition between them for all the conversation they were having.

He gave a quiet sigh of relief when he finally pulled up to the inn. He helped her out and began removing the bags from the trunk.

"I can get those."

"It's no problem."

They walked up the steps onto the porch, and Mia held the door open for him. Grace was behind the front desk, wielding a duster, and Molly was watering the peace lily just off the foyer. He happened to know both chores had been done the day before.

He scowled at his sisters as Mia closed the door.

"Hello," Molly greeted Mia, her smile wide, her eyes a little too excited.

"Hi," Mia said.

"Hi. We met earlier. I'm Grace, one of the owners."

"I remember. Breakfast was great, thank you."

"I'm Molly!"

Levi recognized that look. *Take it down a notch or ten, Molly.*

"Nice to meet you," Mia said cautiously.

Molly was biting her lip, making her face twist in a weird way, and her cheeks were slightly flushed.

He rolled his eyes at his sisters. "She knows we know."

Molly slumped. "Oh, thank God."

"And even if she hadn't, she would've known now. You two are about as transparent as plastic wrap."

"I'm such a fan!" Molly said. "Can I hug you? Man, you don't even need makeup; you're so gorgeous."

"Um, thank you . . ." Mia graciously accepted Molly's hug.

"You were so awesome in *Into the Deep*! Your hair's really grown out." Molly lifted the honey strands that flowed past Mia's shoulder.

"Molly," Levi chided.

"Hey," Molly said, staring closely at Mia's

63

face. "You have green eyes, not blue like you did in the movie."

"Contacts," Mia said.

"Pardon my sister," Grace said. "She means well."

Levi cleared his throat. "So listen, Mia would like to maintain her privacy while here, so of course I assured her we'll be very discreet."

"Of course!" Molly said. "That's part of our job. We won't tell a soul, will we, Grace?"

"Not a single word," Grace agreed.

"And really," Molly said, "you look so different from the way you looked in the movie. Grace actually recognized your voice before your face."

Mia's eyes toggled between the three of them. "Um, thank you. I appreciate your discretion."

For an actress she had a transparent face, and right now she seemed overwhelmed and not a little wary.

"Why don't we get these bags upstairs?" Levi ushered Mia toward the steps.

"It was nice to meet you," Mia said as she headed up.

"Our pleasure!" Molly said. "Really, it was great meeting you. And if there's anything we can do to make your stay more enjoyable, just let us know!"

On the turn to the second floor Levi gave Molly a look. *Chill out.*

What? her look said.

He followed Mia up the stairs, hoping his overenthusiastic sister hadn't completely scared her off. But he forgot about Molly soon enough as he got caught in the sweet waft of Mia's perfume. He dragged in a breath. Man, she smelled like heaven. And those jeans . . .

He directed his gaze to the stairs. The plastic bags crinkled as they continued upward.

"Your sisters seem . . . nice," Mia said as they reached the top.

"You really don't have anything to worry about. I know Molly seemed a little excited to meet you, but she's the soul of discretion."

"Good to know."

It was a throwaway statement. But he'd done everything he could to assure her. He got it. Actions spoke louder than words.

Mia glanced around the hallway. "Is this a slow time of year for you or something?"

"What do you mean?"

"I haven't seen any other guests. Not that I'm complaining."

Levi studied her as they neared her door. She didn't know? "Um, you booked the whole inn."

She stopped so suddenly he almost ran into her. "I what?"

Levi flinched. Her turd of a fiancé had obviously handled all the arrangements. He tried for diplomacy. "You have the inn all to yourself this week."

Hurt flashed in her eyes as if she just remembered the broken engagement. But she quickly blinked it away and gave a wry laugh.

It sounded so jaded he had the absurd notion to pull her into his arms and comfort her. What kind of a jerk asked a girl to marry him, planned a honeymoon and a wedding, then dumped her?

"Well, I guess that works in my favor now, doesn't it?" She unlocked the door and slipped inside, letting him pass. "Roses, champagne, flower petals, room service, chauffeur, and a rented-out inn. Any other little surprises I don't know about?"

He gave her a dry grin. "I think that about covers it."

"Thank you for your help. And the ride."

"That's my job. Let me know if you need anything. I can recommend some places for dinner if you'd like."

"Thanks, but . . . I think I'd better just order takeout—assuming you have that here."

"Of course. And I can intercept it at the front desk for you."

"That would be great. Thank you. And if you wouldn't mind, I think I'd rather come down in the mornings for breakfast."

"No problem. I'll let the others know."

Somehow even after he left her room he couldn't forget that flash of pain or the mocking tone she'd used to mask it. Mia Emerson was much more than a pretty face. She was a woman who'd been hurt. A woman with her guard up. He felt a sudden desire to tear down all those walls.

Then he gave his head a hard shake. He had quite enough people to take care of at the moment, thank you very much.

When he reached the main floor, Molly silently took his arm and dragged him through the living room into the dining room.

"Don't you have something productive to do?" Levi asked. "Like helping Adam with his research?"

Once inside the dining room, Grace pushed the French doors closed.

"What is it now?" Levi asked.

"Shhhh!" Molly hissed.

Levi rolled his eyes. "Can we just handle this like mature adults, please?"

Grace lifted her index finger. "I'd just like to point out that the youngest one here is not the one who lost her cool with our celebrity guest." She fixed Molly with a superior look.

"Duly noted." Levi's gaze drifted to Molly. "You'd never know you're dating a famous author."

"Hey, I really liked that movie!"

Grace waved off her words. "Back to the subject at hand . . . I have the lowdown on Mia, and I think you're going to want to hear this."

Molly glared at her sister. "She wouldn't tell me until you got here."

Levi gave Grace a tolerant look. "Please tell me you didn't Google our guest again."

"There's a scandal, Levi. You know Jax Jordan from the spy series you like?"

He had the absurd urge to cover his ears. "I don't want to hear any more."

"You don't want to hear why she came on her honeymoon alone? Why she had no luggage? Why she's hiding out in Bluebell, North Carolina, where she literally knows not a single soul?"

"Those sites are just a bunch of gossip." And yet, he couldn't make himself simply turn and walk out of the room.

"There are pictures." Grace withdrew her phone. "I have to say it's pretty convincing."

"Let me see," Molly said.

"Our guests' private lives are *private.*"

"We're in a need-to-know situation here, Levi." Grace handed the phone over to Molly.

She looked at the screen, wincing. "Yikes."

Grace continued in a whisper. "There's a new Hollywood scandal brewing, and Mia's at the center of it. Everyone's looking for her, and she's *here.*"

"She's right," Molly said. "This looks pretty bad."

Levi couldn't take it anymore. "Give it here," he said reluctantly.

Molly handed over the phone. He couldn't miss the all-caps headline. The pictures below it made his gut tighten. There was Mia in the arms of Jax Jordan, in what seemed to be a very steamy kiss. He didn't follow much when it came to Hollywood, but everyone knew Jax was married to Emma Taylor.

"She's broken up Jemma!" Molly said.

Levi frowned. "Jemma?"

"Jax and Emma—Jemma," Grace said. "You do live under a rock."

"Couldn't these just be photoshopped? I mean, otherwise, explain all the alien pictures I've seen at checkout counters."

Levi wondered why he was so reluctant to believe the reports. Maybe he'd only just met Mia, but he didn't want to believe she was capable of carrying on with a married man.

"There are too many pictures and too many reputable sites covering this," Grace said. "They apparently aired it on *Entertainment Tonight* last night."

Levi thought back over the twenty-four hours he'd known Mia. The look of vulnerability on her face when she'd checked in. The hint of tears in her puffy eyelids this morning. The guardedness and flicker of hurt in her eyes only moments ago. Maybe it wasn't just the broken engagement. Maybe she was upset about having been caught in an adulterous affair. But she just didn't strike him as a home wrecker.

"Well, I don't believe it," Levi said firmly.

Two pairs of eyes swung his direction and held there for a long moment.

All right, he could see why his adamant defense of Mia might be out of character. But she just didn't seem the type. And for some reason she brought out all his protective instincts.

"Levi . . ." Grace said. "You don't even know her."

"Oh no." Molly touched his arm. "Please don't tell me you're getting a crush on Mia Emerson."

"Of course not."

"I know we've been pestering you to date, but she's a celebrity, Levi. Every man in America wants her, including Jax Jordan, apparently, and she's in the middle of a huge scandal, not to mention fresh off a broken engagement."

He shrugged off Molly's hand. "Stop it. I don't have a crush. Maybe I just want to believe the best about somebody. Ever think of that? She's our guest. Our loyalties lie with her. Besides, she told me something today that you might be interested in . . ."

He waited until he had their attention.

"She's the Livingstons' granddaughter."

"Paul and Dorothy Livingston?" Grace asked.

Molly was shaking her head. "They didn't have any children."

"They apparently had an estranged daughter—Mia's mom. That's why she wanted to come here

70

on her honeymoon to begin with. She wanted to see where her family came from. So, for all kinds of reasons, we need to have her back while she's here."

"Well, you can believe her all you want," Grace said. "But there's a whole bunch of media who aren't giving her the benefit of the doubt, and they're not going to give up until they find her."

Levi frowned. "Then we'll just have to make sure that doesn't happen."

eight

Mia shifted on the chaise in her room, the new memoir propped on her lap. She was having trouble focusing tonight. She'd turned down lunch, and now she was starving.

There were few restaurants that delivered in this town, so she'd settled on pizza. She knew Levi would be glad to run and grab her something, but even though she was paying for his services, he was an innkeeper, not an errand boy. Besides, she didn't like owing people. Didn't want to feel obligated.

As they had so often these past couple days, her thoughts turned to the scandal. She'd buried her head in the sand long enough; she was going to have to call Jax. This scandal wasn't going away, so she needed the truth to be exposed. And that started with Jax.

A tapping sounded on the door, and she set aside her book and answered.

"Pizza delivery." Levi smiled over a small cardboard box. He'd added a plate and silverware rolled inside a napkin.

Mia opened the door for him, and he slipped past and set the box on the table beside the chaise, then handed her a brown leather volume. "Dorothy's journal."

Heart dancing a jig, Mia took the book. Her grandmother's diary. She traced her fingers over the word *Journal* etched into the material.

After arranging the plate and silverware Levi asked, "What can I bring you to drink?"

"I'm all set. Thank you, though." She walked him to the door. "I keep feeling like I should tip you or something, but I've always been told you don't tip the owner."

"You were told right." He stopped in the doorway. "So listen. I wanted you to know we've stepped up security a little around here. We'll be keeping the doors locked so people can't just drop in. Your room key will get you in and out, of course."

"Well, I can't exactly be wandering the streets anyway, can I?"

"I'm always available for transportation. You mentioned hiking before, and we have some great trails around here. I can drive you to the trailheads. There are other hikers, of course, but if you wear your disguise, I think you'll be all right."

"I might do that. I'm already going a little stir-crazy. I'm not used to having so much time to think." She gave him a conspiratorial grin, and he met it with one of his own. His eyes were a beautiful shade of clear blue, and though he couldn't yet be thirty, he had little crinkles at the corners of his eyes.

"Well . . ." He shifted awkwardly, his cheeks going pink. "I don't want your pizza getting cold."

"Thank you, Levi." Mia gave him a genuine smile. "For everything. I really do appreciate it."

"My pleasure, Mia."

She pushed the door and it closed with a soft little *knick*. Her heart was beating too hard for someone who'd only gotten up to answer the door.

Get it together, Mia.

Sure, the innkeeper was too cute for his own good, but what could they possibly have in common?

What was she saying? She had an ex-fiancé and a married supposed-lover. She didn't even need to be thinking about another man right now.

Mia ate an extra slice of pizza not because she was savoring the taste of the treat—although she was—but because she was dreading what she had to do next. She closed the empty box and set it aside.

It was nine o'clock on a Monday night, a good time to call Jax. He had a standing poker night with his buddies when he wasn't filming. It would be best to catch him when he wasn't with Emma. Would he even answer her call? She briefly thought of using the inn's phone, but the area code would show up.

She could block her number, but the chances of his answering were better if he knew it was her rather than some obsessive fan. He was a nice guy, after all. She'd considered him a friend after working on the film with him all these weeks. They'd had some great times together, some good conversations. She didn't know what was happening on his end since the scandal had broken, but she thought he'd be willing to discuss it with her.

She grabbed her phone and stood, needing to pace. Actually, she needed fresh air and lots of it. She slid open the balcony door and stepped outside. The sultry breeze hit her flesh, but it felt good after the too-cool room. The wind whispered through leaves, carrying the smell of burning wood. Some family must be enjoying a bonfire.

For a moment she let herself envy the imagined family—a tight-knit unit, sharing a lakeside vacation, their biggest worry if someone had brought the Hershey bars for the s'mores. She tried to imagine her mom and grandparents in that scenario, but the image didn't quite gel.

Her eyes drifted to the horizon as she let loose a sigh. The sun had recently set over the lake, and the darkening sky was swathed in hues of pink and purple. It was a beautiful sight, and she took a moment to appreciate it.

Oh, who was she kidding? She was just stalling.

This was so awkward. Jax had kissed her, after all, and she'd rebuffed him, and now it had turned into this huge *thing*. This huge, *public* thing.

Please, God. I know I haven't given You much time lately, but please give me the words. Work this out. Let the truth be revealed.

She located his phone number, blew out a deep breath, and tapped it.

Her heart pummeled her ribs as she waited. She'd find common ground with Jax. He was a victim of this scandal too, after all. The media were the enemy. The two of them could join forces and eradicate this scandal, and then everything could go back to normal.

His phone had rung at least four times. Maybe he was busy. Or maybe Emma was right there. But no, it was poker night.

Should she leave a message?

The ringing stopped. "Hello?"

"Jax. Hi. I wasn't sure you were going to answer."

A beat passed, and she opened her mouth to confirm he was still there.

"Why are you calling?" He sounded distant— and not in a geographical way.

"I'm calling because of the scandal, Jax. We have to do something. This is going to wreck my career, and I can't imagine it's doing much for yours either. Can you talk right now? Maybe we can put our heads together and—"

"I really don't have anything to say to you, Mia. You're not only wreaking havoc on my career but on my marriage, and I take that very personally."

"Wh-what?"

"I told you I wasn't interested when we were filming. But you just couldn't take no for an answer. Now that picture has been spread across every tabloid in the country! How do think Emma feels, huh? She's wrecked. Our marriage is in jeopardy because of you."

Mia's fingers tightened on the balcony railing. "Now, wait just a minute. You know very well that's not—"

"Did you tip off the media? Was it a setup? Because I am going to get to the bottom of this."

"Are you serious right now? You're the one who couldn't take no for an answer. You kissed *me* and I pushed you away. Why are you saying all—" Mia huffed out a breath. Emma was there. Of course. He was making this look like it was all her fault. All her doing.

"Don't call me again, Mia."

"You can't do this, Jax. You have to tell the truth. This isn't the kind of man you—"

A click sounded in her ear. She stared at the phone, gaping. Anger boiled inside. Helplessness, she was drowning in it. Is this what Jax was going to tell the reporters? Was he going to make it look like she'd been trying to seduce him?

This could not be happening.

Levi stacked the paid bills on the corner of his desk and stood. He'd put off the ones they couldn't afford to pay yet. It killed him to pay late fees, but it couldn't be helped. He had to leave some room on the credit card for emergencies. He left his room and wandered to the other side of the inn to the library.

He scanned the titles for something to read. Something with a lot of action to keep him engaged. To keep his mind off Mia.

"Whatcha doing?"

He turned at the sound of Molly's voice. She'd just come in from out back and was cradling her laptop.

"Looking for a book. How was the sunset?"

"I got caught up in my research for Adam and missed most of it." She unshelved a Tom Clancy novel and handed it to him. "Here, you'll like this one. Did you know the average orchard size is fifty acres, and it takes at least one colony of bees—that's roughly twenty thousand bees—per acre to pollinate the trees?"

"Did not know that."

"And only one-fifth of the bees in the colonies are actually pollinators."

"What do the rest of them do?"

"I have no idea."

"All these factoids—you've been hanging around Adam too much."

Just the mention of his name brought a goofy smile to her face.

Ever since Adam had moved here from New York in January the two had grown closer. Levi thought he was an all right guy—even if he couldn't throw a football to save his life. Long as he treated Molly right, Levi had no beef with him.

"When does his new book come out?" Adam's new release was more or less his love story with Molly. Levi didn't think he could stomach the read.

"In August. I can't wait."

"Coming up soon."

"Well, he got so much publicity last fall, and they wanted to build on it. He's got another big tour too."

"Makes sense."

Molly's eyes sharpened on the bookshelf. She frowned at a gaping hole. "Where's Dorothy's journal? Oh, you gave it to Mia, didn't you?" Molly was looking at him, her mouth twisted in that funny way that told him she was biting her tongue.

"Stop it, all right? I'm just being a good host. It wouldn't hurt if she went back to Hollywood and told all her friends about us, you know."

"I wasn't going to give you a hard time. It's just—" She turned abruptly and closed the library door, then faced him again. "While I was outside Mia was on her balcony, and I overheard a phone call."

He huffed. "Molly, you and Grace have to stop butting into her business. That's terribly unprofessional, and if she were to find out—"

"She didn't do it," Molly blurted.

"Who didn't do what?" He gave his head a hard shake and started for the door. "Never mind. I don't want to know."

"You were right."

Of course she had to go and say his three favorite words. He turned and gave her a long look, his hand squeezing the doorknob.

"She didn't do what she was accused of. I heard her talking to Jax Jordan on the phone. She accused him of putting the moves on her, but it was obvious he was having none of that. Levi, that is not a woman in love with a married man. It's a woman fighting to save her reputation after said married man Me-Too'd her."

Levi wasn't one bit surprised. But he was torn. He shouldn't encourage his sister's snooping, and he definitely shouldn't involve himself in a guest's personal problems.

But man, did he want to know what was really going on in Mia's life.

"It sounded like Jax might be blaming it all on her. You know, making it look like Mia came on to him."

Levi gave a wry huff. "He's just trying to save face with his wife."

"Not to mention his career."

"At the expense of Mia's." And man, if that didn't just tick him off. Especially when she was fresh off a broken engagement. To think he'd ever held Jax Jordan in high esteem. Right now he wanted to lay the man flat.

"We need to be even more careful around here."

"We're already on lock-down, and I'm driving her everywhere she goes. What more can we do?"

"I don't know . . ." Molly shifted. "Maybe we can help somehow to prove this wasn't her fault—that she was the victim of Jax's unwanted advances."

Levi held up both hands. "That's going too far. This is none of our business, and I'm sure Mia can handle herself. She probably has a whole staff of people looking out for her public relations."

"I guess you're right."

"I am." His gaze sharpened on Molly. "So let's just leave this alone."

nine

Levi put up a jump shot, but it bounced off the rim and dropped into Erik's hands. Didn't matter. They weren't keeping score anyway. But he sure was stinking up the court this morning.

Pawley Park was quiet, the temperature comfortable. A morning fog still hung over Bluebell Lake. The fresh air felt invigorating, as did the bit of exercise.

Erik dribbled the ball out and turned back toward the hoop. "Your shot's off today."

Levi put a guard up on him. "Just distracted."

"Everything okay at home?"

"About the same."

"I'm sure things will get better now that the season is in full swing."

Erik faked to the right, but Levi was right there. "What about you? Everything all right with Karli?"

The ball smacked the pavement rhythmically. "Yeah, it's just getting a little old—the long-distance thing." He'd met his girlfriend on a business trip.

"You could always move to Knoxville if things get serious enough."

Erik made a fadeaway shot that arced through the air and sank through the hoop with a *swoosh*.

"I don't know if I could leave my dad, you know?" Bill owned the local garage, and Erik was his right-hand man. When he wasn't working on cars, he was a volunteer firefighter.

Levi grabbed the ball and took it out. "Right. And with her son in Knoxville, Karli's not leaving anytime soon."

"Seems kind of doomed, huh? Maybe we should just call it quits before it gets too serious."

"Well, you can't ask her to leave her kid."

"I know. She'd never do that anyway."

"So I guess the question is, would you ever move there?"

Erik winced. "I don't know. It'd kill my dad."

Levi moved forward, dribbling with ease. Erik was scrappier, but Levi had the height advantage. Of course, that didn't matter if he couldn't even sink a shot.

"So how are the honeymooners? Or have you even seen them since they checked in?"

Levi took a second to consider how much he wanted to say. "Actually, it's just the woman. Apparently the wedding never happened."

Erik straightened. "She came on her honeymoon alone?"

Levi was no fool—he took advantage of Erik's distraction. Dodged him and put up a lay-up. The ball bounced off the board and dropped through the basket.

Erik made a face. "Cheap shot. But seriously,

some chick is there on her honeymoon alone? With the whole inn empty?"

"That's about the size of it."

"What's she look like?"

"What does it matter? She's a guest."

"Adam was a guest, and that didn't stop Molly from going after him."

"And I disapproved—for all the good it did me. We need every satisfied customer we can get right now."

Erik darted by Levi and went in for a lay-up. The ball sank through the hoop.

"Money still pretty tight, huh?"

Erik was the only one he'd told about the financial struggles, although even he didn't know just how bad things were. "Something's got to give, man."

"Can't you just borrow against the equity?"

"My parents took out a second mortgage, remember? All of it was used on the renovations."

"Well, I'm sure your marketing plans will pan out. Hopefully you'll be full up all season."

"That would help me breathe a little easier."

"You know, you should probably level with your sisters. They're owners too. They'd be ticked if they found out you weren't shooting straight with them. And you shouldn't have to carry this burden alone."

Erik tossed Levi the ball.

Maybe his friend was right. That would at least

keep them from unnecessary expenditures. He was getting tired of being the bad guy every time one of them wanted something for the inn.

Levi took the ball out, moving slowly, catching his breath. But this was his responsibility. He was the oldest. He'd been told from the time his sisters were born that he was the big brother and responsible for taking care of them when his parents weren't around.

"Look out for your sister," his dad had said on Molly's first day of school.

"Look out for your sisters," he'd said when Levi was a teenager and his parents left for the evening.

Look out for your sisters.

And just like that, the night of the accident flashed in his mind. The dark night, silent but for the terrible metallic screech the Jaws of Life made on the wreckage containing his parents.

He'd been home for a vacation when his buddy Erik called. He made it to the scene before the ambulance left. It took a while for them to pry his parents from the car.

It was too late for his mom.

That terrible truth still hadn't sunk in as Levi followed his dad into the back of the ambulance and squeezed in by his stretcher. His dad's eyes were closed, but there were tears on his cheeks. His face was pinched as if he was in pain. He seemed to struggle just to draw a breath.

Mom's dead. It didn't seem real. He couldn't think about that right now.

Levi grabbed his hand. "Dad, I'm right here. Everything's going to be all right."

Levi glanced at his medic buddy who was taking Dad's vitals from the other side of the bed, but the look on Erik's face wasn't encouraging. The ambulance took off, the siren splitting the night.

"Le-vi . . ." his dad said through a moan of pain.

"I'm here, Dad. I'm here. What is it?"

"Love you . . . all."

"We love you too, Dad. But everything's going to be all right."

"Take . . ." His Adam's apple bobbed slowly. "Take care . . . of your sisters."

Levi's stomach bottomed out. A chill swept through his body. His throat closed. "Don't talk like that, Dad. You're going to be just fine. We're on the way to the hospital. They're going to take really good care of you."

Dad's eyes opened just then, the clear blue of his irises clouded by pain or something worse. Levi tried to brace himself for what might happen. For what had already happened. But his pulse was pounding in his ears. He couldn't seem to think.

Dad gave his hand a weak squeeze. "Promise . . . me."

He looked into the suddenly old face of his dad. A tear leaked from the corner of his father's eye and trickled down into his salt-and-pepper hair.

Levi brushed it away. "I will, Dad. I promise."

"Hey, you all right, man?"

Levi blinked. He was still dribbling the ball. He had yet to make his way back toward Erik and the basket.

He gave his head a hard shake, dislodging the memory from his mind, but a headache beat in its place.

"I'm fine. Just fine. Let's play ball."

ten

Mia had slept horribly. She'd started on her grandmother's journal before bed, but had quickly given up. She wanted to give it her full attention.

And try as she might to fall asleep, her phone call with Jax had her keyed up. She tossed and turned all night, his words ringing in her ears. Finally she drifted off in the early morning hours and awakened to a bird tweeting outside her window. The clock read 10:17. She was still on Pacific time.

A shower rejuvenated her. But she was starting to feel cooped up, and she wanted to get her mind off her problems. A hike might be just the ticket today. She dressed in workout gear—yoga shorts, a long T-shirt. She pulled her ponytail through a ball cap, and after she'd tied her tennis shoes, she was drawn downstairs by the fragrant aroma of something sweet and yummy.

The lobby was deserted, so she went through the French doors to the empty dining room and seated herself at a table for two by the window. There was a clanging noise in the kitchen, and a few minutes later a middle-aged woman with dark skin and kind eyes peeked out. She had very short salt-and-pepper hair that made Mia think she must be a confident woman.

"Oh hi, honey. Didn't hear you come in. You must be ready for some breakfast."

"Yes, please."

A moment later she reappeared, carrying a tray. "I just assumed you wanted the full menu—orange spice muffins and yogurt with fresh fruit and homemade granola. I'm Della, by the way."

"Mia. Nice to meet you. The full menu sounds good, and it smells divine."

"Well, I guess I know my way around a kitchen. Been cooking since I was barely able to reach the kitchen counter."

"If you made yesterday's breakfast, I believe it."

"I make all the breakfasts around here." Her smile widened. "If I can get you anything else you just let me know. I'll be in the kitchen cleaning up."

"Do you know if Levi's around?" Mia blurted. She'd need that hike to burn off all these calories.

"He had to slip out for a little bit, but he'll be back soon. I can give you his—"

A clamor came from the lobby—the sound of the door opening and closing, footsteps on the floor.

"I'll bet that's him now," Della said as she disappeared into the kitchen.

Sure enough, a moment later Levi entered the dining room in a pair of basketball shorts and a white T-shirt that clung to his muscular shoulders. His hair was damp, his cheeks flushed.

"Good morning," he said when he spotted her. "I see you found breakfast."

"I did."

"What are your plans for today? Would you like to go anywhere?"

"Actually, I was thinking a hike might be nice. Something fairly rigorous, maybe a few miles long?"

"I know just the trail. And the view from the top is amazing. Let me just grab a shower and I'll be right out."

"Take your time. I'm going to enjoy my breakfast."

Levi disappeared through the kitchen doors, leaving her to her breakfast and thoughts. Last night's conversation with Jax still plagued her. She felt betrayed and hurt by his response. She tried to look at it from his side—with the pregnant wife and the marriage to safeguard. But nothing could excuse his deceitful behavior. He'd blamed her for something he'd done.

She'd called Nolan soon after waking, though it was still pretty early in California, and he promised to come up with a plan to handle this situation. She had a feeling his plan would involve a press release that would publicly pit her against Jax, and she hated that. She'd considered them friends. But maybe she had no real choice in the matter. She had to repair her reputation if she hoped to make it in this business—and keep her role in *Lesser Days*.

She finished her breakfast—which was delicious—and Della cleared her dishes away.

Mia answered Brooke's text from late last night. She'd filled her friend in on her call with Jax. It was gratifying that she was as outraged as Mia at his response. And a text had come in from Lettie, who reminded her she was storming the gates of heaven on Mia's behalf. She could always count on Lettie to have her back.

"Ready to go?" Levi wore a friendly smile and business casual apparel. The light blue polo bearing the inn's logo matched his eyes and made his shoulders seem even broader.

"Sure." Mia pushed back from the table, giving him a smile that felt thin.

As nice and well-meaning as the innkeeper seemed, she needed to keep her guard up. She didn't know Levi or his sisters. They could turn on her just as easily as Jax had. She'd only be here a week anyway. What was the point in making friends?

Once she settled into the sedan he closed her door. She still felt ridiculous sitting in the back, but maybe having some boundaries was smart. Because if she were honest, she felt drawn to Levi.

It wasn't just his good looks, though he had

those in spades. It was something less definable. He was obviously a leader, professional and competent at what he did. She sensed he was a little tightly wound, but that wasn't her problem.

He slipped into the front seat and started the car.

Mia pushed her sunglasses into place. "Where are you taking me?"

"There's a trail on the north side of the lake," he said as he pulled onto the street. "It goes onto state property and weaves back and forth on the way up to Summit Ridge. It's 3.4 miles, all uphill, but the trail is well marked. How does that sound?"

"Perfect."

"The more obvious choice is the trail up to Stone Gap Bridge. It spans a gorge and has great views. But it's also popular with tourists, and on a morning like this you're likely to find ten or twelve people up at the bridge."

She didn't need that. "Yeah, I should probably avoid the popular trails. Should I call you when I'm finished?"

"Reception's pretty spotty around here. I'll just wait for you."

She was anticipating Nolan's call, but she supposed it could wait a couple hours. "It's going to take me a while."

"No worries. Take your time. I brought some work to do."

"Is it a lot of work, running an inn?"

He briefly met her eyes in the rearview mirror, and she felt the hum of attraction. Just as quickly he looked away.

"It has its challenges."

She wanted to ask what they were. If he'd always wanted to run an inn or if his parents' death had completely derailed his plans. But she didn't need to get drawn into Levi's life. She had enough problems of her own. So she stifled the questions and let silence fill the car.

Levi made himself comfortable on a shaded bench as he waited for Mia to return from her hike. No one had gone up the trail after her, so he hoped she wouldn't run into anyone up there. The last thing she needed was to be recognized.

Time to get down to work. He used his phone to look over the proof of an ad he was running in *Blue Ridge Country*. He noted a few changes, all the while praying the fortune he was spending would pay off.

Deep South Magazine had a write-up on the Bluebell Inn that was being published in July's edition. It wasn't *Southern Living*, but he didn't take the free publicity for granted. The inn had a unique and colorful history, and he was glad he'd been able to find one magazine that thought it was worthy of exposure.

He grabbed his phone to write the editor about

the ad proof, and his eyes caught on the email from Thomas at FC. He'd have to write him back today and turn down their offer. The thought hollowed his stomach.

Couldn't be helped though. While they'd all stepped up to the plate in running the inn, it was up to Levi to make sure the inn was solvent. Only then would it be attractive to a prospective buyer. Then they'd have money to invest in Molly's and Grace's futures. And then Levi could return to his life in Denver, knowing he'd done his job.

A long while later Levi's eyes caught on something red. Mia emerged from the heavily wooded trail. Her cheeks were flushed with a healthy glow, her long ponytail swinging with each step. She'd ditched the sunglasses and was carrying the water bottle he'd sent with her—now empty.

As she hit the level ground she searched him out and found him on the bench not far from his car. Twigs snapped under her light step as she approached him.

She seemed invigorated by the exercise. It was fair to say he'd been a little worried about her. He wanted all their guests to enjoy their stay even if, in her case, that might be asking too much. She still looked tired, but it was the good kind of tired.

He stood, smiling at her. "How was it?"

"Great. Just what I needed." She pulled out her

phone. "Are you getting a signal out here? I only have one bar."

"Like I said, pretty spotty. But you'll pick up a signal as we get back into town. Ready to head home or is there someplace else you'd like to go? It's after lunchtime. I could run in someplace and grab food. I was going to fry up some bologna for myself, but you'd probably rather have something else."

She shelved her hands on her slim hips, still breathing hard. "You can fry bologna?"

"Sure can. It's pretty tasty, too, especially with cheese and a slice of fresh tomato. You look skeptical though, so we can stop somewhere, no problem."

"No, no, not skeptical. I just don't want to put you out. A drive-through is fine."

"It's hardly putting me out to throw a couple extra slices in the pan."

"Well . . . if you're sure. I'd appreciate it. Might as well embrace the Southern way."

He tossed her a smile. "Might as well."

eleven

Mia knew something was wrong the moment she got a cell signal, because her phone blew up with texts. From Brooke, from Nolan, from Lettie, and from several other friends and acquaintances.

What is going on?

She opened Brooke's texts and began reading—and gasped.

"Everything all right?" Levi asked from the front seat.

Mia continued reading until she'd finished the long line of texts from her friend.

Then she opened Nolan's first text.

> As I mentioned this morning, we need to put out a press release ASAP. I'm having one drawn up. Should be ready for release by noon.

And his next text:

> Jax beat us to the punch! Call me!

There was a link, but Mia scanned his other texts, dread snaking up her spine.

You there? We need to get on this, quick.

Where are you, Mia? This is bad.

"What now?" she whispered, her heart beating up into her throat. But she knew. All the things Jax had said on the phone last night he'd now said to the world at large.

"This can't be happening."

"Mia?" It was Levi again. "What's wrong?"

She tapped on the link on Nolan's text, and a celebrity website opened. She read the headline: JAX JORDAN BARES ALL, "MIA WOULDN'T TAKE NO FOR AN ANSWER." She scanned the article, in which Jax had divulged the details of her so-called unwanted overtures. He painted her as a desperate and pathetic woman who was obsessed with him. He painted himself as a loyal husband, simply trying to protect his family.

And worst of all—it came off as completely believable.

"No, no, no." Tears stung the back of her eyes. She couldn't believe Jax was doing this to her. But why not? This seemed to be the way of the world she lived in.

She dashed away a tear, angry with herself for crying.

Levi turned in his seat, his arm across the back. The car had come to a stop, she realized. They were in the marina's parking lot, at the back.

"What's wrong?" he asked again. "What can I do?"

The compassionate look in his eyes drew her in. There was so much sincerity in those blue depths. As though he'd like nothing more than to solve all her problems or at least comfort her. No doubt she could use a hug about now. But she hardly knew Levi. And he was only doing his job.

"Nothing, I—it's just business. I have to make a phone call."

She didn't want him to overhear her conversation with Nolan. She looked around the lot. It was empty here at the back, but there were a lot of people up toward the docks, and cars coming and going. She couldn't be seen here, much less take the chance of being overheard.

"Just take me back to the inn, please."

He was still studying her with that unfathomable expression. As though he wanted to say something but didn't know if he should. Growing uncomfortable with his scrutiny and the silence, she dropped her eyes to her phone.

Nolan had tried to call twice, and there was a voicemail.

"I already know about the scandal," Levi said softly.

She sucked in a deep breath as her eyes locked with his. He'd read all those headlines. Not today's, she was sure. But the others were bad enough. Her face filled with heat.

But why did she even care about some back-woods innkeeper's opinion of her?

She knuckled off a tear. "Of course you do."

"Did the media find out where you are? Is that what's wrong?"

"No." She sniffled. "But hey. Maybe you can just tell them and put us all out of our misery."

He tilted his head. "I'm not going to do that."

"Oh, why not, Levi? You could make a lot of money, you know. One simple phone call and you'd have a nice fat check."

He gave an audible sigh. "That's not my style. I wasn't trying to pry into your personal business, and I'm not trying to pry now. But I am trying to keep you safe, Mia, and I need your help in order to do that."

Another tear leaked out. This one because she was being such a jerk, and he didn't really deserve it.

"Do you need to leave Bluebell? I have a friend with a floatplane. We can get you out of here without anyone knowing."

She gave that some thought. She didn't think she needed to leave, but it was nice to know she had a discreet way out of town if she needed it.

"I need to call my agent and figure things out."

"All right. Whatever you want. We'll head back to the inn." He put the car into Reverse and pulled from the lot.

Her mind was spinning with everything she'd

just read. If only they'd jumped on this sooner. Now anything she said was only going to seem fabricated. She should've come out with the truth from the beginning instead of hoping all this would just blow over.

A few minutes later Levi was pulling into the slot in front of the inn. Mia put her sunglasses back on and stepped out when he opened the door.

She stopped, staring at the inn. "Do the others know too?"

When he didn't answer, she sneaked a peek.

His lips pressed together.

Of course they did. Great.

She walked past him and up the walk. If there were any inkling of a chance they'd believed in her before, it had just died with today's press release. They thought she was some sleazy, obsessed seducer of married men.

She almost laughed, because that's just the kind of character she'd played in *Into the Deep*. Then she realized it wasn't funny at all. Because America, who'd already seen her play that role so convincingly, would have no trouble believing that's exactly what kind of person she was.

Things were quiet at the inn after Levi brought Mia back. Miss Della had already left for the day. Molly was probably at Adam's house. Grace had cleaned Mia's room while she was hiking, but his little sister seemed to have disappeared too. She was probably off enjoying the great outdoors.

He gave a hard sigh. Getting that girl to sit down and fill out college applications was becoming a real bear. He knew it could be a little daunting with the essay questions, but Grace was a good writer—even a bit of a perfectionist. And computers were her second language. He felt like a nag, but he had to keep after her until she got it done. Fall would be here before they knew it.

He made two fried bologna sandwiches, even though he didn't know when Mia would come downstairs, and scarfed his down.

When he was finished he considered replying to Thomas at FC. But he couldn't focus on that right now when he was on standby, waiting to see if Mia needed to leave.

He felt a pinch in his chest at the thought of her departure. He was just feeling protective because she was his guest, that was all. When she was there, under his roof, he could keep the outside world out.

But he couldn't protect her from the ravages of gossip.

He couldn't imagine having his reputation wrecked for the whole world to see. Not to mention the havoc it could wreak on her career. She was a strong woman to hold up under all that. No doubt she had a supportive network of people: friends and professionals. But here she was all alone, and that had to be hard.

His fingers twitched to Google the scandal and see what had her so upset. What they were up against. But he wouldn't do it. If she wanted him to know she'd tell him.

Instead he went to the front desk to check on next week's reservations. Mia would be gone by then. The sudden thought made him feel flat. But he pushed through. He had bigger worries.

The inn was only half full next week. Those ads couldn't hit soon enough. He would've scheduled them earlier in the year, but his maxed-out credit card hadn't allowed the expenditure.

The floor creaked above him, and footsteps sounded on the stairwell.

His heart stuttering, he ran a hand through his hair and leaned on the counter in a way that flexed his biceps. Then he rolled his eyes.

She's Mia Emerson, idiot. She could have any guy she wanted. Including Jax Jordan, apparently.

He didn't have much time to castigate himself because she rounded the corner, her hand still on the newel at the bottom.

Her hair was down around her shoulders now, but it was her face that drew his attention. Her eyes were bloodshot and puffy, her lashes still damp. Despite her distress, her shoulders were straight, her bearing almost regal.

He came around the counter. "You all right?"

"I'm fine. We'll get it all sorted out eventually."

"Do you need to leave?"

"Nolan thinks it's best if I stay—if that's still all right."

"Of course. You've got the whole place until Sunday."

She looked down then, her long lashes brushing the tops of her cheeks. When she looked back at him, he got caught in those mossy green eyes. He could see why she'd made it so far in the business. She was beautiful, yes. But there was something beneath the beauty . . . vulnerability. She was also a little guarded. He sensed she had layers like an onion, and it made him want to peel them away one by one.

"I didn't do it," she said softly.

It took him a minute to get on the same page. The scandal. Jax Jordan.

"I know you don't know me, but that's not who I am."

He was surprised she even cared what he thought. But maybe she could use someone in her corner. Someone who wasn't a world away in Hollywood.

"I believe you," he said.

She searched his eyes for a long-drawn-out moment. "Why?"

He couldn't exactly tell her Molly had eavesdropped on her phone call with Jax Jordan. Anyway, he'd believed Mia even before that.

"I'm a good judge of character. And you don't

strike me as the type of person who'd try and seduce another woman's husband."

"I played exactly that type of person on the big screen, you know. Anyway, I'm an actress. Maybe I can make you believe whatever I want you to believe."

It was the guardedness talking. But it didn't put him off. Only made him more curious about why she kept that wall so high.

He tried to lighten the moment. "And maybe you're underestimating my astute powers of intuition."

A bit of rigidness left her shoulders, her lips curling in an almost-smile.

He felt like he'd won a race. "Hungry? There's a fried bologna sandwich with your name on it."

"Actually, I am. Thank you."

"Right this way." They passed through the French doors to the dining room. "You can have a seat anywhere."

But as he slipped through the kitchen door, she was still on his heels. They'd made some commercial upgrades when they'd remodeled, including a large butcher block island, complete with two stools. Molly could often be found in the mornings sitting here chatting with Miss Della when she was supposed to be manning the front desk for checkouts.

Mia set her hand on one of the stools. "Mind if I just eat in here?"

"Make yourself at home."

She settled on a stool. "I used to eat in the kitchen when I was a kid. Our housekeeper and cook, Lettie, was like a second mom to me."

"That's pretty much how Miss Della is to us."

"I can see that. I love Lettie so much that when my mom passed I hired her. I'd want her around even if she wasn't so good at what she does."

"She sounds great." She must be special indeed to have gotten inside Mia's fortress.

He took the tinfoil off the plate he'd made and added some fresh fruit from this morning's breakfast. He set it in front of her and added a water bottle from the fridge.

He felt her appraisal as he moved about the kitchen and resisted the urge to flex. Since when was he such a poser? He was a decent-looking guy, and he worked out several times a week. That plus all the work around here kept him in shape. But she was used to the likes of . . . Well, he didn't know many actors by name. But she was out of his league—he knew that for sure.

And why was he even going down that road?

"Sorry I snapped at you earlier," she said quietly. "It had nothing to do with you."

He gave her a tentative smile. "No worries. You were upset."

"I was more angry than anything. I cry when I'm angry." She took a bite of the sandwich.

"My sister Molly does that. She hates it."

"This is good," she said when she swallowed the bite. "I hate it too. Everyone thinks you're hurting when really you just want to throat punch someone."

His lips twitched at the thought of Mia getting violent. She was a nice person, likeable, and definitely not inclined to punching.

He leaned against the kitchen counter opposite her, a little amused at how much she seemed to be enjoying the food.

"Jax put out a press release this morning. He claims I was pursuing him for months and just grabbed him and kissed him that night."

"Let me guess—it was the other way around."

She did a double take. "How'd you know?"

He winked at her. "That intuition of mine."

Did he really just wink? He was getting awfully comfortable with Mia. Too comfortable? He was always after Molly for lacking boundaries with the guests. But those lines, always so obvious before, seemed fuzzy with Mia. It was the vulnerable situation she was in, along with his desire to protect her.

"I'll be putting out a press release through my agent, Nolan, but it's probably too little, too late."

"What does he advise beyond that?"

She lifted her slim shoulders. "We'll have to play it by ear. See how people respond to the releases. He thinks it's best if I stay put for now, stay off social media, and let the press release do its job. Fans will take sides. I'm not sure how this is going to impact the film we just wrapped. Nolan's also working on that. We're supposed to do a publicity tour when it releases to theaters."

"That might be a little tense."

"I'm sure Emma wouldn't be too crazy about the idea either. Not that I blame her."

"They say there's no such thing as bad publicity."

"The production company can sort it out. But my reputation has taken a hit. And if people believe what Jax is saying now, it's only going to get worse."

"Will that affect your career?"

She gave him a wan smile. "Well, it's not going to help. Jax and Emma are a force to be reckoned with. They've been in this business a long time, and they have loads of fans. I'm just a newcomer. The media has already weighed in, and apparently I'm the bad guy."

"Maybe you should give an interview and tell your side of it."

"That came up. Problem is, he never sent inappropriate texts or anything, so I have no proof to back it up."

"Neither does he."

"No, it's a 'he said, she said' situation."

A text came in from Molly. It was just a photo of a shirt she thought he'd like, but it made him squirm a little. He felt like she'd caught him consorting with a guest in the kitchen. And after all the times he'd gotten after her for much the same thing, he felt a pinch of guilt.

"I'm really sorry you're going through this." He gave Mia a polite smile and straightened from the counter. "I should get back to work. But I hope you'll let us know if we can do anything to help."

She blinked, caught off guard, no doubt, by his sudden slide into professionalism. Maybe that was how it felt when you crossed a line. He'd have to ask Molly. Not.

twelve

Mia set her laptop aside and blinked against the tears. She shouldn't have done it. She knew better. People could be brutal, especially when they hid behind a screen. But she just had to know what everyone had thought of her press release.

And now she did.

She got up from her bed, the walls of the honeymoon suite pressing in on her. It was late, almost midnight, but she slipped on the white terry robe with the inn's logo and left her room. The inn was so quiet she was surprised when she met Molly on the stairs.

"Hey, Mia. You're up late. Is there anything you need?"

Sweet of her to offer, since she was obviously heading to bed. Thankfully Molly had settled down since they'd first been introduced. Mia had become used to a certain amount of fangirling, but here in this tiny town it felt different somehow.

"No thanks. I just wanted to get out of my room for a while."

"I don't blame you. Help yourself to the TV in the living room. Or there's a beautiful full moon tonight right over the lake. I saw a falling star out back the other night."

"Sounds great. Thanks, Molly." She passed the innkeeper.

"Mia?"

She turned, looking up at Molly.

"I just wanted to reiterate that you're in good hands here. We'll do everything we can to keep your whereabouts under wraps."

"Thanks. I appreciate that." Mia gave her a smile and continued on.

"And Mia?"

She turned again.

"Sorry. I don't mean to be a pest. But I want to say that I think you're getting a really crappy deal in all this. I'm thoroughly ticked at Jax Jordan, and I'll never watch another one of his films. Except the one you're in, of course," she added hurriedly. "I'm sure you've got a million people in your corner—I just wanted you to know I'm one of them."

It felt good to be so easily accepted. Mia gave her a warm smile. "Thanks, Molly. That means a lot to me."

"I'll let you get on with your night. If you get hungry there are cookies and muffins in the kitchen."

Mia thanked her again and continued down the stairs. Molly's words were soothing after the diatribes she'd just read online. And it made her feel at home to know the kitchen was open if she had the midnight munchies. But she wasn't hungry and had no desire to watch TV.

The darkness beyond the windows beckoned. She followed the hall around the check-in desk and past the library. The lock turned easily, and she stepped outside into the mild evening. The scent of a wood fire carried to her on a breeze as she made her way down the sloped lawn to the neat row of Adirondack chairs. She settled into one of them, curling her feet underneath her.

The lake was pitch black except for the cone of shimmering moonlight reflected on it. On the distant shoreline house lights gleamed here and there. Overhead, beyond a canopy of leaves, the stars twinkled on a black canvas. She leaned her head against the chair's tall back and snuggled in, watching for a falling star. She could use a free wish about now.

At times like these a girl was supposed to be able to call her mother. But Mia's mom was gone, and she'd never been that kind of mother anyway. She hadn't been much on advice—unless it related to beauty and fashion. At those things she'd been very good.

Mia wrapped her arms around her body. It was almost chilly with the breeze coming off the lake. But still she couldn't make herself go back inside. She thought of the handsome innkeeper and his earlier kindness. She liked that he believed in her even though he had no real reason to. She also liked the way he'd kept her company in the kitchen while she'd eaten. He seemed like a capable man—the kind who looked out for others and took his responsibilities seriously. Maybe too seriously.

She smiled as she remembered the way he'd been with his sisters. She'd always wanted siblings. A younger sister to mentor, an older brother to look out for her. She'd be willing to bet Levi had a bossy side that drove his sisters crazy. But then he must've had a lot of responsibility foisted onto him when their parents died. Good thing he had those strong shoulders.

"Mia?"

She jumped at the sound of the male voice. Footsteps brushed through the grass. She scanned the darkness. Only as he neared could she make out his familiar silhouette in the moonlight.

"Levi?"

"Didn't mean to disturb you. I was working in my room and saw someone out here. Wanted to make sure we didn't have a trespasser."

"Nope." She sank back into the chair, her heart settling. "Just me."

He stuffed his hands into his khaki pockets. "Couldn't sleep?"

"Still on Pacific time."

"Are you warm enough? Let me grab you a blanket."

"No, that's okay. I'm comfortable."

"Would you like some tea? I think Molly has one that functions as a sleep aid."

"No thanks. I'm not much of a tea person."

"Don't say that too loudly. You're in the South now."

"Good point."

"Well . . ." He took a step back. "I don't want to disrupt your evening."

She was loath to get wrapped up in her own thoughts again. "I wouldn't mind the company—unless you're heading to bed. Sorry, you probably have to be up early."

And she was supposed to be more careful about who she let in. But she'd only be here a few more days. What could it hurt? She was getting lonely, with Brooke and Lettie so far away and a million fans turning against her. At least Levi and his siblings seemed to be on her side.

"I'm not really tired yet." The chair beside her groaned as he eased his weight onto it. "I've always been a bit of a night owl. I can function pretty well on six hours' sleep."

"Lucky you. I need a solid eight."

"Tell me about your work. How'd you get into show business?"

"My mom. She was an actress—Katherine Emerson?"

"Right. I should've put that together."

She smiled. "I guess you really *didn't* know who I was when I checked in."

"Sorry," came his sheepish reply. "My sisters

filled me in quickly enough. Told me I live under a rock."

"I don't mind. It's kind of nice." Somehow it was easier conversing with him under the cover of darkness. Also, it made her aware of how deep and lovely his voice was.

"It must be a pain to be recognized wherever you go. Molly's boyfriend is a famous writer, so he deals with that too."

"What's his name?"

"His pseudonym is Nathanial Quinn, but his real name is Adam Bradford."

"That sounds familiar. But yeah, being recognized can get a little intrusive. Most people are pretty cool about it, though, and I do enjoy meeting fans—usually," she added, thinking of the last few days. She pulled the robe tightly around her chest.

When Levi had seen the shadow moving across the yard, he immediately thought of all the people looking for their guest. He half expected a flash to go off when he opened the back door. Once he saw it was only Mia he hadn't intended to stick around. He'd had a little talk with himself after their chat in the kitchen. But when she asked him to stay he detected a hint of desperation in her tone. Maybe she was lonely. All her friends were on the other side of the country, and she was alone on what was supposed to have been her honeymoon.

"Have you always lived in Bluebell?" she asked, breaking the silence. She really did have a distinctive voice. A little throaty. Very sexy.

"I went away to Colorado State, and after I graduated I got a job in Denver. I lived out there for several years—until I came back here to run the inn."

"That surprises me."

"Had me pegged for a country boy, did you?"

"Caught me." He heard the grin in her voice.

"I like Denver, traffic notwithstanding. I had a great job there with growth potential, an apartment I loved, and a . . ."

He didn't finish the thought, hadn't meant to go there. It might be late—and dark—but Mia was still his guest.

"And a girlfriend?" she asked when he left the sentence hanging. "Did you leave behind a special woman, Levi?"

Her tone was teasing, almost flirtatious, and it made his pulse kick up. It was easy to see why she had so many male admirers. "Sure did."

"Was it serious?"

"Not especially. We'd only been going out several months."

"But it had potential." She was looking toward him now, her head resting against the chair back. He could feel her perusal.

"Who knows? I thought it might. But then I

was needed here. I believe things happen for a reason."

"Do you believe in God, Levi?"

The personal question surprised him. He turned toward her, even though her features were murky in the shadows. "Faith is a big part of my life, and part of the reason I was able to accept moving back home and ending that relationship. God has a plan, and He was directing my steps. How about you?"

She was quiet a moment. The leaves rustled overhead and water rippled against the shoreline.

"Lettie took me to church as a child. It seemed—out of step with the rest of my life. It wasn't until I was older that I saw it was the only part of my life that was real and normal. So yes, I believe in God. He's been a constant. If I didn't have Him in my life, I don't know how I would've held on to any sense of normalcy."

"He's blessed you with a lot of success."

"And I'm grateful. It's a competitive world, acting. People scrambling for parts, jealousy, backstabbing. It's vicious sometimes. You think someone's your friend, but they're just using you. Everyone I knew was praying for their big break, and I was always praying that God wouldn't give me more than I could handle."

Interesting. He tilted his head. "Why do you think that is?"

"It's not that I'm not driven or competitive. I

just saw how it—fame—affected people in my life. I didn't want that happening to me."

"Your mom?"

"My mom most of all. But I do love acting—the actual work of it. I love exploring different characters and trying to become them for a little while, trying to portray them accurately. I've always felt called to acting, but I was happy just making a living at it. I didn't need to be a Hollywood sensation."

"Too late," he teased.

He thought she smiled back but couldn't be sure. He was enjoying their chat. And, he noted, since he'd come out here his stress level had seemed to drop tenfold. Maybe Mia just had that effect on him.

"So," she said after a moment's quiet. "Why didn't you try the long-distance thing with your Denver friend? Or are you staying here indefinitely?"

"My plans are to make the inn profitable, at which point we can sell it as a viable business. Our mom and dad dreamed of turning the place back into an inn, but they wouldn't have wanted us to give up our own dreams to follow theirs."

"Dodging the subject?"

"Darn." His lips twitched. "Didn't work."

"At least you don't have your love life splashed across every celebrity magazine nationwide."

"I can't even imagine."

"What was her name? What did she do?"

"You're not going to let me off the hook, are you?"

"You already know all about my love life."

"Fair enough." He didn't even know why he was reluctant to talk about it; there was no big story here. "Her name was Gretchen, and she was an admin assistant. And to answer your question—"

"Finally."

"I wasn't sure how long I might be here. I didn't feel it was fair to leave her hanging."

"Do you miss her?"

Mia was very direct out here in the dark. He thought about her question, wanting to be honest but needing to clarify things in his own head. "I missed her for a while, but now I think I just miss having someone special. My life's too full for that right now though. I have responsibilities that need my full attention."

"The inn, you mean?"

"That and my sisters. Speaking of which—they don't know about Gretchen, so I'd appreciate it if we kept that between us."

"You're keeping my secret, so I can certainly keep yours. But why don't you want them to know, if you don't mind my asking?"

He lifted a shoulder. "I guess I don't want them feeling guilty about what I gave up."

"It was an unselfish thing you did."

"We all made sacrifices. Molly gave up a great internship in Italy that she'd worked hard for. Grace gave up a lot of activities at school her junior and senior years."

"It was all for your parents?"

"That and also for Grace. We wanted her to be able to finish high school here, and the inn seemed like the only viable way to do that."

"I think it's really special what you're doing—all of you. Your parents would be really proud of you."

He heard a wistful tone in her voice and wondered again about her own family. "I hope so."

"You seem close. I never liked being an only child. Other kids have imaginary playmates; I had imaginary siblings."

He chuckled, easily able to picture little Mia having tea with her "sisters."

"The reality is probably less appealing than the fantasy. Believe me, we fuss and argue and annoy each other, even now. Running a business together hasn't been easy. If left to her own devices Molly would spend us out of house and home. She's all about whatever it takes to make the guests happy. Grace is more low-key, but the inn is just a means to an end for her. She wanted to finish school here, and she did. Not that she doesn't care about our parents' legacy."

"Sure, but she's only, what, eighteen? I was pretty self-absorbed at that age."

"She's nineteen, but yeah, I get it. She'll be heading off for college in the fall and everything. Following her own dreams."

"Will you hire someone to fill her spot?"

"Yeah." He winced at the thought. He'd have to pay someone more than the piddly sum they were paying Grace, and he wasn't sure where that money would come from.

"I'm glad you turned the place back into an inn. In a way, you're keeping my grandparents' legacy alive too."

Levi hadn't thought of it that way. But it made him feel good to please Mia. "The place has a rich history. I like sharing it with others."

"It's an awesome place. I'd be happy to recommend it to my friends and fans."

He stared across the space between them, wishing he could read her features. "Really? You'd do that?"

"Of course. Although right now, I don't think my recommendation is going to help your cause much."

"This scandal must seem pretty awful at the moment, but I'm sure it'll pass in time. People have short attention spans."

"You sound like my agent."

"Must be a smart guy."

He felt, more than saw, her responding smile. "I hope you're right."

thirteen

After Mia finished breakfast she continued reading her grandmother's journal. The small deliberate script was easy to read, as was her natural style of writing. Mostly she wrote about their guests, about her husband, about the daily life of an innkeeper. She obviously cared about people and even seemed to grow attached to her guests.

Although she had a positive attitude, there was an underlying sadness to her entries that Mia couldn't put her finger on. Maybe her estranged relationship with her daughter? She hadn't mentioned Katherine at all, but maybe it was too depressing to even journal about.

The page blurred as Mia's thoughts turned to Levi and their late-night conversation. He'd opened up a little, and that felt good.

Her offer to endorse the inn had been spontaneous. She hadn't realized it would mean so much until she heard the hope in his voice. The memory of his reaction made her uneasy. Was he only being kind in hopes of getting something in return? He was personally invested in this inn, after all. More on his parents' behalf than his own, but still. It was reason for caution.

"Got you hooked, has she?"

Mia jumped as Levi appeared at her side. She closed the journal. "I'm only a little ways in, but I'm really enjoying it. It's like getting a peek inside my grandmother's mind."

"She seems like she was a special woman."

Mia tucked the journal into her purse. "I wish I'd had the chance to know her, but she died before I was born."

"That's unfortunate." His eyes raked her form. "You're dressed to hike."

"I'd love it, if you have time to drive me."

His eyes smiled. She'd never known blue could look so warm. "At your service."

She stood, feeling the stretch from having sat on the wooden chair so long. "I need the exercise. And the change of scenery."

"All right." He started through the French doors. "Need anything from your room before we go?"

"I'm all set." She put her sunglasses in place and tugged the brim of her cap down. Overly cautious was better than careless and caught.

She followed Levi out the door, which he locked behind them. Halfway to the car she bit her lip. After their talk last night, sitting in the back seat seemed silly. He was sort of a friend, albeit a short-term one.

When he reached out to open the back door, she set her hand on his arm. Warm flesh stretched tautly over hard muscle.

She drew her hand away. "Do you mind if I ride up front with you?"

"Of course not."

"It just—it seems silly to ride in the back like you're my chauffeur or something."

"Whatever you want." He reached for the passenger door.

A moment later he got in on the driver's side, seeming to shrink the sedan in half. There was only a narrow console separating them.

She shook away the thought. "Where are you taking me today?"

"I guess that depends on how adventurous you're feeling." He spared her a smile as they pulled out onto the street.

"That sounds like a challenge . . ."

He chuckled, a deep, rich sound that made her insides twist. "We can stick to the touristy trails if you prefer, but there are some lesser-known ones outside the state park. There's another waterfall—not as big as Lone Creek Falls, so it's usually overlooked. It dries up in late summer, but this time of year it's nice, and sometimes you can get a glimpse of wildlife up there. The trail's not marked well, so it's easy to take a wrong turn, but I brought a map."

She gave him a wry grin, appreciating his nice profile. "I'm not exactly known for being good with maps. I get lost in public parks. It's too bad though. Sounds really pretty." She bit her lip, feeling uncharacteristically shy. "Unless . . ."

"Unless . . . ?" he prompted when the silence dragged on.

She shook her head. "I was going to ask if you wanted to come along. But you're not really dressed for it. And anyway, that's not part of your job. I'll just take a different trail. There are plenty to choose from."

"I don't mind coming along. In fact, I'd actually feel better about it. You really shouldn't hike alone on deserted trails. As you discovered last time, reception isn't good up in the mountains."

She glanced down at his khakis and boat shoes. "Are you sure you don't mind?"

"Not at all. It's not that hot." He tossed her a smile. "Besides, now I can pass up the gym today—at least the cardio part."

Levi told himself he was just being a good host. He told himself again as he took Mia's hand to help her over a wet gully. And when he steadied her as she climbed over a fallen tree.

It wasn't too hard to convince himself. After all, even though this wasn't normally a part of his job, Mia wasn't the average guest. She—or rather, her fiancé—had paid a lot of money to make sure the staff of the inn were at her beck and call. Entertaining her was part of making sure she enjoyed her stay. And after she'd promised an endorsement, how could he do anything else?

They climbed steadily upward through the thick woods. He'd let her take the lead, wanting to be as unobtrusive as possible. The path was trampled down but not covered with mulch or gravel like the well-known trails. This was actually a deer trail, leading to Lone Creek. He held tree limbs for her, ducking under low-hanging branches. The woods were thick with pines, the ground beginning to level out.

"So what kind of wildlife do you have around here?"

"Let's see . . ." They'd been mostly quiet so far, enjoying the scenery. "We have raccoons, groundhogs, deer, wild turkey, black bear, bobcats—"

She stopped so suddenly he almost slammed into her back. He steadied her with hands on her sides as she whipped around. Her green eyes were wide, her pupils large in the shadowed forest.

"Bears? You're just now telling me you have bears?"

"We're in the mountains, Mia."

"I'm a city girl. What do I know about mountains? Or bears?"

His lips twitched. "We're fine. That's why we've been making plenty of noise—to avoid surprising them. If we come upon one, we just slowly back away. Bottom line, they're more afraid of us than we are of them."

"Speak for yourself."

"They're rarely even sighted. There's no need to be afraid—unless there's a cub present."

Her eyes widened even more. "What do we do then?"

"Get the heck out of Dodge."

She elbowed him. "Why didn't you tell me this before? I was hiking alone!"

He couldn't hold back the smile. "You were on a public trail before. They tend to stay away from people."

"Have you ever seen one?"

"Couple of times. And look . . . I'm still alive to talk about it. Relax. You should probably be more concerned about the rattlesnakes."

"Rattlesnakes!"

He chuckled at the adorable look on her face. "Didn't you read that pamphlet I gave you?"

"I guess I misplaced it."

Something scuttled in the underbrush.

Mia squealed, all but leaping into his arms. "What is it? Is it a snake? Be careful!"

"Mia. It's a squirrel."

"Are you sure? How do you know?"

He laughed. "See it? Right there?"

"Oh. Yeah." She looked back at him and seemed to realize she was practically hanging from his neck. One hand grasping his shirt, one knee tucked up against his stomach where he'd caught it.

She gave a sheepish laugh as she disentangled her limbs. "Whoops. Guess I got a little spooked. My heart is beating so fast right now."

Hers wasn't the only one. "See how much more fun it is hiking with someone?"

"You mean more terrifying?"

"I've lived here most of my life, and I know how to handle myself. I wouldn't let any harm come to you."

"Great, well . . . maybe you can just take the lead then."

"Happy to." He squeezed around her on the narrow path, pausing to pull a leaf from her ponytail. His eyes met hers. "You have a great laugh, by the way."

Levi set off on the trail again, wincing.

You have a great laugh? She's going to think you're hitting on her.

Never mind that she'd just been in his arms. Never mind how good she'd felt against him. Or how reluctant he'd been to let her go.

But the look in her eyes when he'd said it. The way they'd warmed. The way her face had softened just before he cleared his throat and passed by. When a man got a reaction like that, it only made him want to do it again.

fourteen

By the time Mia heard the rush of water she was out of breath, and sweat beaded on the back of her neck. She and Levi broke through the dense forest. A small waterfall plummeted into a shallow creek that was about thirty feet wide.

"Here we are." Levi walked to the edge where the grassy bank flowed right into the water.

Rocks poked up through the shallows like turtlebacks, the water flowing by, heading to the lake somewhere down the line. The air was heavy with the fresh scent of pine.

"This is pretty. And so peaceful. What is it about rippling water?" Mia sat on the bank and pulled off her tennis shoes.

"Makes you want to take a nap, doesn't it?"

She took off her socks and pulled up her leggings to her knees. "Feels great," she said as she stepped into the water, which was deliciously cool. She began picking her way across the rocks. "Aren't you getting in?"

"In a minute. Hey, be careful, those rocks are—"

Mia's foot slipped. She squeaked.

"Mia!"

Her foot hit the water, found purchase on the

mushy bottom. Her ankle turned out with the weight, and she gasped at the pain.

Levi was there in an instant. He took her elbow, a frown creasing his brow. "You all right?"

"Your shoes . . ."

"Are you hurt?"

She shifted her weight, wincing. "I think I might've twisted my ankle."

"Can you walk on it?"

She put a bit of weight on the foot. Pain shot up her leg again, and she sucked in a breath. "I—I don't think so."

"Here, let's do this." He swept her up in his arms as if she weighed nothing.

She grabbed onto him. "I can't believe I did this. What if I can't walk back?"

"Slow down. You might've just wrenched it." He set her on a mossy log and knelt down by her foot. He ran his fingers gently along her ankle.

It was really throbbing now.

"It's already starting to swell," he said.

"It hurts pretty bad."

He looked up at her. "You should get an X-ray just to be safe."

"I'm not going to a hospital. I don't want to take that risk."

He nodded thoughtfully. "Well . . . I have a buddy who's an EMT. He could probably stop by the house."

"That would be great. But . . . how am I going

to get back down? You can't carry me all that way, Levi."

"Sure I can. We'll take it slow."

She tilted her head, giving him a skeptical look. She might be thin, but at five foot ten she was no lightweight.

"See, I'm going to have to prove myself now."

Her laugh was pinched off by the throbbing in her ankle.

He looked down and brushed the side of her foot. "It's starting to bruise. We'd better get you back."

Levi grabbed her shoes, stuffed her socks inside, then tied the shoestrings together. He draped them around his neck, then squatted in front of the log, his back to her. "Hop on, gimpy."

Clinging to Levi's back, Mia gritted her teeth against the pain in her ankle. She knew without looking it was swollen and bruised. She couldn't wait to get back to the house, where she kept a couple painkillers in her purse.

Levi had been trudging carefully along the trail for fifteen or twenty minutes, his arms locked around her knees. But even at this pace the movement jostled her ankle.

"I knew I was supposed to be your transportation this week, but this is taking things a little far." He sounded winded.

Of course he was. He was carrying her down

a *mountain.* "I'm so sorry. This definitely goes above and beyond."

"I aim to please."

"I'm such a klutz."

"Those rocks are slick as ice. Should've warned you."

She thought of the last four days and gave a dry laugh. "What a week. I've been publicly maligned, betrayed by a so-called friend, taken a honeymoon alone, and sprained my ankle. That takes a special kind of talent. Good thing the paparazzi aren't around. I can see the headlines now: 'Mia Emerson, distraught from rejection, tries to drown herself in creek, winds up in hospital.'"

He chuckled. "Or 'Emma Taylor, in jealous rage, pushes Mia Emerson down stairs.'"

"Oh no, America's sweetheart would never do such a thing." She winced at her bitter tone. "Sorry, that was harsh. This isn't Emma's fault."

He paused to hitch her weight up.

"Do you need to stop and rest? Your back must be killing you. Not to mention your arms." Although they felt pretty darn nice, she had to admit. He wasn't big and bulky, but he was strong and solid with capable broad shoulders.

"I'm all right for now. I'm just glad you weren't up there alone. And it could be worse; at least it's downhill, huh?"

"I didn't take you for such a Polly Positive."

He huffed. "Molly must be rubbing off on me. I'm usually the pragmatic one."

"That's something we have in common then. And where does Grace fall? Is she a pessimist? Sorry, you should probably save your breath for important things like surviving."

"Yeah, Grace is more of a pessimist—and I can actually use the distraction."

"From the pain of carrying me down a mountain on your back?"

He chuckled. "You do realize I'm the envy of every guy in America right now. You could sell tickets."

She laughed. "Oh, you flatterer, you."

"It's the truth, and you know it. How does it feel to be so well loved?"

"A little creepy sometimes, actually. And let's be honest. It's not really me they love, just their idea of who they think I am or who they want me to be. That's not love. They have no idea who I really am."

"And who are you, Mia Emerson?"

He'd certainly picked right up where they'd left off last night. Then again, she was riding on his back. And maybe he was too distracted by his physical efforts to weigh his words carefully.

"I think," she said, "that's something you only learn by spending time with a person."

"True enough. I've only had a few days to form an opinion, but so far I'd say you're strong, resilient, and down-to-earth—for a Hollywood type." The last part was said in a teasing tone.

Warmth flooded her at his complimentary assessment. She didn't always feel so strong and resilient. "You forgot clumsy."

"Trying to be nice. How's your ankle?"

"Not great. I guess I need a distraction too. Do you think your friend will be able to see me right away?"

"Unless he's out on a call. He's actually a mechanic by trade, but he's also a volunteer on the fire department."

"Known him all your life?"

"Pretty much. He was the one who called when my parents had the accident." He paused to shift her weight and gave his head a shake before starting off again. "Don't know why I just told you that."

She didn't either, but she liked that he was opening up to her. "It must've been a terrible shock."

A moment passed before he answered. "It was. I was home for a week to visit. Mom and Dad had an estate sale they wanted to go to—they were buying things for the inn—but Mom didn't want to take time away from our visit. I encouraged them to go."

"Oh, Levi." Her heart ached for him. "I hope you don't blame yourself."

"How can I not, to a certain degree? I know—

everything happens for a reason, and God has His reasons, and He calls us home when He wants to. Believe me, I've heard all the platitudes."

"I'm sorry." She tightened her arms around his shoulders and leaned her head against his, as much of a hug as she could give him at the moment.

"Thanks. But maybe we could talk about something else. Like . . . what's next for you? Your next role?"

"I'm shooting a film called *Lesser Days* starting in late July. It's a relationship drama with some strong female leads."

"Is that what attracted you to it?"

"That and the fact that it's the role of my dreams. It's a multigenerational thing. Really good script. I sure hope this ankle heals up in time."

He brushed too close to a tree, and her foot caught on the trunk. She sucked in a breath.

"I'm so sorry." He paused, looking over his shoulder. "You all right?"

"I'm fine. You must need a break by now." Her own arms were aching.

He looked around. "I think there's a log up ahead. We'll take a little break there."

He marched on, ducking low under branches, careful to shield her foot. When they reached the fallen tree, he lowered her onto it and straightened, shelving his hands on his hips.

"Better prop that foot. It must be throbbing."

She set it on the log. It had swollen more and turned bright red around the ankle.

"Here." He extended his water bottle, which he'd tucked into one of her shoes. "You can have the rest."

Her mouth was dry, but there was only an inch or so left in the bottle, and he'd just hiked all this way, carrying her.

"I'm okay. You can have it."

"You need to stay hydrated. Drink up."

She reluctantly did as he suggested. When she was finished he took the empty bottle and stuffed it back into her shoe.

"What kind of preparation do you do before you film? Other than memorizing your lines, of course."

"Depends on the role. For the last one I had to learn how to use a firearm, so I took lessons. It took a while to get comfortable with it—to look comfortable."

"And for the next one?"

"I do a lot of physical labor, so I need to be in shape, and I need to stay slim. It's set in Ireland, so I've been working on my Irish brogue."

"Let's hear it."

She cleared her throat, got into character, and rattled off one of her favorite lines from the movie.

He listened intently, and when she was finished he chuckled. "That was really good."

She beamed. "Thanks. I worked on it with a dialect coach back home."

"I'm impressed. What do you do back home, when you're not filming a movie or preparing for a role?"

"Oh, let's see, there's premieres and speaking engagements. Sometimes I make appearances. I also have a 'little sister' named Ana Marie. She's eleven and a real cutie."

"I'll bet she's completely starstruck."

Mia laughed. "Not at all. She keeps me quite humble, in fact."

"Well, I think it's great that you give back." Levi looked down the trail, then at her. "You ready to hit it?"

"Whenever you are."

fifteen

After a brief conversation at the front door, Levi thanked Erik and let him out. Fortunately his friend hadn't seemed to recognize Mia. He had, however, given Levi a raised brow at having such an attractive guest under his roof.

Levi glanced up the stairs, wondering where his sisters had gotten off to. Was anyone even around to answer phone calls?

He went back into the living room. Mia was reclined on the sofa, her foot propped on a pillow with a cold pack, waiting for her medication to kick in. She'd taken off her cap, and her ponytail was askew, her face fallen.

"At least it's not broken," he said.

"Four to six weeks—why do I have to be such a klutz?"

He rounded the couch. She looked cute when she pouted, her lush lower lip turned out just a bit.

"You'll be on your feet in a couple days. We need to get you a pair of crutches until then. Too bad your room's upstairs. Maybe I could switch with you. Mine's pretty small though, and when Miss Della starts breakfast in the morning, your sleep is pretty much over."

She met his eyes. "That's sweet of you, but I think I'll just stay put."

"At least you'll be off the crutches by the time you leave." A sound of the door opening pulled Levi's gaze.

Molly was home. She caught sight of Levi standing beside the couch, then Mia, sprawled on it, foot propped.

"Oh no, what happened?" Molly rushed over. "Is that why Erik was here? What's wrong?"

"Mia took a little fall up on the trails," Levi said. "She's going to be fine though."

"I'm so sorry. How bad is it?"

Mia filled her in on the details, and Molly made a fuss over her, fluffing pillows and bringing her a glass of fresh lemonade. She thought she knew someone who had crutches that would work for Mia and promised to check.

When Molly was finished mother-henning, she turned to Levi. "Can we talk if you have a minute?"

"Sure." He looked at Mia. "I'll be right back."

Levi headed to the front porch, where they could talk in private.

Molly pulled the door closed behind her and took a seat on the swing, a serious expression on her face.

He wondered if she was going to chastise him about all the time he was spending with Mia. He had a list of excuses at the ready. Plus, who was Molly to talk?

138

"Will you sit down?" Molly said. "You're making me nervous."

Levi took a seat and regarded his sister silently. She was biting her lip, making it twist.

Then she took a deep breath and let it out. "I think it's time we expand in the restaurant area. I know. I know. We'd need extra licensing and all that, but we can handle it, and I think it would be worth it in terms of guest satisfaction. We might even be losing customers because we have no way of feeding them in-house. And you know how businesses are around here. Sometimes it's tough to even find a restaurant open off-season or when it's storming or when the owner feels a headache coming on."

It was true, and he'd taken that up with the Better Business Bureau. It was hard enough to draw guests without the mom-and-pop places closing shop on a whim. But so far he'd gotten nowhere.

"You aren't wrong. But we have to consider the bottom line."

"It was always the plan to add a dinner menu. I've already talked to Miss Della and—"

"You what?"

"She said she's on board. She said she'd actually welcome the extra hours."

Yeah, if only we could afford to pay her. He scowled at Molly. "You shouldn't have gone to Miss Della. This is between us. And we said we'd expand when the bottom line allows for it."

She huffed. "Well, we're doing fine, aren't we?"

No. No they weren't. Levi ran his hand over his face. "It's not the right time for this, Molly."

"It's what Mom and Dad planned. They were going to open with a full restaurant. I know I agreed to wait, but we've been open a year and we're not even offering a full breakfast. I think it's time to expand our menu."

"This is my area of expertise, not yours. Let's see how this season goes. And then maybe next spring—"

"Next spring!"

"What's going on?"

He hadn't even heard Grace pull up. His eyes narrowed on the sister who was supposed to have been covering the inn all morning. "Where've you been?"

"Out boating with Sarah." She exchanged a look with Molly. "Sheesh. What's his problem?"

"My problem is nobody's treating this place like a business. I know we're on lock-down this week, but we can't all just be leaving willy-nilly. Somebody needs to be here to answer calls and take reservations while I'm shuttling our guest around." He nailed Grace with a look. "And how are those college apps coming along?"

Grace's spine lengthened. "I haven't had time to work on them."

"Yet you have time to go boating with Sarah? You could've been finished by now if you'd just buckled down."

Her jaw set. "That's the last thing I want to do right now. I just finished finals. I need time to decompress."

"You mean procrastinate. You promised to do it this week, Grace, just like you've been promising since the fall. You're running out of time."

"I'm nineteen. I can handle my own future."

"Apparently not. It's June, Grace, and you don't even know where you're going to college. All of your friends are already enrolled, aren't they?"

"Just leave me alone, Levi!" Grace spun on her heels, heading inside.

"I'd love to do that, Grace," he called after her, "if you'd just get with the program."

The door slammed behind her, and he could practically hear her stomping up the stairs from the porch. He closed his eyes and blew out a breath. If everyone would just pull their weight around here maybe he wouldn't be feeling so much pressure.

That familiar band had tightened around his head, and he massaged the back of his skull where a headache throbbed.

"Don't you think that was a little harsh?" Molly asked.

"Come on, Molly, you know she's been putting this off for months."

Molly stood, the swing moving behind her with a squawk. "Maybe there's a good reason for that, brother."

His gaze sharpened on Molly. "Do you know something? Has she said anything to you? She's going to college and that's that."

Molly turned at the door. "I don't know anything—except that maybe we should be asking questions instead of making demands."

Levi frowned after her. Sure, that sounded simple. Grace was a smart and capable girl, but she was only nineteen. What did she know about real life? He knew she had no interest in working at the inn long term, and the only jobs she'd had were babysitting and the Dairy Bar.

Their parents had encouraged all of them to get degrees, and if they were here they'd be urging Grace to finish those applications. He had to look out for his sister, even if she didn't want him to. That was part of being a parent—and he had to face it. That's more or less what he'd become when their parents died.

A text buzzed in, and he checked his phone. It was Molly's boyfriend, Adam, asking if Levi would be around later that evening. He responded in the affirmative. He couldn't imagine Mia would want to go anywhere tonight. He should probably go check—and maybe grab some painkillers for himself.

He slipped into the house, locking the door behind him. When he rounded the couch he saw Mia lying just as she'd been when he'd slipped out. But now her eyes were closed, her lips parted. She didn't stir even as he covered her with a throw.

sixteen

Molly entered Firehouse Coffee, scanning the place for her best friend, Skye. She drew in the wondrous aroma of java and artificial stimulation. What more could a girl ask for?

She was running a little early for a change. She'd been annoyed with Levi and wanted to get out of the house. He could be so bossy—and he was such a bean counter! She understood the need to turn a profit, but things were fine. She wished he'd just relax about the money already.

She stepped up to the counter and ordered an iced latte for herself and a green tea for Skye, making small talk with the baristas. Drinks in hand, she found some comfy chairs on the patio.

The old fire station had been renovated into a coffee shop several years ago. On nice days the old doors were rolled up, creating an open-air environment. It was a popular place for locals and tourists alike.

"You beat me," Skye said with surprise. She was obviously fresh from her yoga/dance studio, her leggings and snug T-shirt showing off a lithe figure.

"Miracles never cease." Molly allowed herself a moment's jealousy of Skye's toned muscles. Then again, the woman basically worked out all day and subsisted on organic squirrel food. Not worth it. Molly took a sip of her cinnamon roll latte, taking delight in its spicy-sweet flavor.

Skye scooted closer to the table and took a sip of her tea. "Thanks. This hits the spot. What's it going to cost me?"

Molly gave her a droll look. "A good ten minutes of listening to me whine about Levi."

"I'm sure you have more than that in you."

"I have book club in an hour."

Skye laughed. "So I take it you pitched your idea for the broader menu."

"If you consider me bringing it up and him shooting it down a 'pitch.' "

Skye gave her an empathetic look. "He tends to forget the inn belongs to all three of you, doesn't he?"

"I mean, I know the business stuff is his area of expertise, but he does update us at the monthly snoozefest, and things are going fine."

Skye's brows disappeared beneath her mahogany bangs. "And you're actually awake for these meetings?"

"Maybe my eyes glaze over at the mere mention of a spreadsheet, but I can read the bottom line easily enough. A full-service restaurant was part of our parents' dream. It would expand the services we offer our guests and maybe even draw in more. I don't see why he's being so stubborn about this."

"What reason does he give for holding off?"

"Just the same old story—the profits, the extra staff, blah, blah, blah. He's such a penny-pincher. I bought a bunch of new towels so we wouldn't have to do same-day washings—and I got a good deal on them too. He made me send them back! I wanted to go with a new luxury line of soaps, and he put the nix on that too. It wasn't even that much more than what we're using."

They talked a while longer about the situation. Skye suggested that Molly start with a smaller request, like a made-to-order breakfast, and work up to a dinner menu. Baby steps. Her friend was good with conflict resolution, so Molly took her advice seriously. She wasn't giving up.

When they'd exhausted the topic, she asked Skye about her love life, which her friend described as deadly dull to nonexistent, so talk turned to the yoga studio. Skye regaled her with stories that had Molly spewing coffee at one point.

Finally, she brought up the real reason she'd asked Skye to meet for coffee today. "So . . . I do have some exciting news to share."

Skye leaned forward. "Whatever it is has your eyes sparkling like Bluebell Lake on a summer day."

Molly drained the last of her iced latte, drawing out the moment. Torturing Skye was always fun.

"Miss Nonnie had her hair done at the Hair Lair the other day by Patty Burkes."

Skye gave Molly a searching look. "Aaaand . . ."

"Patty's daughter, LeeAnne, works at the Crow's Nest."

"I know . . . She's a hostess."

"Yes, and she takes reservations." Molly gave her a pointed look. "And *someone's* boyfriend made reservations for two, a week from this Friday."

"Oooh . . . that'll be nice. You should wear your red sundress. I love that on you."

Molly quirked a brow. "He asked for the best seat in the house—the corner booth for two right by the window. And he said"—Molly emphasized the words—"that it's a *special occasion.*"

Understanding registered in Skye's expression. Her lips curled coyly. "I take it this is not a birthday celebration."

"His birthday is in February. But it is the anniversary of a certain first kiss."

Skye pressed her palm to her heart. "The one in the boat in the pouring rain? Be still my heart. That one still gets me, and I wasn't even the recipient."

Molly leaned forward. "I think this is it, Skye. He's going to propose."

Skye squealed and grabbed Molly's hand. "I think you're right. I'm so excited for you."

"I know. I can hardly believe it. We haven't

been dating that long, but I've never been so sure of anything. And he's so romantic—of course he'd pick the anniversary of a special moment. It's just like him."

"You're so lucky. He's wonderful. And he's good for you too—so level-headed and thoughtful."

"He is all that and more. He still writes me love notes. I've saved every one."

"You lucky dog. Meanwhile I'm subsisting on a steady diet of 'Hey' guys on Instagram."

Molly laughed. "You should totally go out with Levi. I keep telling you."

"You also keep telling me what a pain in the rump he is!"

"Oh, you know I love him. He has a lot of good qualities too. I may take those for granted. But he's solid, dependable, and he has an actual plan for his life."

"Yes, a plan that puts him squarely back in Denver as soon as possible. No thanks. Besides, I've never viewed him as anything but a friend, and I'm pretty sure he feels the same."

Molly considered that. As much as she'd like her best friend and brother to hook up, it seemed someone else had caught his eye. "I think he's got the hots for our new guest anyway. It seems like he's with her all the time."

"The honeymoon woman?"

"That's the one." It was killing her to keep quiet about Mia's identity, but she'd promised.

148

"Isn't she fresh off a heartbreak?"

Molly shrugged. "I think the wedding was canceled a while back."

Skye's eyes suddenly lit up. "Before long you'll be planning *your* wedding."

Molly squealed. "I know! I can hardly believe it. Do you think he's gotten the ring yet?"

"I'm sure he has. It's probably a zillion carats!"

"I don't care about that. I just want to be his."

"Spoken like a true romantic. You guys are perfect for each other."

Molly squeezed her hand. "I'm hoping both you and Grace will agree to be my maids of honor . . . ?"

Skye's eyes went glossy. "I'd be honored. You're the best friend ever, Molly. This is going to be so amazing. I can give the two of you dance classes so your first dance is like a dream."

"I'd love that!" Molly would have to do some real talking to get Adam to agree, but she thought she could pull it off. "I don't know how I'm going to wait more than a week. This is going to be torture."

"One day at a time."

Molly checked her watch. "I've got to run. Hey, didn't you read *Where the Crawdads Sing*? I don't suppose I can talk you into book club?"

Skye laughed. "You're still calling it that? You're the only one who reads the books."

"The others read the books. Sometimes." Molly

made a face. Mostly the hour consisted of the ladies gossiping while Molly tried to drag them back on subject.

Skye pushed back from the table. "Yeah, I think I'll pass this time. But good luck with that."

seventeen

The dull throbbing in Mia's ankle awakened her. The sun had shifted, giving way to indirect lighting. She peeked at her foot. The cold pack was gone, and someone had covered her with a quilt.

Levi. Her lips softened into a smile as a warm, fuzzy feeling flooded through her.

A phone rang in the lobby, and she heard Levi's low voice as he answered the call, even though the pocket doors between the rooms were closed. She recalled the way he'd carried her down the trail this morning. It seemed almost like a dream now. But the throbbing in her ankle assured her it was not.

What was she going to do if it didn't heal in time for filming? There was no way she was passing up this role.

She reached for her own phone, checking the texts that had come in. She responded to Ana Maria's first, then others from Brooke and Nolan. There was apparently a Where's Mia? meme going around that mimicked the old Where's Waldo game. They were also having a little fun with the acronym for "missing in action." #MIA was apparently trending. These people needed to get lives.

She ignored the other texts, mostly from seemingly concerned acquaintances. It was hard to know which of them were genuine and which were prodding for gossip they could share with their friends or, worse, the media. The world she came from wasn't exactly an authentic one. Was it any wonder she had trust issues? This place she'd landed in, Bluebell, seemed to have authentic people in spades—and she'd only met a few of them.

She closed her eyes and focused on Levi's deep voice. He was apparently still on that phone call. A customer or something more personal? He hadn't said anything about a current girlfriend, but then she'd only asked if he'd left one behind in Denver.

That was the last thing she should be dwelling on. She needed something else to keep her occupied, or the next few days were going to drag. There was always her grandmother's journal. And if she had to lie low for a while, she had the ideal situation for it: a quiet inn, a flexible schedule, and abundant help.

The door slid open, and Levi appeared. "You're awake. Let me get that cold pack for you."

He returned in a couple minutes with a fresh glass of lemonade as well. "How's the ankle feeling?"

"Better. The painkillers helped."

He set the cold pack on her ankle and met her gaze. "How's that?"

The soft lighting made the most of his features,

deepening his eyes to the color of the ocean. She'd seen worse-looking men in starring roles. "You have a face for film, you know."

He gave a half smile that only proved her point. "No thanks."

She'd been thinking that since they'd met, but she hadn't meant to tell him. "Painkillers make me a little loopy."

He tucked the blanket around her foot, then sat on the coffee table opposite her. "And sleepy, apparently."

"That too. Have you ever done any acting?"

"Not unless you count my third-grade portrayal of Abraham Lincoln."

Her lips twitched as she envisioned him in a tall black hat with a fake beard. "I'll bet you were a real cutie. You probably had all the little girls wrapped around your finger."

"Nah," he said. "They were most impressed with my mad math skills."

"What were you like as a kid? Was your upbringing as wonderful as I'm imagining?"

"Sure, it was pretty great. What was I like? I don't know, I guess a lot like I am now. Just shorter and with less body hair."

She smiled lazily. "The oldest child is often a natural leader. They tend to be independent achievers. I study these things for roles I play."

"I'd say that's a pretty accurate assessment. My sisters would add 'uptight' and 'bossy.' "

"See, that's what wrong with being an only child—no one to boss around."

"Was it lonely, being an only—when you weren't playing with make-believe siblings?"

"Sometimes. Yes, often, actually."

"No neighborhood kids to pal around with?"

She gave a wry laugh, thinking of the gated community and the rolling acres surrounded by high brick walls. "It wasn't really that type of neighborhood."

"What about your parents? Did they play with you?"

"My mom really wasn't like that. My dad left when I was five."

"Must've been hard."

Her dad had left so easily, it had seemed. And here was Levi, staying with his sisters, putting his own dreams on hold until they'd settled into adulthood. She could only admire such loyalty and devotion. Not only that, but Levi was clearly a hard worker, steady and dependable. When a person's childhood lacked those traits, they came to mean a lot.

"I barely remember my dad," she said. "If I asked my mom about him she'd give me the silent treatment, so after a while I stopped asking. She was angry with him for leaving, I guess." Man, she was like a bubbling fountain today.

Levi gave her an empathetic smile. "That's too bad."

"I've never told anyone that—not even the counselor my mom sent me to as a teenager."

"Why not?"

"I don't know. I guess I can be a pretty private person. It's hard to know who to trust in this business."

"I'm sure it is. I'm glad you feel you can trust me."

She gave him a long, steady look. She did, she realized. At least, more than she usually trusted people. She wasn't sure why. Or even if it was smart. But she couldn't seem to help opening up to him. It was like this place had cast some kind of spell on her.

She grasped the quilt, feeling snug despite her throbbing ankle. "Thanks for covering me up earlier."

His voice was rough as his eyes pierced hers. "You're welcome."

Her honesty seemed to have deepened the intimacy between them. A pleasant fluttery sensation bubbled in her stomach.

She pulled the quilt up to her chin. "I don't know what I'm going to do about my career."

"What does your agent say?"

"He thinks we should wait it out a bit."

"Why not do an interview like Jax did? You have the truth on your side—surely that'll come through on camera."

"It'll also feed the beast. Nolan thinks it would

155

be better to let it die down. Also, going public would further pit me against Jax, and he has a lot of fans. More than I do. Nolan knows what he's doing. He's been in the business a long time."

Levi leaned forward, elbows on knees. There was something about his eyes that drew her. They had so many looks: calm as the deep blue sea; twinkling with humor and crinkled at the corners; and as she'd seen him up at the falls, filled with concern.

They talked about the business a bit, and he shared about running the inn. He entertained her with guest stories. Some of them funny, others, like the couple who'd come to the lake to spread their son's ashes, more poignant.

Her ice pack had long since warmed to room temperature when a knock came at the front door. Grace was still upstairs, and Molly had left a while ago, so Levi jumped up to answer it.

Levi opened the door, prepared to turn away a potential guest. The vacancy sign wasn't always enough. He blinked at the sight of Adam standing on the porch, then remembered he'd asked to come by this evening.

"Adam, come on in." He glanced at his watch, surprised to see it was almost six.

"Hi, Levi." Adam spotted Mia on the couch. "Hello."

"Hi there," she said.

Levi diverted his attention. "I'll grab us some drinks and meet you out back?"

"Sure."

Levi grabbed the cold pack, returning it to the freezer, and promised he'd go for takeout in a while. He made sure Mia was comfortable before joining Adam on the back lawn.

Molly's boyfriend came by every so often just to chat. He was new to the area and didn't have any siblings. His best friend—and agent—Jordan lived in New York, so Levi was probably the closest thing he had to a friend in Bluebell. They didn't have much in common, but what Adam lacked in conversational skills he more than made up for with his sincerity and intellect.

The day was winding down, only one boat out on the lake, the sun low in the sky. A squirrel nattered from a nearby tree, and the smell of freshly cut grass hung heavily in the air, reminding Levi that it was time to mow again.

He handed Adam one of the cans and sank into the Adirondack chair. "Molly at book club?"

"Yes. They were reading *Where the Crawdads Sing*, though in all fairness, Molly's probably the only one who finished it."

"It's not really about the book, you know," Levi said.

"I gathered as much. She keeps begging me to go with her."

Levi chuckled. He'd bet the old biddies would love that.

"Yeah, that's not happening. Even if I have already read the book."

"Did you mention that to Molly?"

"She didn't ask."

Levi laughed again. He liked to read, but his sister was a total book nerd. Stood to reason she'd hook up with another one, an author no less.

A moment of silence passed as they enjoyed their cold drinks. A breeze came off the lake, fluttering the leaves overhead and cooling his skin. His headache lingered, but it wasn't as bad as it had been earlier.

Adam shifted in his seat.

Levi was starting to sense he had something on his mind. Adam was always a little awkward, but he seemed even more so today. Levi wondered if everything was all right between him and Molly. His sister didn't really talk to him about guy stuff—for which he was grateful.

Or maybe it had to do with his family. Adam hadn't really opened up about that, but Levi knew he was close to his mom and gathered he hadn't had the best relationship with his dad.

Adam cleared his throat. "So, um, listen, Levi . . . I wanted to talk to you about something."

His intuition had been spot-on. He held back a smug grin. "Sure, what is it?"

"Well . . . it's about Molly." He shoved his glasses up with a finger.

"Everything all right?"

"What? Oh, yes. Everything's good. Great, actually." A flush crawled up his neck and into his cheeks. "We're coming up on an anniversary in a couple weeks."

Levi gave him a questioning look. "You didn't get together till August or September, right?"

"August, yes, but this is more—it's an anniversary of, well, our first kiss."

"Say no more." *Please. Say no more.*

They'd first kissed mid-June of last year? Levi wasn't sure what had gone on between June and August to delay progress. He supposed he could read all about it in Adam's new book if he wanted. And he definitely didn't.

"Right." Adam cleared his throat again. "Well, so that was a beginning, of sorts. And we've come a long way in the past ten months, obviously."

"Sure, sure."

"I guess what I'm trying to say, and not very articulately, is that your sister has come to mean a great deal to me. I'm sure you realize I'm in love with her—and she with me. We're in love with each other."

"Well, sure." Levi shifted in his seat, the heat of the sun making a sweat break out on his skin.

"With your parents gone and you being her older brother, for whom she has a great deal of respect, I wanted to ask you . . . I'd like to ask Molly to marry me. I'd like to ask if I have your blessing on that."

Levi's mouth parted as he stared back. Adam's words whipped through his mind. Maybe this shouldn't seem like such a curveball, but it did. It seemed so fast. Maybe Adam had kissed Molly a year ago, but they hadn't gotten together until months later.

"I can see I've caught you off guard."

"No, not—" Who was he kidding? He gave a wry laugh. "Well, yeah, actually. I guess you have."

"Do you, um, have concerns about me? I guess I wouldn't blame you. I wasn't honest with Molly last summer. But that's not who I am. Molly and I have done a lot of talking, and I've been very careful to—"

"It's not you, Adam. I mean, yes, that was a concern initially, but I can see that's not who you are."

"Then what is it? Do you have concerns about the two of us together?"

"No, that's not—it just seems kind of sudden. I wasn't expecting this."

"We've been together since August. That was ten months ago."

"Right, right. But you had a long-distance relationship until January."

"That's true. And yet, I feel as though I've

known Molly forever. I'm wholly devoted to her, Levi—I want you to know that. There's no one else for me, and I believe she feels the same about me."

"I don't doubt that. And as much as I sometimes like to think I can control Molly's life, she's made it clear that's not my place—and she's right. She's an adult, and so are you."

A long, uncomfortable silence hung between them. Levi hated to disappoint Adam, but he didn't see what the big rush was. Ten months was nothing. And only five months living in the same town. How could they possibly know each other well enough to commit to a life together?

"But you have reservations . . ." Adam said.

Levi thought about that. What would his dad say if Adam were asking for his blessing? The image of his dad on that gurney in the ambulance was the only thing that came to mind.

Take care of your sisters.

Levi's headache pulsed in his ears. Adam was patiently waiting for a response. "My only reservation is the length of time you've been together. And during that time, Molly's had a lot to deal with—we all have. The trauma of our parents' sudden death hasn't been easy to recover from. Making a go of this inn has been an additional pressure because it's deeply personal to all of us. Add to that, her previous relationship with Dominic messed her up for a while."

"I'm aware." Adam's brows pinched in a frown. "She has been through a lot."

"It's been a lot to process. And falling in love on top of it . . . I just wonder if a little more time might be in order. This is a lifetime commitment you're talking about."

Adam looked crestfallen. "Right."

Levi hated to burst his bubble, but he had to think of what was best for Molly. And he knew without a doubt that more time would be wise. They had the rest of their lives to be married. On the other hand . . .

"As I said though, you're both adults. You have to do what you feel is right."

Adam seemed to gather the disappointment and shove it somewhere deep. His shoulders straightened, and he gave Levi a brave smile. "I value your opinion. It's why I came to ask for your blessing. And if you feel Molly needs more time . . . I'll respect that."

Relief flooded through Levi. He couldn't stand the thought of watching Molly make a huge mistake—not on his watch. He stretched out a hand.

Adam grasped it.

"You're a good man, Adam. A little extra time never hurt anything."

eighteen

Mia's breakfast plate had been cleared for a while. Her foot sat propped in the chair opposite her. Della had fussed over her ankle, bringing a pillow from the living room and tucking the cold pack around it just so. There sure were a lot of caregivers around this place.

She opened up the journal and picked up where she'd left off last night.

August 1957

Dear Diary,

We've been so busy! Lake season is in full swing. Paul and I are two ships in the night lately. But tonight we're going out to celebrate our fifth anniversary. Paul is taking me to the same restaurant he took me to on our honeymoon, and I'm going to wear his beautiful wedding gift, the blue diamond.

I have named my necklace Carolina Breeze. Paul laughs at my silliness, after all the diamond is hardly substantial enough to warrant a name of its own, but it is still rare and precious, all the more so because it was a gift from Paul.

I feel bad for not wearing it more often, but I'm afraid it'll fall right off my neck. When we bought the inn I worried even when it was put away, because we house so many strangers. But Paul finally arranged a safe spot in which to store it, and now I can breathe easy, knowing that Carolina Breeze rests in safety.

Mia read the last entry again. She hadn't misread it—a blue diamond! She was no expert on jewelry, but she knew blue diamonds were rare and valuable. She'd known from previous entries that her grandfather came from an affluent family, but she had no idea he'd been that kind of wealthy.

Mia wondered what had become of the necklace. Her mother hadn't received any of their belongings, so where had they gone? She read the last line of the entry again.

A safe spot. Was it possible the necklace was still here, hidden away in the inn somewhere?

Her heart stuttered at the thought. She was probably getting worked up over nothing. But she had to ask Levi about it. He'd already read the journal. Maybe he knew what had become of the necklace. She momentarily forgot her injured ankle and banged her foot on the chair as she got up, wincing in pain.

She grabbed the crutches and made her way as

quickly as she could through the dining room and foyer.

At the back door, she fumbled with the lock and made her way clumsily down the two steps. The roar of the mower quickly alerted her to Levi's whereabouts. He was swiping a path toward the neighboring property.

Mia made her way across the patio and down the slope of the lawn. The journal was tucked under her arm, making the crutches even more awkward. Her ankle was pounding, but she was too excited to care.

Levi made a turn at the edge of the property. As he was coming back toward her, he caught sight of her and turned off the mower, removing his earbuds.

He was off the mower and at her side in seconds. "You all right? You should slow down on those things—you don't want to fall again."

"I was reading the journal and came upon the part about the blue diamond necklace. Do you know what happened to it?"

"Come sit down before you fall." Levi took the journal from under her arm and led her back up to the patio.

When they reached the patio he took her crutches. "Have a seat. Let's get your foot propped up."

She did as he said, watching as he grabbed a low table and set it in front of her. "Do you know what happened to the necklace after Dorothy passed away?"

"No idea."

"I know it didn't go to my mom. They were estranged."

"Don't ask me. Before you showed up I thought they didn't even have children. Maybe it went to another relative. Or got pawned."

"Oh, I hope not. Do you have any idea what blue diamonds are worth?"

"I assumed they had the same value as regular diamonds."

"Not at all. They're extremely rare and precious. You've heard of the Hope Diamond?"

"Of course."

"Well, that's a blue diamond. Granted, it's huge, but even a small one would be quite valuable. We have to figure out what happened to it. The entry I just read said Paul made a safe spot for her to tuck it away in. What if it's still in the house, Levi? That would mean it belongs to you."

Surprise registered on Levi's face. He seemed to process that thought for a long moment. "Well, let's see. The Livingstons lived here until they passed away. I think the place was auctioned off after that, and the state's governor purchased it as a summer home."

"But what would've happened to the Livingstons' personal effects?"

Levi shrugged. "Molly might know something.

She's obsessed with the history of this place. Do you need your cold pack? Your ankle looks a little puffier than it did yesterday."

"Forget my ankle, Levi. We have to find that necklace."

He straightened, hands on hips. He wore a baseball cap, and a sheen of sweat made his arms glisten. "Why?"

"Why?" There were lots of reasons, including the tug at her heart to find this little piece of home, this tangible symbol of her roots. But that wasn't the reason she mentioned. "Because it's worth a lot of money to whoever has it. And what if it's still here, Levi?"

Levi was already shaking his head. "This place has been through multiple renovations, Mia. The governor converted it into a house. Then we turned it back into an inn. It's been emptied out a few times over. We've taken down walls and put up new ones. It would've been found."

"Are you sure? Don't you think a blue diamond turning up in Bluebell would be newsworthy enough you would've gotten wind of it?"

He seemed to weigh her words. "That's a good point."

"Is there anything left untouched in the inn? What about an attic?" Maybe she was grasping at straws, but she couldn't help it. She felt like an archaeologist making a rare discovery.

• • •

Levi's eyes slid over Mia's face. Her eyes sparkled with excitement. The tense look she'd worn since she'd arrived was gone. She didn't look tired anymore. She looked . . . alive.

All of this over a lost necklace. It was kind of cute. "You're obsessed," he teased.

She narrowed her eyes at him playfully. "You're not taking me seriously." Mia whipped out her phone and started tapping the screen.

Levi sat down on the chair next to hers. He could only imagine that this was a nice distraction from the messy state of her life right now.

"Here, right here." She shoved the phone under his nose. "Blue diamonds can easily be worth one hundred thousand dollars *per carat*."

Levi read the information, then sat back, blinking. He let himself think about it for just a moment. Let himself dream that Dorothy had tucked the necklace under a secret floor panel somewhere and it could still be there all these years later.

That was about as long as he could push back his pragmatic side. "Chances of it still being here are pretty slim, don't you think? Dorothy had to know the value of that necklace. Wouldn't she have left it to someone in her will?"

"I don't know, but it's at least possible, isn't it?"

"It's probably long gone. And I have no idea how we'd even go about finding out."

She bit her lip, drawing his attention to the pink lushness. She was a beautiful woman, no doubt. And he sure wasn't the first to think it. But he wondered how many had seen her this intent. He could almost see the wheels spinning.

"Is there a way to get hold of that will and find out if someone inherited the necklace?"

"I don't see how. Wills are private, and besides, that was a long time ago."

"Maybe there's a statute of limitations on those records."

"I guess it's possible. The will's probably long gone by now though. There's only one law firm in town, but I'm not sure how long it's been around. I could check on that, I guess."

"Would you?"

The grateful look she gave made him willing to do much more than run downtown and ask a few questions. Did she know the kind of pull she had? He gave his head a shake. What was getting into him? She was a guest. Just a guest.

But her excitement was contagious.

"Sure, I can do that."

Mia shifted forward, closer. He caught a whiff of her soap or shampoo. Something clean and feminine. He drew in a lungful.

"Can you imagine what that kind of money could do for your inn, Levi? For your future?"

He loved that she was so excited for him. But he was afraid to even think about getting that kind of windfall. He didn't like getting his hopes up needlessly. Life didn't just go around handing you priceless treasures. He'd rather focus on the facts and maintain a realistic attitude.

Besides, Dorothy and Paul were Mia's grandparents. Wouldn't that make the necklace an heirloom that belonged to her? "You know, in the event we did find the necklace, it's probably more yours than mine."

She waved him off. "While it might be cool to have something of my grandmother's, if we found it in your house it would rightfully belong to you."

"I appreciate your generous spirit. And your enthusiasm," he told Mia with a smile. "But one thing at a time. Let me check at the law office and see what I can find."

"Can we go today?"

He quirked a brow. "Aren't you afraid of being seen?"

"I can wait in the car." She was already grabbing her crutches.

"You mean now?" He looked back at the Toro.

Her whole body seemed to sink in the chair. "Oh, right. Sorry. You were in the middle of mowing."

He supposed the lawn could wait. "Come on. I'll finish later."

Her bright smile was all the thanks he needed. He helped her to her feet. Her arms were slim but strong, and he found himself reluctant to let her go as she balanced on the crutches.

"You're supposed to be resting that ankle."

"I can rest it in the car," she said with a saucy smile and hobbled away before he could argue.

nineteen

It was taking Levi forever. He'd parked in the shade behind the law firm and left her the keys. Mia put down the window and propped her foot on the dashboard.

Maybe it was good news that it was taking so long. On the other hand, he probably just knew the people inside. Small-town folks often liked to stop and shoot the breeze. Not like in LA, where you passed only strangers on the street, and when you did run into someone you knew, it was all polite smiles and promises of lunches that were never fulfilled.

Mia pulled out the journal and continued reading. Who knew, maybe her grandmother would mention the necklace again. Several entries later, the driver's door opened and Levi slid inside.

Her eyes raked over his face for any clues as to his success. "What did they say?" Mia pulled her foot down from the dashboard.

He started the car and buckled himself in before answering her. "Well, for starters, I was wrong."

"I've never heard that roll off a man's tongue so easily," she said playfully.

He gave her a wry look and adjusted the air conditioning. "Sorry it took so long. I ran into a buddy from high school."

Levi put the car into Drive and pulled from the parking spot.

"Well, don't keep me in suspense," she said. "What did he say?"

"It's good news, actually. Wills do become public after the estate is settled. And they're stored at the clerk's office. Although Robert said with this one being kind of old he didn't know whether they'd still have it on hand. It might take a bit of patience to retrieve it."

"But that's great news! Can we go there next?"

"I'm one step ahead of you. I already called down there, and Connie's looking for the record now. She said it would be in the basement, so she's trying to hunt it down."

Mia could hardly sit still. "We could have that will in our hands in a few minutes."

"Provided she can find it. And even so, keep in mind, it might not tell us a thing about the necklace."

She gave him a pointed look. "That would be good news though."

Levi's lips twitched. "Fair enough. Just trying to temper your enthusiasm with a little realism."

Mia clutched the journal. "I haven't found another mention of the necklace, but I'm not done yet. I hope it's in the house somewhere. Wouldn't that be something?"

"That it would. But chances are she left it to a friend or relative."

"I hope not."

"Well, we'll know more soon enough."

It only took a few minutes to get to the courthouse.

Levi reached for his door handle. "I'm not sure how long it'll take."

"I'm coming too." Waiting wasn't her strong suit, and she was tired of sitting in the car.

"You sure?"

She tugged her ball cap down. "It's just the one woman, right?"

"Yeah, she pretty much has the run of the place."

"All right then."

The clerk's office was a two-story brick building on the other side of town. Levi held open the door and Mia stepped inside, the air conditioning cooling her skin. The main room was small, containing only a few seats, a big table, and a mammoth-size copy machine.

To their left was a window that opened into an unoccupied office, bright with florescent lighting. The building smelled of old documents and burnt coffee. Dust motes danced in a beam of sunlight shining through the front window.

"She's probably still downstairs." Levi crossed the room and began looking at the old photos on the walls.

Mia followed on her crutches. There was a photo of an old mercantile with a couple standing out front. A black-and-white beach shot from the forties. An old dance hall, its parking lot packed with cars from the sixties.

"Look," Levi said from the adjacent wall. "I forgot these were here."

Mia hobbled to him and peeked over his shoulder. She smiled as her gaze scanned a collage of photos of the historic inn over the course of time.

Levi pointed to a photo of a young couple on the porch. "That's your grandparents, right there."

Mia gasped, leaning in close. She wished the photo were larger. But even in black-and-white she could see that her mom bore a great resemblance to her grandmother. And her grandfather was quite the looker, with his dark hair and confident smile.

Mia placed her palm on her chest. "I'd never seen them before. What a handsome couple."

"I think you resemble her. Your hair color and the shape of your eyes."

She took out her phone and snapped a couple photos. A few moments later she moved on to peruse the other photos, standing close to Levi.

His masculine scent enveloped her. Just a hint of wood and leather. Nice. She leaned forward a bit, drawing in a deep breath, then she lost her balance and toppled forward. She grabbed Levi's arm.

He whirled, steadying her. "Careful there."

"Stupid crutches." Was that her voice, all breathy? His arm was thick and muscular under her palm. She should let go. She really should.

Let go, Mia.

He was close. So close the brim of her hat only allowed her to see as high as his lips. They were nice. Dusky mauve. The top one bowed nicely in the middle. He hadn't shaved this morning, and that was nice too. She could almost imagine the bristly scratch of his jaw against her bare cheek.

He hadn't moved back, and neither had she. Tension crackled between them. Her skin tingled, and her palms grew damp. His arm beneath her hand was hard and warm and—

"Sorry it took so long!" A short, round woman barreled into the room.

Mia jumped back, wobbling, and Levi steadied her again. She shot him a grateful look even as her pulse raced at the moment they'd shared.

"Howdy-do. Oh dear, what happened to your foot?"

"I slipped and fell yesterday."

"You poor thing." Connie waddled over to the table and set a bulky binder on it. She had a kind smile and cheeks that bunched when she smiled. "You'd better have a seat, dear. I just hate using crutches. Got new knees in 2012, and getting around was such a bear."

Levi pulled out a wooden library chair for Mia.

"Connie, this is a guest from the inn . . . um, Mia. Mia, this is Connie Harmeyer, our town clerk."

Mia smiled and tugged her brim down. "Nice to meet you."

"You too, honey. You in town doing some family research?"

"I'm just taking a little break from work."

"Well, where better than the Blue Ridge Mountains? It's so lovely here in the summer." She pushed up her glasses. "So, I brought up the records from 1986–1989. Paul preceded Dorothy in death, and she passed in '86, so I think it would've been out of probate by '87."

The phone rang in the office.

"Excuse me," Connie said. "You can just look through those—they should be in alphabetical order."

"Thanks, Connie." Levi took a seat next to Mia while the clerk went to answer the phone. "Sounds like we should start with '87."

Mia opened the large binder, setting it between them. The musty smell of the basement clung to the hundreds of papers filed inside. They were organized by month, then alphabetical order.

"April," Levi said after a few minutes of browsing. He pulled a file. "Here it is. Dorothy Livingston."

Mia made room on the table. There were several documents in the file, but it only took a moment to locate the will.

"It's pretty thick." Levi began reading, and a moment later he said, "It doesn't look like the legalese was any clearer back then than it is now."

"Will she let us take it?"

"I can make you a copy." Connie was already bustling back into the room. "Will that work?"

"Yes, ma'am," Levi said. "Thank you."

Ten minutes later they were walking out with a copy of the will.

"Bye, y'all," Connie said. "Tell Molly it was great seeing her at book club."

"Will do," Levi said.

"And tell her to bring that boyfriend of hers next time."

"I'll tell her. Take care now."

When they reached the car they got in, Levi storing the crutches in the back seat.

"I don't think she recognized you," Levi said a minute later as he pulled out onto the street.

"Me neither." Traffic was light. The sun glistened brightly off the lake, and the marina's slots were filled with boats of all shapes and sizes.

Mia looked at the papers sitting on the console. She was dying to get at that document. She reached for it.

Levi snatched it up, his eyes still on the road. "Oh no, you don't. We'll read it together once we get home."

She huffed, half impatient, half amused. "You are bossy. I'm the one who brought this whole thing to your attention."

"And I'm the one who tracked down the will."

"Only because I asked you to."

"Well, it's my necklace—or might be."

Mia chuckled at the stubborn set of his chin. "And I'm sure it'll look very nice on you."

He gave her a droll look, but his lips were trying to smile. "I know just the outfit I'll wear it with."

The thought of that necklace around his very masculine neck made her laugh. "You wouldn't be caught dead in that thing."

"Maybe not, but it wouldn't hurt my pride to auction it off."

"So you're admitting it could be in your house somewhere."

"I'm admitting I'd be a fool not to find out for sure. We have the will, and we'll know soon enough."

"Don't you ever like to dream?" she asked playfully. "It's fun. You should try it sometime."

"Somebody has to be realistic."

Truth be told, she found this practical side of him kind of sexy. It was a big change from the actors she worked with. Most of them were more like her, in need of a good director to keep them all on track.

Plus, he had that crinkly eye thing going for

him. She found herself looking for opportunities to provoke it.

Levi slowed as they approached the inn. "Uh-oh."

Mia's eyes followed his. A handful of people stood out front, cameras around their necks.

Her stomach dropped like an anchor. "Oh no."

"Get down."

They were too close. No choice but to drive by. "Ugh! How did they find me?"

"Duck down."

She bent in half, muttering, "Déjà vu."

He drove on, keeping a steady pace, his hand on her back. "Stay there. We're almost past. They're watching, but they can't see you."

Mia's heart rate had tripled. She clenched her fists. What was she going to do now? Her respite was over. She had to deal with reality now, and she wasn't ready for it.

"Let me get around the corner." The car slowed and swept in a wide arc that followed the lake's shoreline. Levi checked the rearview mirror. "All right, I think we're safe."

Mia came upright as Levi pulled over to the side of the road, a turnout for tourists who wanted to take in the beautiful lake view.

"What do you want to do?" he asked. "We could hang out someplace else for a while. Maybe they'll give up."

"They're not going away, Levi. They wouldn't

have come all this way unless they were sure I was here, and they're going to camp there till I come home." She felt trapped. Tears pressed the back of her eyes. She couldn't breathe.

"I'll call the police." He was already taking out his phone.

"There's nothing they can do. They're not breaking any laws. They're allowed to stand on the sidewalk and shoot pictures and ask anything they darn well want."

"That doesn't seem right."

"Tell me about it."

He set down his phone and put his hand over hers. "You don't have to go back at all, Mia. I have that buddy of mine with the floatplane. He can whisk you right out of here. I can mail your things to you."

She looked out at the vast lake and on to the blue skies beyond. What he offered was tempting. But where would she even go? The thought of going someplace new, starting over, was exhausting. And besides, what good would it do?

"They'll only find me again," she said softly.

If she went back to LA they'd be there all the time, everywhere she went. She knew how these feeding frenzies worked; she'd seen other actors go through them. At least here they were on a deadline. They'd have to get back home eventually.

She looked at Levi. His steady gaze was calming. His presence was soothing. The thought of leaving him made her feel a little hollow inside. She liked the Bluebell Inn. She liked being where her grandparents had lived. She liked the little family that lived there now. And yes, she liked Levi. It felt as if she'd found a little piece of home—the kind she'd never had. And she was loath to give that up just yet.

Besides . . . she hadn't done anything wrong. In her efforts to evade the vultures she kept forgetting that. And really, that ought to matter most of all.

Her chin came up as she focused on Levi's piercing eyes. "I'm not going to let them intimidate me. I didn't do anything wrong. Let's go home."

Levi's mouth tipped in a grin. "Thatta girl."

She drank in the approval in his eyes. It felt good to make him proud. But her ankle chose that moment to let itself be known. It throbbed with each beat of her heart.

Her ankle. The crutches.

"Ugh. I don't want to hobble past them. It'll start a whole new thread to this stupid scandal." Exactly the opposite of Nolan's advice not to feed the beast.

Levi glanced in the back where the crutches lay. He gazed out the window thoughtfully for a moment.

"I have an idea," he said. Then he put the car into Drive.

twenty

Levi was a genius. He drove them to Adam's house, borrowed his boat, and brought Mia back to the inn by way of the lake.

Once they arrived at the inn, Molly ushered them inside. "If only you'd answered your phone an hour ago," she said to Levi. "I tried to warn you."

Molly had already pulled all the blinds. The phone had been ringing off the hook too. Levi was returning Adam's boat now, which meant he'd have to come up that sidewalk. Mia hated that she was putting them all in this position.

She propped her foot on the coffee table and listened to Nolan's monologue on the phone. He'd been surprised that the vultures had found her tucked away in the Blue Ridge Mountains.

"It's your call, Mia," Nolan was saying. "You can come home now and face them here if you want. Either way I advise you to avoid answering their questions. We need to let this die a quiet death."

She made herself at least consider leaving Bluebell. Levi's buddy could fly her to the nearest airport, and she could literally go anywhere in the world. Maybe someplace in Europe: Paris, Barcelona, Rome. They wouldn't find her over there, surely. She wasn't well known globally. Parisians wouldn't give a hoot about her.

But then everyone she knew would be halfway around the globe. Suddenly it sounded like a very lonely escape.

And going elsewhere meant leaving Bluebell behind. Leaving this inn behind. And then there was Levi. She really liked him. And even though she'd known him less than a week, she'd come to trust him—against her better judgment. But he'd proven himself trustworthy, hadn't he?

As much as she wanted to escape the press, she couldn't bring herself to leave. Not yet.

"I think . . ." Mia said. "I want to finish out my week here. Maybe the press will get bored with me and leave soon."

Plus, she was dying to figure out what had happened to that necklace.

Levi pushed back the lobby drapes and grimaced. Darkness pressed in on the front yard, but he could see the shadows skulking near the curb. Those hounds were still out there. When he'd returned home they'd crowded him, shoving microphones in his face.

"Is Mia Emerson staying here?"

"What's your name?"

"Do you know Mia Emerson?"

"Is she in contact with Jax Jordan?"

"What can you tell us about their relationship?"

Levi had pushed through the crowd, not making eye contact, not responding, but by the time he closed and locked the door, his blood was boiling. He didn't want Mia or his sisters facing this every time they left the house.

He called Chief Dalton and asked him to stop by. Maybe he couldn't do anything, but his presence would at least alert the group that one violation of their so-called rights, and Levi would gladly have them hauled away.

Please. Cross the line.

The phone had been ringing continuously, but they'd stopped answering it hours ago. He hoped they weren't missing many actual customers. He'd changed the voicemail, directing potential guests to their website. Still, not answering the phone was never good for business.

Molly had ridden back to Adam's with Levi, and she'd stayed there. Grace was upstairs, hopefully working on college apps. *Please, God.* Mia had been on her phone all afternoon, doing damage control. She'd gone upstairs before he returned from Adam's.

Levi felt keyed up, like he'd had too much caffeine, when he hadn't had any at all. What if Mia took him up on his offer to get her out of town? She could fly off into the great blue yonder, and he'd never hear from her again.

That shouldn't bother him. Guests came and went all the time. It was part of the business. But this wasn't his first clue that she'd come to mean more to him than she should. She'd gotten under his skin. Maybe it was best that she did leave.

His chest tightened at the thought. What was happening to him?

He needed to find something productive to do. He took a seat behind the front desk and called Skeeter to see if he was available for a flight tonight if that became necessary.

Next he replied to his former boss at FC. He'd put it off too long, reluctant to turn down the job offer. He hoped it wouldn't ruin future opportunities at the company. He'd loved his job. He'd even loved the city. So much to see and do.

Success there hadn't come easily. The firm hired him fresh out of college, and his youth and Southern accent didn't exactly charm the subcontractors. He worked hard to prove himself, and they came around eventually. By the time he'd left they'd been coming to him for advice.

Levi leaned back and sighed. No use dredging up all that. He needed to focus on making the inn profitable. A buyout would give his sisters a nice start in life. Get Molly closer to her dream of owning an inn in Tuscany. Pay for Grace's college. He had to take care of his sisters before he could even think of going back to his old life.

Thumping on the steps—the slow, deliberate thumps of a person on crutches—diverted his attention.

"Need some help?" he called.

"I've got it." Mia turned the corner on the landing, and he caught sight of her for the first time since he'd gotten her home safely. Weariness lined the planes of her face, and hopelessness shadowed her eyes.

"What did your agent say? Do you need to leave?" His lungs seized in his constricted chest as he awaited her reply.

"He left that up to me. But no, I'm staying put for now—if you guys will still have me."

And just like that the tightening in his chest gave way. He breathed. "Of course. You're welcome to stay as long as you want. But you should probably get your foot up. What else do you need?"

She gave him a wry look as she negotiated a step. "I need a new life, is what I need."

He guessed being famous wasn't all it was cracked up to be. There was a great discrepancy between fantasy and reality.

"This too shall pass," he said gently.

"That's what I hear." She tilted her head and gave him a sheepish look. "I'm really sorry for the inconvenience, Levi. First you had to lock your doors, and now you have to pull all the blinds, and everyone's going to get ambushed every time they walk out the door. I know this is really disruptive to your business."

As if to prove her point the phone pealed again.

Levi grinned. "What's a few extra phone calls?"

"And a few vultures on your doorstep? I hope they didn't harass you too badly."

"Don't worry about me. I can handle myself." He steadied her as she reached the bottom.

She looked up at him, an enigmatic smile hovering around her lips. "I'll just bet you can. You're kind of good in an emergency, you know. That's a handy skill to have."

He gave her a wry grin. "You wouldn't believe the situations that can arise around here. Experience is a good teacher."

"I don't doubt it. Still, the ability to think on your feet isn't necessarily a learned one. If it were, I'd be Wonder Woman by now."

He grinned. "Are you hungry?"

"I'm fine. Grace made me a salad earlier. I actually came down to ask what the will said. I've been dying to know."

"No idea. Haven't read it yet."

Her eyebrows jumped even as her face softened, and a look of gratitude danced over her features. "You waited for me?"

That she could be so grateful for such a small thing was a wonder. Not exactly the spoiled princess he'd expected. "We were supposed to read it together. Do you want to do that now?"

"Um, yes, I want to read it now," she said in a *duh* tone that reminded him of Grace.

He laughed, stepping behind the front desk and

reaching under it. "Well, I just happen to have it handy."

They settled in the library, where they could hunker over a desk. The window above it had a stunning view of the lake when the blinds weren't pulled.

Levi waded through the legalese of the first page, Mia leaning in close. He was usually pretty good with contracts, but the sweet scent of her was a major distraction. He missed having a woman in his life. He missed the quiet conversations, the subtle touches, the stirring of want.

He tried to remind himself it was the famed Mia Emerson inspiring these cravings, but his heart didn't care. Never mind that she was so far out of his league she might as well be in a different galaxy.

"Finished?" Mia asked softly.

Levi was only halfway done, but obviously she wasn't having the same difficulties.

He flipped the page and redoubled his efforts. But this page was only about the executor of the will. "We could probably just skip this section."

"I'm all for that. I'm about to doze off. These lawyers, yeesh."

He flipped the page. "Here it is: Distribution of Personal Property."

He read the paragraphs detailing the Livingstons' property. They'd wanted the inn sold at auction and the proceeds to go to First Community Church. The contents of the inn were to be auctioned off separately, the proceeds going to Bluebell Baptist Church Camp, a ministry that was still situated on the lake.

He flipped the page, ready for more, but there wasn't anything else about their assets.

He sighed. "That's it, I guess. They didn't have an itemized list at all."

"Are you sure?"

He skimmed the rest of the document. "Yeah, it's a pretty simple will as far as the assets go."

"So there's no mention of the necklace at all? How could that be?"

Levi lifted a shoulder. "There must not have been anyone she had in mind for it. Are you sure she didn't give it to your mother?"

"I'm positive. They wrote her off after she left home. Besides, if my mom had a piece of jewelry that rare, she would've worn it every occasion she could."

"The necklace must've gone in the estate auction then."

"I guess that's possible. But what if that's *not* what happened? Think about it. They were running an inn. With all the strangers coming and going Paul found a place to hide it away somewhere. Levi . . . the necklace really could still be in this house somewhere."

He didn't want to get his hopes up. But he

had to admit he'd expected to find the necklace listed in the will. Would Dorothy have hidden it somewhere on the property? And wouldn't they have come across it in the renovations?

"Is there any part of the house you didn't remodel?" Mia was obviously on the same wavelength.

"Very little, and that's only accounting for the changes *we've* made. My sisters' room is original. Also my parents' room—where you're staying. It already had an en suite bathroom, so we only did cosmetic things in there. The library wasn't touched or the basement. And there's an attic."

"But it was cleared out?"

"Yes, we store Christmas decorations and junk up there." He scratched the back of his neck, something coming to him. "There is another section of the attic. I never really noticed it until we were renovating upstairs. It's accessed through the girls' bedroom closet. I don't remember anyone ever going up there though."

Mia's eyes lit up. "Let's go look!"

Levi looked at her crutches. "No way you're getting up a ladder."

"Well, I'll shine a light for you or something."

She was smiling that pretty smile of hers and looking so hopeful. So different from the weary look she'd worn when she'd come downstairs.

Well, what else was he supposed to do? "All right. I'll sneak out to the shed for a ladder."

twenty-one

Grace's bedroom door was closed when Mia and Levi reached the top of the stairs. Mia was high on hope. She just knew that necklace was somewhere in this house, and the attic seemed like their best shot.

Levi rapped on the door. "Grace? Can we come in?"

There was a shuffling sound. Then a moment later the door opened. Grace was wearing plaid pajama bottoms and a T-shirt that read *If you say so.* Her long blond ponytail trailed over her shoulder.

"Hey." Grace's gaze swung between the two of them. "What's up?"

"First of all," Mia said, "I want to apologize for all the hoopla outside. I'm so sorry for bringing my crazy world to your doorstep."

"It's not your fault. I wonder who squealed. It wasn't us."

"I believe you." Mia was a little surprised how true this was. Trust had never come easily to her, yet this little family had quickly earned it. It said a lot for the Bennetts. "It could've been anyone I passed on the trails or who saw me around town in the car or who caught me coming or going. It doesn't matter anymore. What's done is done."

Grace gave Levi a look. "Well, you wanted the inn to get national attention. Mission accomplished."

Mia gave a rueful smile. "Be careful what you ask for."

"That's not quite the kind of attention I was after."

Grace noticed the ladder. "Um, what's that for? Something broken?"

"We need to get up in the attic through your closet," Levi said.

"Ooo-kay . . ."

"You're not going to believe this," Mia said. "Have you read Dorothy Livingston's journals?"

"Um, yeah . . . A long time ago."

Mia went on to explain that the blue diamond necklace was worth a fortune and that Dorothy had said she kept it tucked away somewhere safe.

Levi took over when she got to the part about Dorothy's will, explaining that the necklace was unaccounted for.

"So . . ." Grace said after she heard him out. "You think it might still be here somewhere?"

She didn't seem very optimistic, but Mia was starting to realize that was Grace.

"It's possible," Mia said. "Isn't that exciting? I can't wait to start looking."

Grace shrugged, opening the door wider. "Knock yourselves out."

They slipped through the door and onward toward the closet.

Levi knew Grace was skeptical they'd find anything more than dust bunnies in the attic. She was just too kind to burst Mia's bubble. He was thankful for that. And glad he could divert Mia's attention from the scandal taking over her life.

He opened the door to the small walk-in closet, his heart sinking. "You've got to be kidding me." The floor was covered with clothes and boxes and who knew what else. He threw Grace a look over his shoulder. "Seriously?"

"On a positive note, I got the college apps done," she deadpanned.

Well, that was something. "All three of them?"

"All three of them. Happy?"

"Ecstatic." He wanted to add *About time,* but he held his tongue. "Now we just have to wait for their response. Did they say how long it would be?"

"Six to eight weeks, but my friends say it doesn't take that long."

"I hope not. That's cutting it a little close." Levi looked at the cluttered closet floor. "Now maybe you can help me make room for this ladder?"

Ten minutes later there was finally enough room to set up the ladder. Levi climbed a few rungs, almost dreading the moment he lifted the hatch. What if the space was empty? He wasn't so much dreading it for himself—although the windfall from such a find would be more than welcome. He was thinking of Mia. She was so hopeful, and he didn't want to let her down.

She stood under the ladder, perched on her crutches, anticipation shining in her green eyes.

"Ready or not," Levi said as he pushed up the drywall cover. Warm, stuffy air assaulted him. The attic was pitch black. He reached for the flashlight in his pocket, clicked it on, and shined it into the darkness.

The space was about ten by twelve, covering the area over his sisters' room. And it wasn't empty. There were boxes, stacked high and lining the walls, and a few pieces of furniture. If nothing else, those might be worth something. They must be antiques by now.

"Well?" Mia asked. "Anything up there?"

"Actually, there is. Some boxes and stuff."

Mia squealed. "I'm coming up."

He scowled down at her. "No, you are not. I don't even know how safe the floor is up here."

"By all means," Grace called, "go ahead and walk right over top of me then."

Levi went up the remaining rungs and stepped into the attic space. The air was thick with old dust and stifling heat. His beam of light caught on a hanging string, and he pulled it. Miraculously the lightbulb still worked. He turned his attention to the boxes. They were pretty heavy and looked full. He couldn't imagine handing them down safely to Mia or Grace.

He spotted a tiny double-hung window on the opposite wall and carefully made his way toward it, hunching over as he went.

"The ceiling's pretty low," he called down to Mia. "Even if you could make it up here you wouldn't be able to use your crutches."

He unlocked the window and struggled to lift the sash. It was probably on the old weight and pulley system and hadn't been opened in years.

"Is there a lot of stuff up there?"

"Tons." He finally managed to lift the sash. He already had a film of sweat on his back. "Too much to tackle tonight."

"But you'll get a start on it, right?"

How could he turn down all the hope in that tone? He shook his head, a wry grin tugging his lips. He was becoming a regular dope.

"Would you tell Grace to bring me a fan?"

She didn't need to pass it on because next thing he knew Grace called out, "Yes, master!"

An hour and a half later Levi was coated in a thick layer of dust plus assorted cobwebs. He'd gone through quite a few boxes, finding all kinds of fascinating old stuff. It was hard to keep from inspecting things. He'd set aside the more interesting items to bring downstairs.

Molly was going to eat this up. She'd returned

home earlier on Adam's boat, sneaking in without trouble, and came upstairs to tell them she'd identified the person who'd given away Mia's location. It was a tourist, a young woman who'd snapped a photo of Mia getting out of the car out front. The Twitter thread, #MiaEmersonSpotting, had already grown long.

When Molly found out what was going on in her room, her eyes lit up. Another lost-and-found mystery—she'd discovered a lost love letter last year during the renovation.

But before she could get too wrapped up in the adventure, Levi shooed her away. This was going to remain Mia's and his mystery to solve, thank you very much. Molly only pouted a little as she went downstairs to make a pot of decaf.

Mia had also left. At his encouragement she'd taken breaks from her vigil and was presently in her room, propping her foot.

Levi focused on his task. The good news was, he knew some of the stuff went back to the Livingston era because the newspapers wrapping some of the fragile items were dated. He brushed a cobweb from his hair and let loose a sneeze. If that necklace would turn up sometime soon that would be just dandy.

Grace called from down below sometime later. "Um . . . hello? I'd really like to go to bed without hearing your big feet tromping overhead."

Levi checked his watch. It was after eleven. His eyes drifted around the attic. He was only about a fifth of the way through the boxes. The rest would have to wait until tomorrow.

twenty-two

It was suppertime when Levi descended the ladder from the attic.

At Molly's insistence, Mia had made herself at home on her bed. She was officially off the crutches, although she sported a limp. The sisters had split for the day, braving the growing crowd of photographers out front.

Mia's flight home was tomorrow, but she hadn't packed yet. She didn't even want to think about leaving Bluebell. Or going home to face 24/7 scrutiny. Couldn't one of the Kardashians just do something outrageous already?

Levi emerged from the closet, carrying a cardboard box. Poor thing had been in the sweltering attic for most of the day. His hair was almost gray with dust, dirt smudged his blue T-shirt, and something that looked like grease marked his cheek.

But the expression on his face said it all.

"Nothing?"

" 'Fraid not."

"And you've been through everything?"

"Every single thing." He gave the box a little bounce. "Found some interesting old stuff though. An oil lantern, photos, and random stuff from what must've been the inn's lost-and-found box."

199

She could tell he was trying to ease her disappointment. A consolation prize. She made room for him on the bed. "That's fun. Let's go through it."

He glanced at the bed. "Molly'll kill me if I set this down here. Why don't we head downstairs, maybe order a pizza? It's getting on toward suppertime."

"Sure." She followed him out the door. "I pity the delivery person, though, having to wade through all the stalkers outside."

"I'll warn them when I order, but I'm sure they already know." He gave her a look. "It was in today's paper. Front-page news."

"Great. Now everyone in town knows I'm here. And I'm sure they probably know about the scandal too."

He gave her an empathetic look as he preceded her down the steps. "There was mention of it in the article."

"Of course there was." She took her time with the steps. Last thing she needed was to fall and hurt herself again.

"Well . . . you'll be out of here tomorrow anyway. I've already talked to Skeeter about flying you to Charlotte. He can sneak you out the back. I'll wait a while, then notify the goons out front that you're gone."

"Sounds like you've got it all worked out." Business as usual. She didn't know why that bothered her so much. She had no reason to complain. He'd taken such good care of her.

"I'm not sure an endorsement from me is going to count for much by the time all's said and done," she said.

"I'm just sorry your trip wasn't more relaxing." He glanced back at her. "At least you won't have to hobble through the airport on crutches."

"There is that." She settled on the living room couch, and Levi set the box on the coffee table, then went to change out of his dusty clothes.

He returned wearing his standard khakis and a black T-shirt that set off his dark hair and blue eyes. "Hungry yet?"

"Let's wait a bit if you don't mind."

He sat beside her. "Not at all."

They began rooting through Levi's finds, the musty smell of the attic filling her nostrils. He'd turned off the phone's ringer last night, so the house was quiet except for the ticking of the mantel clock. It was probably going to take hours to weed through all the voicemails.

The oil lamp looked really old, and it was in perfect condition. There were pillbox style hats that were popular in the '50s. She modeled them for Levi. When he came across a black fedora he set it on his head, making Mia wish men's hats were all the rage again because, mercy.

"Ooh la la," she said. "Very Frank Sinatra."

He left it on as they continued their exploration.

Mia pulled out a gold woman's watch and turned it over. An inscription read *All my love.*

"Look, it's engraved."

"Nice."

Mia wondered if her grandfather might've given it to her grandmother, but it could've been anyone's. It could've been left at the inn by a guest.

"Look at this." Levi showed her several photos taken inside the inn back in the days of black-and-white. "I wish we'd had these for the remodel. Would've been fun to recreate some of this."

"You did a great job with the place. It's so warm and inviting. Despite the circumstances, I've loved staying here." And she was feeling more than a little depressed at the thought of leaving.

His eyes searched hers for a long-drawn-out moment. It was a thing of wonder that his mere look could make her body hum.

"I've loved having you." The low thrum of his voice strummed a chord inside her. The vibrations spread throughout.

I've loved having you, not *we've.* She shouldn't make too much of that, but the way he was looking at her made it all too easy. Those eyes, warmer than blue had a right to be. His bone structure was the handiwork of God Himself, a masterpiece.

Of its own volition, her hand lifted to thumb away the streak of dirt from his cheek.

At her touch his eyes flickered with surprise.

She jerked her hand back and showed her thumb, clearing her throat. "You—you had a streak of something on your cheek."

"Oh. Thanks." He rubbed the spot.

Had she mistaken the moment for more than it was? Her face warmed.

Since they'd gone through all the goodies from the attic, they started loading the box back up.

Levi topped the pile with the fedora. "Ready for that pizza?"

Actually, the very thought of pizza made her stomach rebel. She'd had pizza three times this week and had hardly had anything but takeout since she'd arrived, and she didn't even want to think about getting on the scale right now.

What she really needed was a nice grilled chicken breast and a side of steamed broccoli.

"Not hungry yet?" Levi asked.

"It's not that. I'm just . . . a little tired of pizza, I guess."

"Okay. Well, we could order wings instead. Or Chinese. Did you like it last time?"

"Yeah . . ."

The truth was, she'd had it with being trapped like an animal. Her travel had been restricted for seven days, and she was ready to go crazy. Of course, she was leaving in the morning anyway, but just now the thought of another takeout meal made her want to vomit.

And even more so . . . She was sick and tired of everyone else dictating where she could and couldn't go. She was a grown woman. She was tired of hiding from the general public and even more tired of hiding from the paparazzi.

She looked at Levi, resolve flooding through her even more strongly as she met his steady gaze. "You know what, Levi? I think I want to go out."

His eyebrows popped. "Really?"

"No, I don't *think* I want to go out. I *know* I want to go out. And not through the back door, either. I want to walk right out of here, past the vultures, and go to a nice restaurant where I can sit down and have a healthy meal that isn't fried twice over or consists mainly of refined carbs— no offense to Southern cuisine."

"None taken."

"And I want to stop hiding—stop acting like I *have* something to hide, because you know what? *I didn't do anything wrong.*"

Levi's lips lifted in a smile of wonder. His eyes softened in approval. "All right then. Let's do this."

twenty-three

R eady?" Levi gripped the inn's front doorknob, adrenaline beginning to surge through him.

Mia had gone to her room to freshen up. No more ponytail. No more ball cap or yoga pants. She was sporting a pair of stylish jeans and a black top with cutout shoulders.

In short, he could hardly take his eyes off her.

"You sure you want to subject yourself to this?" Mia asked him. "You could just loan me your car. I'm a good driver."

No way was he sending her out there alone. "At least let me get you safely to the restaurant. I can wait for you in the car."

She looked at him like he was a big dope. "I wasn't trying to ditch you. I'd love to have dinner with you. It's just that you're not used to this, and it can be a little daunting."

"I think I can handle it."

"If you're sure." She drew a deep breath. "All right then. Here we go."

Levi exited first. The little horde of photographers snapped to attention at the sound of the door closing.

Ever since the press had shown up they'd kept the porch lights off, so it wasn't immediately apparent who was coming out.

But the photographers figured it out soon enough. Cameras began clicking in rapid-fire staccato. Flashes lit the night. Levi averted his eyes from the blinding glare.

"Mia, what do you have to say about Jax Jordan's allegations?"

"What are you doing in North Carolina, Mia?"

"Mia, do you have feelings for Jax Jordan?"

"Mia, did you hurt your foot?"

"Why are you limping, Mia?"

"No comment," she called in a clear, confident voice, several times. Nonetheless they continued their queries.

Levi led her down the walk toward the group. There was no way around them, so he aimed at a gap closest to his car.

When they reached the throng the reporters pressed in.

One of them got in Mia's face with his microphone. "Mia, can you tell us—"

"Back off!" Levi blocked the man with a shoulder. He pulled Mia close and barged through the group, shoulder first.

And then the horde was at their backs, following them like stink on a monkey.

"Who's your friend, Mia?"

"Mia, where are you going?"

"Are you coming back?"

They fired questions one on top of the other.

Levi made a beeline for the passenger side,

ushered her in, and got the door shut as quickly as he could. As he jogged around the car the photographers swarmed outside Mia's window, snapping shots. She stared out the windshield, looking cool and calm, wearing a pleasant smile.

He started the car and put it in Drive, not bothering with his seat belt yet. The vultures surrounded the car, their flashes going off. He should just run them all down. He couldn't believe this was legal.

He continued forward slowly as the crowd morphed to allow room for his progress. A couple of them hung around after the others moved aside.

"Idiots." Levi laid on his horn and pressed the accelerator until finally he broke free of them.

He checked the rearview mirror, hoping they wouldn't follow. But they must've gotten what they wanted because they seemed preoccupied with their cameras. They'd probably race to see who could get their shots up on their websites first.

"They're not following." He looked over at Mia, but it was too dark to see her expression. "You all right?"

"I'm fine. I'm glad I did it." She gave Levi a wry grin. "This week's starting to feel less honeymoon-for-one and more DEFCON 1."

The humor in her tone relieved him. "That was insane. Is it always like that?"

"Sometimes. Though my life mostly doesn't beg that kind of attention, thank God."

"Did you hear the one guy? 'Mia, did someone hurt you?' "

"I've heard worse," she said. "But now that they got what they wanted maybe they'll go away."

It was obvious that pushing through that barricade had been a sort of breakthrough for her. She was almost aglow.

The thought of her leaving tomorrow wasn't something he wanted to entertain. Somehow, in only a week, he'd gotten used to having her here. And, he admitted wryly, he'd definitely managed to develop a little crush on her. And he'd always said Molly was the fanciful one.

Mia chose an Italian restaurant situated on a quiet lot outside of town. It was a little late for supper, so there were only a few other guests. The hostess seated them at a booth for two in a private corner.

She ordered a chicken Caesar salad, and Levi couldn't resist the baked mostaccioli. She laughed at their hasty exit from the inn, but Levi was still a little too irritated by the reporters' nerve to take it so lightly.

When their breadsticks arrived Mia tucked into them, despite her earlier complaint about refined carbs. "Totally worth the calories," she proclaimed.

"The best in town."

There was still so much in Bluebell he wanted to show her. Not only restaurants she hadn't gotten a chance to sample, but some of their popular attractions that had been too touristy for her to risk: Stone Gap Bridge, Pineview Bay, Summit Ridge. She was leaving Bluebell without having really seen it.

"I'm sorry we didn't find the necklace in the attic," she said, breaking the moment's quiet. "I thought for sure it would be up there."

"At least we found other interesting things."

"They're probably worth something, especially the furniture. Still, I really wanted to find that necklace. You should keep looking. It's a big house. It might be somewhere else."

"Maybe." But the thought of continuing the search without Mia left him ambivalent.

"I've been wondering though . . ." Mia said. "Could the Livingstons have had a safe deposit box at the bank?"

"Didn't the journal say that Paul made a safe place to keep it?"

"It said 'Paul finally arranged a safe spot.' If they'd put it in a safe deposit box she probably would've just come out and said so."

"I agree. And I can't see Dorothy putting it in a bank anyway. She seemed like the kind of person who kept the things she valued close to her."

Mia looked thoughtful for a moment, and Levi

wondered if she was thinking about her mother, clear across the country from Dorothy.

"I think you're right," she said finally. "But what about a safe in the house?"

"I'm sure we would've come across it by now."

He finished his breadstick and washed it down with Coke. Mia sure was intrigued with that necklace. He wondered if that was all she was searching for. Or if finding her grandmother's necklace was important for reasons other than the sheer value.

He had to admit he was enjoying this little project. Not just spending extra time with Mia, but also working as a team with her. It felt good to have a partner, especially when it seemed he was flying solo in so many other areas of his life.

"Will you keep looking after I leave?" Her eyes shone with too much hope for the question to come off as a mere inquiry.

He leaned his elbows on the table, the breadsticks forgotten. "Why does that necklace mean so much to you? I mean, I know it's worth a lot of money, but . . ." He wasn't sure how to tactfully point out that she probably had more money than Oprah.

"I know I seem a little obsessed. But I don't know . . . The idea of finding something rare and valuable . . . It energizes me. Gives me hope."

She was rare, Levi thought. *She* was valuable. Sometimes he wondered if she realized just how much.

• • •

Mia changed into her pajamas and readied for bed, exhaustion settling over her like a lead blanket. When she and Levi had returned home from dinner, there'd only been a few photographers in front of the inn. She was tempted to check the online coverage, but that usually only led to frustration.

It was late when she finally got into bed, but her floatplane didn't leave until ten o'clock. This was her last night at the Bluebell Inn. It was bittersweet. She'd entered this room full of self-pity about the non-honeymoon. But after only a week she could honestly say she was glad Wesley had broken their engagement. Something had been missing.

She gave a wry laugh. Yeah, like love. He'd just been a user, riding on the coattails of her success. As soon as he'd scored a big role he hadn't needed her anymore.

She waited for the ache of regret, but it never came. Hmm. She must be getting over him.

Mia rolled over in bed, thinking again of Levi and the good conversations they'd had tonight. It seemed easy, opening up to him. Maybe because he was a temporary fixture in her life. Someone she would say good-bye to tomorrow. Her throat went tight at the thought.

How had she gotten attached to him in only a week? She was usually slow to let her guard down. Maybe just knowing the relationship was temporary had led to her being less careful. It was probably best she was leaving now before any real damage could be done.

But the punch in her heart made her realize that she'd already done some real damage. Levi was an extraordinary guy. If he lived in LA she could see the relationship developing into so much more.

But he didn't. He was determined to make a go of this inn, and when he was finished here, he had his life waiting for him in Denver. There was no future with Levi.

Yes, it was definitely best that she was leaving.

The vibration of her phone woke Mia some time later. She grabbed it and winced at the bright screen. Nolan was calling.

"Hello?" she croaked.

"Hey, Mia, did I catch you at a bad time?"

"It's after midnight here. I'm in bed."

"Sorry about that. But I thought you'd want to hear the latest."

"I hope they didn't make my injury into something more than it is. They probably already have me and Emma in a catfight over Jax."

"Not at all. In fact, the narrative has completely changed, Mia. All they're talking about now is the guy you were with tonight."

Now she was awake. She sat up on her elbow. "You mean Levi?"

"There's no name, just photos of you and him."

"He's the innkeeper here. He escorted me to the restaurant last night. What do you mean the narrative has changed?"

"Everybody's wondering who your new boyfriend is. More importantly, they're wondering how Jax's statement can be true if you're secretly seeing someone else."

"But he's just the innkeeper. For all they know he's my bodyguard."

"Uh-uh. Perception is everything, remember? Have you seen the photos?"

"Um, no. Because you always tell me not to look."

He chuckled. "I'll send you a couple."

"What are you laughing about?"

"Just take a look at the photos. And Mia . . . you should probably stay put for a while. Let's keep this narrative going as long as we can."

"You think?"

"I know. Get some rest, kiddo. I'll touch base with you again tomorrow."

"Wait, what do you mean, 'keep the narrative going'?"

But he was already gone.

Mia ended the call and lay back against the pillow. Was Nolan right? Were things swinging the other way just because of a few photos of her and Levi?

The reporters had probably tried to get his

identity, but she didn't imagine the folks around here had been very helpful.

The phone buzzed an incoming text, then another. She checked the screen. Nolan's photos had come through. The first picture was an image of Levi pushing back the photographer who'd gotten too close. She enlarged it with her thumb and forefinger, trying to see it objectively.

She was turned away from the camera, but still recognizable. Levi's brows were low and tight over his eyes, his jaw knotted. She wouldn't want to mess with that guy.

The second photo had been snapped after he'd put his arm around her. She was tucked into his side, her face turned into his shoulder. He was shielding her from everyone, his face intense and protective.

It was obvious he was no bodyguard. They didn't wear their emotions on their sleeves.

Mia shut off her phone and settled back in her bed, still seeing the image of Levi's fierce expression. She had a feeling sleep would be a long time coming.

twenty-four

After a poor night's sleep Levi awakened bleary-eyed to his seven o'clock alarm. He got showered and ready, the scent of apples and cinnamon drawing him to the kitchen. He found Miss Della washing up in the kitchen, her hands dark amidst the soapy bubbles in the sink.

He drew in a breath of scrumptiousness. "I could eat a dozen of your muffins this morning."

"Well, you'll have to wait till they're out of the oven at least." Her eyes narrowed on him. "You look tired. Headache again?"

"Just didn't sleep well." Although, now that she mentioned it, he did already have a headache blooming at the back of his skull. He helped himself to coffee.

"Our girl's leaving today?"

He liked how Miss Della had taken to Mia. But Mia was easy to take to. "Skeeter's picking her up at ten and flying her to Charlotte."

"You must be awful sorry to see her go."

"Why would you say that?"

Della pursed her lips. "That innocent look don't fool me. Buzzer's about to go off. You mind pulling the pan from the oven?"

"Sure." Levi grabbed a potholder and did as she asked. "Are those vultures still out front?"

"More than before, even."

His spirits sank. "I hope they didn't bother you on your way in."

"No, sirree. Came in the back way. Maybe it's best things get back to normal. A body can't even come and go around here."

"Mia and I stepped out for a while last night. I was hoping they'd get their fill and leave."

"Just gave 'em a little tease, and now they want more." She shook her head. "Mmm, mmm, mmm. Don't know how they live with themselves, disrupting folks' lives like they do."

The ceiling creaked overhead, a sign Mia was up and about. She usually slept later, but maybe she'd finally adjusted to Eastern time—just in time to go home.

He grabbed four muffins and set them on a plate. "Thanks for breakfast. I'm going to go listen to our voicemails."

There were seventy-two messages. Levi went through each one, painstakingly deleting the press calls and saving the others. There was definitely an uptick in the number of inquiries, and a quick check showed a substantial increase in online reservations.

This was great. Awesome. Probably not the results of his marketing plan, but hey, he'd take it.

He heard noise on the staircase and recognized

Mia's careful stair-by-stair descent. His heart quickened. This might be the last time he heard her come down those stairs. From now on he'd only see her on TV or at the movies—and online because, let's face it, he was going to look her up.

A moment later she rounded the corner, and her eyes brightened as they settled on him. "Good morning."

That smile hit him like a blow to the chest. "Morning, Mia. You're up early."

She wore a casual red shirt that looked amazing on her and a pair of white shorts he hadn't seen before. If she hoped to get through the airport unnoticed in that, she was going to be disappointed.

"I didn't sleep very well. I made myself stay in bed until I heard others up and about."

"I'm sorry. I thought you might sleep better after facing down the reporters last night. Are you hungry? Miss Della's apple cinnamon muffins are incredible."

"That sounds great, but . . ." She stepped up to the desk, tucking her hands into her back pockets. "Do you have a minute to talk?"

"Sure, of course." He placed his hands on the desktop and leaned into them, trying not to let his gaze stray from her eyes. "What's on your mind?"

"I was, um, wondering how you might feel

217

about me extending my stay. I mean, feel free to say no, because I know my being here causes a major problem for you with the crowd outside, but I'm willing to continue paying for the whole inn so the press wouldn't be an inconvenience to your guests."

She wanted to stay. Surprise battled with joy for top billing. He tried to fight back the optimism, but it was pointless. The thought of Mia staying made him ridiculously happy.

"Of course you're welcome to stay. But we couldn't let you keep paying for the whole place—you could rent out a mansion for that rate, you know."

"Yeah, but then I wouldn't have my own personal chauffeur." Her smile ticked up at one corner, her eyes flirting. "And who else is going to bring me cold packs and carry me down mountains when my clumsy side makes an appearance?"

It didn't escape his notice that those were all things he'd done. She hadn't even mentioned Della's muffins or Grace's way with a dust rag or Molly's gift of gab—not that *he* considered that a positive trait.

And the way she was looking at him, he'd move heaven and earth to do her bidding. "I do aim to please. But we really can't let you rent out the whole inn—we actually have other guests on the books already."

"Oh! Of course you do. I wasn't thinking. Well, that won't work then."

He tempered the disappointment that welled up. "I'd be happy to find you a house to rent. There are some nice secluded ones over by Pine Bay." Although he didn't like the thought of her staying alone with those hounds stalking her.

"Do you have space for me here?"

"I'm sure we do." He stepped over to the computer and opened up the schedule. "Let me see . . . Yes, the suite is actually available until July eighth, when we're hosting a wedding party. How long are you thinking of staying?"

She shifted. "I'm not sure—a couple weeks? Can I just . . . play it by ear?"

"Of course."

"And . . ." She tilted her head, giving him a hopeful look. "Maybe we can keep searching for the necklace? I mean, when you have spare time?"

And have more opportunity to spend time with her? "I think I can make that happen. But are you okay having other guests in the house? They very well may recognize you."

She lifted a shoulder, a beautiful smile lighting her face. "Well, I'm just going to have to get over that, aren't I?"

Mia shifted, biting her lip. She had one more item to address with Levi, but this one was trickier. More personal. She'd texted Nolan this morning, asking for clarification on his advice about continuing the narrative. His direction had been crystal clear. And it made all kinds of sense.

She was a little uncomfortable with it, however, as she had an aversion to deception. But Nolan's argument made sense—she'd actually be doing this in service to the truth.

She lifted her eyes to Levi's questioning gaze.

"Is there something else I can help you with?"

She gave a nervous chuckle. "You could say that." The only problem was her request went above and beyond the call of duty. Way above.

"What is it?" Those darn crinkly eyes would be the death of her.

"So, um, Levi, I don't know if you've gone online and looked at the pictures from last night."

He shook his head.

"Right. Well. It seems the press was very curious . . . about you."

His brows jumped. "About me?"

"Well, specifically . . . your relationship to me."

"Aaah. Well, they've surely figured out I'm only the innkeeper."

"Not yet, actually. But . . ." She wasn't sure how to say he'd put off a very protective vibe last night. She'd just show him instead. "Here, maybe if you take a look."

She pulled up the photos and handed her phone to him. Would he see what others had seen in his expressions? That he looked like an avenging angel? That his protectiveness seemed . . . personal?

As he studied the photos a flush crawled into his cheeks. He handed her phone back and scratched the back of his neck. "So . . . what are you saying exactly?"

She cleared her throat. "Nolan thinks the speculation about our relationship is a good thing. It's changed the narrative from Jax and me to . . ."

"You and me." Realization dawned in his eyes. "That's why there are more of them out front today."

"Right. And I'm so sorry about your picture being spread all over creation—I guess I should've warned you about that."

"I figured as much when we walked out the door last night. I just didn't think—"

"Me either. But the press have inventive ways of stirring up talk, and Nolan would much rather that they were talking about us than the scandal. He asked if we might be willing to, um . . . continue the narrative."

"Continue the narrative . . . like be seen together as though we're . . ."

"In a relationship, yes. And feel free to say no, because I realize this is a huge ask. I wouldn't blame you for not wanting the public scrutiny. Believe me, I know what a pain that is. But the thing is, not only are people speculating about our relationship, they're wondering how Jax's version of what happened can be true if I'm involved with someone else."

Levi's head tilted back in understanding. "Ah, makes sense. That's a good thing then."

Mia winced. "Except it's not really true. And I don't want you to do anything you're uncomfortable with. I'm extending my stay regardless, and I honestly wouldn't blame you if—"

Levi hit the counter with his palm with a decisive smack. "Count me in."

The smile blooming on Mia's face was unstoppable. "Really? I mean, you won't have to, like, lay it on thick or anything. Just being seen out and about together is enough. They'll do the rest."

She loved the formidable look that came over his face. The determined thrust of his chin. "Know what? It's time Jax Jordan was put in his place. He spread blatant lies about you, and if I can help expose him for the schmuck that he is . . . I'm all in."

twenty-five

Molly was already seated in the library when Levi entered with the financial folder. He'd been a little scattered since his conversation with Mia earlier in the morning. She'd gone upstairs to unpack, and Levi had texted his sisters, moving up their financial meeting. He had items to go over, and they wouldn't be checking in guests until later this afternoon.

Levi turned the desk chair to face the small sofa and was just sitting down when Grace entered.

"Why'd we move up the *board* meeting?" Grace asked.

Molly chuckled and gave Grace a high five. "Nice one."

Levi's gaze toggled between them. "What? Oh, *bored* meeting. I get it. Very funny. Sit down, both of you, and try to stay awake this time."

"Yes, master," they said simultaneously.

He sighed as he passed out the spreadsheets.

"Before we get into this exciting stuff," Grace said, "I'd just like to say I'm really overdue for a raise."

Levi rolled his eyes.

"I'm serious. I'm making minimum wage here."

"As I said—last month and the month before

and the month before that—we're all making minimum wage here, Grace. Until the bottom line improves it will continue that way. Speaking of which, I have a potential solution I'd like to propose—"

"Wait," Molly said. "I'd like to address the restaurant situation."

"We don't have an actual restaurant," Levi said. "And again, we can't afford one."

"Well, I think we should at least extend the breakfast menu, Levi. I'm tired of hearing about—"

"If you'd just wait a minute, Molly, I have an idea that will increase our profits and maybe take care of all our problems." *Please, God.* Why did his sisters have to be so difficult?

Molly crossed her arms. "Fine. I'm listening."

"I've been doing some research, and I think we should increase our rates."

"What?" Molly said. "No. That doesn't make sense."

"We're already pretty empty through the week," Grace said. "Isn't raising the rates just going to scare people away?"

"Not at all. We're the only inn in town, and we're almost full up on the weekends. That's where our rates could go up. By my calculations we can increase the price by 8 percent and still remain competitive."

"I don't like it," Molly said.

"That's not really a valid argument," Levi said. "And we need to do something to increase our bottom line. I think this would go a long way toward growing the business."

"I thought that's what your marketing plan was for," Grace said.

"Yes, but that costs money, and those dollars come straight out of our bottom line. Unless you want to charge for the extras like internet and breakfast, we're going to have to raise our rates."

"We're not nickeling and diming our guests to death," Molly said. "Inns are supposed to have extra amenities. This is not a Motel Six."

"Then we need to raise the rates. You're just going to have to trust me on this. I know what I'm doing. We'll honor the prices for those who've already booked, of course. But new bookings get charged our increased rate."

"Repeat customers are going to love that," Grace said.

"We've been open a year. How many repeat customers could we have? They probably won't even notice, and if they do, we could give them a one-time reduced rate to mollify them. Agreed?"

Grace and Molly looked at each other, then back to him. "Fine," they said simultaneously.

"Great," he said on a sigh. That had been easier than he'd anticipated. And he wasn't nearly as certain as he'd made it sound that the risk would actually pay off. "Now let's go over last month's numbers."

He talked them through the income and expenditures listed on the Excel spreadsheet. As usual he hoped his sisters wouldn't notice that the numbers didn't quite add up. The spreadsheet didn't account for the fact that all the marketing dollars had gone onto Levi's personal credit card.

No worries, though. As usual their eyes remained good and glazed over throughout the meeting. Forty minutes later he was finished.

Levi closed the folder. "And that's about it for this month."

"Thank God," Grace muttered, pushing up. "It's been real."

"Wait up," Levi said. "Before you go there's one more matter I want to discuss with you guys."

The girls groaned as they sank back into their seats.

There it was—the reason he personally referred to the meetings as the monthly Moan and Groan.

"Before you slip off into dreamland again, this isn't regarding business per se. It's about Mia."

"I just love that girl," Molly said. "I'm so glad she's staying on a while."

"Me too," Grace said. "I never dreamed she'd be so down-to-earth."

"Right? She's so considerate. And she plays a mean game of five-card draw."

"Anyway," Levi continued, "it seems that when she and I slipped out last night the press took some photos and posted them online."

"The paparazzi?" Grace deadpanned.

"Unheard of," Molly added.

He gave them both a look. "Anyway . . . Since then there's been some speculation about our relationship, and that scrutiny has kind of changed the subject, if you will, in regard to Mia's situation with Jax Jordan. Her agent thinks that if we— No phones during our meetings, Grace."

Grace's eyes remained glued to her screen. "Relax, brother dear, just looking up those photos you— Oh. My. Gosh."

"What?" Molly leaned over. "What is it?"

"Look at these. Look at this one."

Molly cut a look at Levi. "Levi . . . you dirty dog. You're totally in love with Mia Emerson."

Heat rushed through his body, shooting down his limbs and up his neck. He wiped his palms on his legs. "She's our guest, Molly."

Grace gave a wry laugh. "You are such a goner."

They were not making this easy. "*Anyway* . . . As I was saying, her agent thinks it would be good for her career if we continued the narrative a bit. So I just wanted you to know we'll likely be seen out and about town the remainder of her stay."

"Otherwise known as 'dating,'" Grace said, still staring at her phone. "Look at this one—look at his face."

"So fierce!"

Levi snatched the phone. "All right already. Can you guys just listen for a change? We're not actually going to be dating. I'm simply helping a guest with a . . ." He searched for the right word.

"Project?" Molly asked, a gleam in her eyes. "Would you say this is a project, Levi?"

He gave her a withering look. He'd been all over Molly for getting into that love letter project with Adam when he'd been their guest.

"I'm pretty sure projects with guests are discouraged," Molly said.

"Frowned upon," Grace added.

"Forbidden, even," Molly said.

Levi glowered. "This is *her* project, not mine. There's a difference. This isn't—"

Grace and Molly traded looks, chuckling.

He clenched his teeth and tossed Grace's phone back to her. "Know what? If you two could just continue saying 'no comment' as you come and go that would be great. Thanks for your support."

He got up and left the room, their laughter following him all the way to the lobby.

twenty-six

The next Tuesday Mia followed Levi down the marina dock. The gaggle of reporters that had followed them from the inn was shooting from the parking lot with their telephoto lenses.

"This is really weird," he said.

"You're doing great." She smiled her thanks as Levi helped her on board the beautiful wooden boat bearing the name *Mystique*. "Just keep smiling. Good news is, we're about to make our getaway." She took the beach bag from him and stowed it on a bench seat.

Levi untied the boat and hopped inside. He'd been busy working over the weekend, so Mia had just hung around the inn. She'd worked on her lines, Skyped Ana Maria, and caught up on emails.

Meanwhile the media had figured out who Levi was, and the speculation that he was a significant other had waned. Nolan suggested that being seen together on an actual "date" would help their cause.

Levi's marina friend had loaned him the boat for the afternoon, and the rest was history. Or soon would be, when the pictures were published. Mia wore her red shorts with a white gauzy top, and Levi wore a pair of navy blue trunks with a white T-shirt. They looked like they were on a nautical dream date.

She settled close to him on the bench seat as he started up the boat, his masculine scent carrying over on a breeze.

"Think they got some good shots?" he asked.

"I hope so."

"Let's get out of here then." He pulled the boat from the slip, going slow through the no-wake zone, and Mia settled back in her seat.

Levi took her across the lake to a private little spit of beach. They lay out in the sun and grazed on the snacks Miss Della had packed them. They talked about his family and his life back in Denver. Mia wondered if he knew that his tone took on a wistful quality when he talked about that life. And she wondered if his sisters knew how much he was sacrificing for them.

With the sun overhead beaming hot, Levi got in the water, swimming out to a submerged boulder and back. Mia, having no swimsuit, simply splashed in the shallows, cooling her feet.

Her ankle was only a little swollen now, and the bruising had faded to a yellow-green. She could walk without limping, though she still took care with her steps.

After three lazy hours they headed back to the marina. Mia slumped in her seat, sun-tired, her hair windblown.

"That was a nice break," Levi said as he steered into the no-wake zone. He perched his sunglasses on top of his head.

White fluffy clouds had gathered overhead, screening the sun, so Mia did the same. "I think I got too much sun."

His gaze raked over her, a flicker of male appreciation in his eyes. "Your cheeks are a little pink, but the color looks nice on you."

At his scrutiny a pleasant shiver passed over her heated flesh. "I should've worn sunscreen—I probably don't look very Irish at the moment."

"That's right. Tell me more about the movie. You said it was multigenerational?"

She loved that he listened to her. She never got the feeling he was daydreaming or thinking of what he'd say next. "It's called *Lesser Days*, and it's about a mother and her two daughters. It's set in Ireland during the potato famine in the 1840s. It's got a lot of grit. The female characters have lost so much, and it really showcases the power of resilience and fortitude. It's so empowering— that's what attracted me to the role."

"Sounds intriguing. I can't wait to see it."

"We have to shoot it first." Her smile wavered. It was still possible the studio would cancel her contract. They had the right to do so with the morality clause, and Nolan had reported that they were nervous about her participation after the scandal.

Mia settled deeper into the bench seat, feeling languid after all the sun. Their bodies touched at the shoulder and thigh. Was she sitting too close? He didn't make room between them.

"You had a busy weekend." She'd missed him the last few days while the inn had been flooded with guests. Though she'd enjoyed seeing the siblings in action, especially him.

"I meant to ask—did anyone recognize you?"

"A couple people. But they were cool." She tossed him a look. But it lingered longer than she'd intended. The bit of color he'd gotten today made his eyes seem even bluer.

"So . . ." She pulled her gaze away. "Have you given any more thought to where we might look next for the necklace?"

"I know the basement is empty. I couldn't see Dorothy hiding valuables down there anyway. I thought we might check the walls for safes, just in case. Maybe look around the main attic, even though I'm pretty sure it was cleaned out. Sorry I haven't had a chance to look yet."

"Understandable."

"I'm afraid we have a large family coming for a reunion tonight and staying through Sunday. Not sure how long you were planning to stay . . ."

It sounded like he was fishing, like maybe he didn't want her to leave. Or maybe he did want her to leave because of all the extra hassle. But then she remembered the way he'd looked at her a couple times today.

"At least another week, if that's okay."

Did the corners of his lips lift just a bit? "Let's plan on getting back to it after they leave then?"

"Sounds like a plan."

The marina was quiet as Levi expertly guided the boat into the slip. Mia found herself reluctant to return to the inn. She'd enjoyed having Levi all to herself. There was something growing between them, and even though she knew it could only be temporary, she couldn't seem to quell the butterflies fluttering about her belly. He'd made her laugh today, made her let down her guard. And it felt good. Right.

Whoa. That was a dangerous thought. Her life was in LA, and his was not. Besides, he wasn't in the business, and that had a way of making relationships difficult.

And yet . . . those butterflies.

He'd turned off the boat, and it bobbed gently in the waves. He made no move to get up, and she could feel his gaze on her.

She looked at him and found him closer than she realized. He was regarding her seriously. His piercing blue eyes making those wings flutter.

"I had a good time today." His words came slow and lazy.

Tension crackled in the air between them. "Me too."

His eyes dropped to her lips, making them tingle with just a look.

And then he was right there, his lips meeting hers. He brushed them once, twice. A hum of pleasure moved through her, making the world disappear.

He moved back just a breath, pausing.

Her heart stuttered as she waited, eyes still closed, feeling his breath on her lips. Then he palmed her face and drew her back to him.

She settled her hand on the warmth of his thigh and gave herself fully to the kiss. And what a kiss it was. She'd had many of them, both on-screen and off.

But this one. She never wanted it to end. Wanted more.

He turned more fully into her, wrapping an arm around her waist, delving his fingers into her hair.

Her heart stuttered. Her breath caught in her lungs. She couldn't get close enough. Couldn't get enough of him, period.

A clicking sound pulled Mia back to planet Earth. A repetitive clicking. Almost like . . .

Levi pulled back.

Over his shoulder she saw the photographer, camera poised.

Levi shot up from the seat, rocking the boat. "Hey, take a hike, buddy! This is private property."

Mia turned from the camera, running her hand

through her tangled hair, her brain still fuzzy with that kiss.

Someone from the marina was already making his way down the dock. "I'll have to ask you to leave, sir."

The photographer was backing away, still snapping photos.

Levi took a few threatening steps toward the man. "Back off!"

"Sir, you need to leave."

Had Levi seen the photographer lurking in the shadows as they'd approached the dock? Had he staged the moment? That amazing kiss?

Think they got some good shots?

Levi's words from earlier flashed in Mia's mind. Those butterflies seemed to sink like lead to the bottom of her stomach.

"I'll tie up for you," the marina guy said to Levi.

"Thanks, Ernest." Levi grabbed her hand. "Come on. Let's get out of here."

The mood had shifted by the time Levi ushered Mia inside the inn. The photographers were still out front, although there were fewer. Mia had been quiet since they left the marina.

He'd been irate when that infernal clicking had interrupted their kiss. But it had only taken about two seconds to start wondering if Mia's generous response had been for the benefit of the camera.

And that had done nothing for his mood.

The quiet drive home provided time for further speculation. This was Mia Emerson he was talking about. The famous celebrity, Mia Emerson, worshiped by every male over the age of twelve. What had he been thinking?

The front desk was empty, but there were noises coming from overhead.

Mia seemed a little shaken.

"You all right?" he asked.

"Yeah, I just . . . I think I'm going to work a while, maybe catch up on emails."

"Yeah, sure."

The phone rang just then. Molly must've turned the ringer back on.

"Guess I better get that."

And then Mia was gone, taking the stairs like she couldn't get away from him fast enough.

What in the world had just happened?

twenty-seven

Molly set her cloth napkin on her plate and pushed it back. The evening was perfect. She and Adam had watched the sun set quietly over the lake, and now the interior of the Crow's Nest glowed dim in the candlelight.

The golden light flickered on Adam's handsome face. He'd worn his charcoal gray suit with a crisp white shirt and the red tie she'd gotten him for Valentine's Day.

She wiped her sweaty palms down the length of her red sundress. She loved him so much, and she couldn't wait for the moment he settled that ring on her finger. She bit her lip. She would not start rambling about nothing. She'd already done that a few times tonight, and she was determined not to ruin everything with her ridiculous blathering.

The server set the bill on the table, and Adam tucked his credit card inside the folder. A moment later the server snatched it up.

Adam leaned in, his elbows on the table, his face growing intent. "I was wondering . . . Do you remember what tonight is?"

Molly sighed. Finally. She leaned forward, falling headlong into his denim-blue eyes. "I was wondering if *you* remembered."

237

He gave a shy smile. "How could I forget the best kiss of my life?"

Her heart squeezed. He said the best things. She winced playfully. "Until I ruined it." They'd gone over that kiss many times. It had been wonderful. But the intense feelings she had for him had scared her silly.

"I admit it felt like rejection at the time. But the explanation you gave me later more than made up for the heartache."

She smiled, the memory of the kiss flooding back. "It was a great kiss, wasn't it?"

"Definitely worth celebrating."

The server smiled as she set the bill folder on the table. "Thank you. Y'all have a wonderful evening now."

Adam responded to the server as Molly bit back an impatient huff. They were just getting to the good part.

He removed his credit card from the folder and tucked it into his wallet, meeting her gaze.

Here it comes. She leaned closer.

He lifted his brows. "Ready?"

Molly blinked. They were leaving? "Um, yeah. Sure."

He was already standing and pulling out her chair. Befuddled, Molly followed him from the restaurant.

All right. He wasn't going to ask her here. She gave her head a shake. Of course he wasn't going to ask her at a restaurant. This was Adam, notable writer of epic love stories. He'd take her someplace special. Maybe to Pawley Park where he'd first told her how he felt about her. Or out in the boat where they'd shared that first kiss. She should've worn a light sweater, she thought, as they made their way to his car.

He helped her into the car, and soon they were making their winding way down the mountain. Quiet settled between them. He was probably as nervous as she was. Of course he was. This was Adam.

She glanced at him out of the corner of her eyes. Although she hadn't noticed him poking his glasses into place even once tonight.

Then again, he'd grown more comfortable around her since he'd moved to Bluebell. He rarely messed with his glasses or spewed statistics anymore. And she'd mostly ceased to babble like a downhill brook. They were content together.

Her lips tugged upward. *Content.* What a lovely word.

A while later they came out of the mountain turns and eased onto the low road that curved around the lake. She held her breath as they neared the turn-off for the park. This could be it. This could be the moment that . . .

But no. The car didn't slow at all.

Okay. All right. A boat ride then. And this way she could grab her sweater from her room before they set off. Aw, this was perfect. A boat ride proposal on the one-year anniversary of their first kiss. He was so thoughtful. She couldn't wait to throw her arms around him and say yes. She clasped her hands in her lap so her response didn't precede the actual question.

A few minutes later he pulled into the slot in front of the inn. Thank God the paparazzi had given up their station after Levi and Mia had given them what they'd wanted.

Molly and Adam were all alone. The porch light glowed, giving the place a homey feel. Her heart pummeled her ribs, and her mouth was a little dry. A bunch of words bubbled up, but she bit them back.

No talking, Molly. Do not ruin this!

He shut off the engine and came around for her door. She gave him her best smile as she brushed past him. The moonlight kissed every surface, giving the night an ethereal glow. The scent of jasmine hung in the air. It was a perfect night for a proposal. For an engagement.

Squee!

Deep breaths, Molly. Settle down. Remain calm.

Her knees felt a little rubbery as she took the porch steps. Adam's hand rested on the small of her back. She had to be careful not to ruin the surprise he'd planned. When was he going to suggest a boat ride?

She reached for the door handle.

"I should probably say good night out here," he said. "I have an early radio interview."

She turned and met his gaze, her heart stuttering. "Oh?"

"Out of New York. One of the largest stations in the country, actually."

"That's great." On the porch then? Was he going to ask her on the porch?

He brushed a thumb across her cheek and looked deep into her eyes. "I had a wonderful time tonight. I always have a wonderful time with you, Molly."

"Me too. Thank you for dinner."

Something shifted in his eyes. But it wasn't something good. More like a dark shadow. Sadness? Regret? He wasn't supposed to be having regret tonight. He was supposed to be—

But then his eyes were closing, and he was brushing her lips softly.

Molly responded to the kiss as her mind spun. What was going on? Why wasn't he asking her? Had she done something wrong?

Maybe . . .

Oh my gosh, was it possible she'd invented the whole thing? Had she completely misunderstood? The dinner reservations could have simply been his way of celebrating their first kiss.

But no. Two days ago she'd seen a call come in on his phone when he was out of the room. It had said Tiffany & Co.

Tiffany! You didn't have to be from New York to know what that was. Of course, they sold more than just engagement rings. But her birthday was a long way off, and Adam didn't wear jewelry at all. What else could it possibly be?

She didn't have to have a Tiffany ring; she wasn't fussy. She'd be thrilled with a ring from Jared's or Kay's or, at this point, a gumball machine.

Adam pulled away, giving her a quizzical look. "Are you all right?"

She forced a smile. "Of course, I'm fine. I'm great. Just peachy. I'm not sure I've ever been better." She bit her lip.

He quirked a brow, giving her a fond look. "You're so cute. Have I told you that lately?"

"Well . . . not tonight. Except you just did. So I guess you did. Say it. Tonight."

His lips twitched. He brushed her lips again. "Good night, Molly. I'll call you tomorrow. I love you."

"Love you too. Good night."

He turned on the way back to his car, giving a little wave. Molly forced a smile as she fluttered her fingers and hoped he couldn't see the sheen of tears in her eyes.

twenty-eight

On Sunday afternoon Levi tapped lightly on Mia's door. He'd hardly seen her since the kiss. On Thursday the photos had hit the tabloid websites—Molly had shown him. He was never going to hear the end of it from his sisters.

He'd had plenty of time to think about that kiss though. Mia had definitely seen that photographer. Why else would she have responded so eagerly? He wasn't sure how he'd gotten up the nerve to kiss her at all, but it was best if she thought he'd simply been playing a role too.

That wouldn't stop him from reliving her passionate response though. He could still feel the softness of her lips on his. The warmth of her hand on his thigh.

The door swung open, and there was Mia—hopefully not reading his thoughts.

"Hi." She smiled at him, looking beautiful in leggings and a pale green tunic that brought out the color of her eyes. Her hair was pulled back in a messy bun, highlighting her cheekbones.

"Hey. So, all the guests have checked out. You have time to look for the necklace?"

Her eyes lit as she tossed the script she was holding onto the bed. "I always have time to look for the necklace."

"I can come back if you're working."

"I needed a break anyway. Where should we start?"

He gestured toward her room. "In there, I was thinking, since that was likely the Livingstons' bedroom."

She opened the door wider with a sheepish smile. "Okay, but I may have already checked behind the wall hangings."

She was so cute. A thought supported by every man in America, he reminded himself. And probably half of Europe.

She kicked a pair of balled-up socks to the side and picked up two soggy towels. "Where should we start?"

Levi glanced around the room. "How about the floor? It's the original wood. We can just go plank by plank and see if anything's loose."

"Sounds like a plan. We should probably roll up the rug first."

They got on their knees and began rolling the floral area rug. He liked the way she dug right in. His initial presumptions about her had sure been proven wrong.

"So . . ." She spared him a glance under those long eyelashes. "Did you see the pictures online?"

"Molly made sure of it." He scrubbed the delicious image from his mind. "I guess we played that off just right, huh?"

Her lashes fluttered down. "Right, yes. That's all they're talking about now—or so I hear. I've learned the hard way to let Nolan filter the gossip for me."

"I can't imagine having my whole life on display. How do you deal with the lack of privacy?"

"It's not my favorite thing, but what are you going to do? It goes with the job. I learned that early on from watching my mom. I think she kind of got off on the spotlight though."

"Liked the attention?"

Mia gave a dry chuckle. "You could say that. I felt more like her showpiece than her daughter sometimes. Even when I was little she dressed me up like we were headed for a photo shoot. Every time we left the house, I was told to smile and stop fidgeting and act ladylike. She just . . . preened for the cameras, and I was her little mini-me."

Levi stopped rolling the rug and looked at her. What kind of mother made her child feel like an accessory?

"Listen to me." She gave an awkward laugh. "I've known you for all of two weeks, and I'm spilling all my secrets."

The vulnerable look on her face tugged at him. She tore her gaze away and continued rolling the rug.

"That must've been very difficult for a little girl to understand," he said when they'd finished.

"A lot of pressure. It's a wonder you wanted to be an actress."

"It's the work I enjoy. Unlike with my mom, the attention is just something that comes with it—something I put up with."

"All things considered, you seem very well adjusted. And I hope you know I'd never share the things you've told me with anyone."

"So you're not going to sell me out to *People* magazine?" she said lightly.

"Never." He gave her a playful smile. "Maybe *Entertainment Weekly* or *U. S. Weekly.*"

Her eyes met his, lighting a moment before she started laughing.

"What?" he asked, bemused. "What's so—?"

Mia snorted. "It's *Us Weekly*, not *U.S.*! United States Week—" She couldn't finish for the laughter.

His face heated. He scratched his neck. "All right, all right. So I don't know my gossip rags. Sue me."

Her cheeks had blossomed a pretty pink color, and her nose crinkled adorably. Her laughter was like a beautiful melody—even if it was at his expense.

"If you're gonna laugh, sweetheart, I'm gonna give you something to laugh about." He poked her in the side.

She squealed and sternly pointed her finger. "Levi Bennett . . ."

He got her again in the ribs, the soft clothing making it so easy to reach his target.

"I'm very ticklish!"

"How lucky for me." He went after her, careful of her ankle, making her laugh hysterically. "Yes, much better than being laughed at."

She rolled onto her back, wiggling and squirming. "I wasn't laughing at—"

He got her other side. "What was that?"

"All right, I was, but it was so—"

"Sweet? Cute? Clever?"

"Cute! It was cute. Let's go with that."

He paused a moment to give her the stink eye.

A snicker sneaked out.

Levi lifted his tickling hand over her in a threatening manner.

The smile dropped from her face. Though her lips may have twitched.

Then her expression suddenly shifted. She widened her eyes, all innocence. She gave a slow blink. "It was *so* cute I could hardly stand it. Cutest thing I've ever heard."

He narrowed his eyes, waiting for a lapse in her expression.

She looked every bit the innocent. Her eyes didn't so much as twinkle.

"Darn, you're good."

She blinked again. "Does that mean I'm off the hook?"

"All right. Fine. As long as you don't tell all

your celebrity friends what I said." He helped her up into a sitting position.

She chuckled.

He could hardly even bring himself to scowl at her, so instead he said, "And you, Mia Emerson, are a snorter."

She gasped. "I am not."

"Like a happy horse."

"A *horse?*" She elbowed him, chuckling.

A tap sounded on the door. It was still open, so he could easily see Molly leaning on the doorframe, arms crossed, a dustrag in her hand. She looked every bit as innocent as Mia had a few seconds ago.

"Need any help with your . . . project?" Molly asked, wide-eyed.

"Are you finished cleaning the rooms?"

"No . . ."

"Then we don't need any help."

"All right then." She gave Levi a knowing smirk before she turned. "Don't do anything I wouldn't do."

"That leaves a very broad gap," he called after her.

Mia gave him a questioning look. "What was that about?"

"Sibling stuff." He grabbed the rug. "Why don't we haul this into the bathroom."

Mia grabbed her end, and they carried the rug into the bathroom, his face heated.

What was he doing, rolling around on the floor with a guest? With *Mia Emerson,* no less? If he'd caught Molly doing that when Adam was a guest he would've sat her down and given her a nice long lecture about boundaries. Of course, he'd apologized to her for that, but he never dreamed he'd find himself on Molly's side of this equation.

What had gotten into him? His gaze drifted to Mia with her pert little nose, creamy skin, and melodic laughter. Mia had gotten into him, that's what. She'd gotten under his skin and right into his heart.

Oh, for crying out loud, he was even sounding like Molly.

They set down the rug and went back into the bedroom.

"I'll start over on that side," Mia said, "and you can start over there."

"Sounds like a plan." Probably best they stay on opposite sides of the room, since he couldn't seem to keep his hands to himself.

twenty-nine

Mia worked on her lines the next day in the shady backyard of the inn, her feet propped on the footrest, her script opened on her lap. The dialogue for *Lesser Days* was terrific. She couldn't wait to read lines with the other actors. Couldn't wait to bring the part of Fiona to life.

Out on the lake a lone boat drifted by, its white sail billowing on a breeze. The leaves shimmied overhead, and the smell of freshly cut grass hung in the air. It was so relaxing here. A nice break from the hustle and bustle of LA, though she was starting to get twitchy. She missed her work.

A text came in from Brooke, who was fretting about a job. Mia texted her back, assuring her it would all work out. Brooke was a pro, but she had a lot of self-doubt.

A sound at the back of the inn made her turn around.

Molly, wearing a white top and khaki shorts, was rolling out the garden hose.

"Hi, Molly."

"Oh, hey! I didn't see you there. Will it disturb you if I water the flowers? Mother Nature's slacking."

"Not at all. I'm just memorizing lines."

"For your next movie?"

"Yeah, we start filming soon."

The faucet handle squeaked as Molly turned on the water. She pulled the hose along with her as she began watering the flowers that lined the walkway heading down to the lake.

"No luck finding the necklace?" Molly asked.

"Not yet. We're going to look again tonight. I'm afraid Levi might be right. It probably got sold in the estate auction."

"Oh, don't let Levi burst your bubble. There's nothing wrong with dreaming. I'm sure that necklace meant a lot to Dorothy. I can't imagine she'd just let it go in some random auction."

"That's what I thought, but we're running out of places to look."

Molly gave her a commiserating smile, then continued a few paces along the walk. "So, I have to ask . . . Those pictures of you and Levi . . ."

Mia wondered if Molly was upset about them, but she wasn't giving off that vibe. "Yeah, they seem to have had the desired effect. It's definitely taken the focus off my supposed crush on Jax Jordan."

"I'll say. Everybody's talking about you and Levi and your 'incredible chemistry.' " She made air quotes around the words.

Mia's face heated at the memory of his kiss. Talking to his sister about it was a little

251

awkward. "Levi's amazing. And he's movie star handsome—in case you weren't aware. The camera loves him."

Molly gave a rueful grin. "If you say so."

"He's very special. So competent."

"I'll give you that one."

Mia searched for a new topic. "And your guy—Adam? He seems pretty terrific." Mia had met him at church on Sunday. She'd met a lot of people.

"Yeah." Molly's eyes seemed to dim, and her smile drooped. "Yeah. He's great."

Mia thought she'd continue, but she seemed lost in thought now. Molly continued watering the same flowers until the soil around them was nearly flooded. One thing about Molly—her every thought was right out there for everyone to see. And coming from Hollywood, Mia appreciated that trait more than most.

She closed her script. "You all right, Molly?"

Molly studied Mia for a long moment. "You've had a lot of boyfriends, right?"

Mia smiled. "Well, I don't know about a lot . . ."

"Right, I just mean, you know, serious relationships. After all, you were engaged—and I probably shouldn't have brought that up. You know what? I shouldn't have brought any of this up. You're a guest and I'm your host. Sorry, just forget I opened my big mouth."

Mia's lips twitched. "Are you having boy trouble?"

Molly dropped the sprayer and rushed over to Mia. "Yes! And I'm about to burst."

Mia held back a smile. "Have a seat. Tell me what's wrong."

Molly plopped down on Mia's footrest. "I usually talk to my friend Skye about this stuff, but she's away at some conference, and I don't want to bug her."

"What is it? Something happen with Adam?"

"Something *didn't* happen with Adam. We had this anniversary of sorts on Friday, and I found out he'd made reservations at the Crow's Nest, and then last week a call came in on his phone from Tiffany jewelers and—"

"Tiffany!"

"I know! The little blue box! I was so excited for our date Friday. I wore my favorite dress and took so much time with my hair and makeup, and I got a manicure—I never get a manicure!— but dinner came and went, and then he brought me straight home and said good night on the porch."

"Oh no."

"I was so disappointed I cried a little after he left. Maybe a lot. And okay, the next day too, but now I'm just confused. I must've done something wrong, but I can't for the life of me figure out what it was."

"I'm sure that's not it. Maybe he's planning to ask you another time."

"But Friday was the anniversary of our first kiss, and the Crow's Nest is *the* special occasion place in Bluebell. I was just so sure he was going to ask me. And ever since then things have been weird."

"How do you mean?"

"I don't know, there's just this . . . strangeness between us that wasn't there before. It's probably me. But he seems distracted when we're together, and he never seemed that way before. And maybe I've been a little quiet, too, since I'm trying to figure out what happened. He keeps asking if I'm all right, but I don't know what to say."

"Maybe you should talk to him about it."

"Tell him I thought he was going to propose and I'm heartbroken that he didn't?"

"You could . . ."

"But then if he really is planning to propose, I'll ruin it. And he knows I love surprises. I can't do that to him."

"Then maybe you should just be patient a while longer and see what happens. I mean, if he bought a ring, he must be planning to propose, right?"

Molly's face broke out into a smile. "You're right. Of course. I should just be patient—not exactly my strong suit, but if I know it's coming I can tolerate the wait." She squeezed Mia's hand.

"Thanks, Mia. I'm glad we talked. I feel so much better."

Mia really liked Molly, liked her authenticity. She was so different from Levi, practically his opposite, although they both shared that particular trait.

Mia smiled. "Glad I could help."

thirty

Levi couldn't sleep. He turned to his other side, bunching his pillow under his head. It was almost midnight, and he had to be up at six. He kept thinking about Mia. They'd rooted through the main attic tonight, and even though they hadn't found anything old or interesting, he'd had a great time with her.

He loved hearing her laughter so much he found himself dropping lines he knew would amuse her. He'd poked her in the side once or twice just to see that stern look come over her face. That elegant finger point at his chest.

And then when he ran out of new imagery, he recalled that kiss on the boat. Would he ever tire of remembering the way her skin had felt beneath his hand? So soft. Or the way her hair had sifted like silk strands through his fingers?

Never mind that she'd only been playing a part. She'd played it so convincingly his heart had been about to pound right out of his chest. He'd only seen the resulting photos in passing when Molly had shoved her phone into his face.

Now he found himself tempted to take another peek. It was him in the photo too, after all. Who wouldn't want to see what the rest of the world was viewing? He'd pushed aside the temptation for five days, but now his laptop seemed to beckon him from the desk.

He heaved a sigh. May as well give into it. He wasn't sleeping anyway. He got out of bed and sank into the desk chair. The bright screen made him squint in the darkness, but his eyes adjusted quickly. He flipped on the desk lamp so he could see the keyboard and typed in both their names. He clicked on the first website that appeared.

There they were, Mia and him, making out in the boat. The photographer had zoomed in close, capturing the moment just after she'd set her hand on his leg. Mia was leaning into him, her eyes closed. She didn't look like a woman pretending for the camera.

But then, she was an actress. She'd probably kissed for the camera many times. There was a thought that rankled.

He clicked on another link and read the article printed along with the photo. The article speculated about their relationship and mentioned their "obvious chemistry." It was a sentence deep into the article that made him frown.

Mia's date, Levi Bennett, has been identified as the innkeeper at the Bluebell Inn in Bluebell, North Carolina, where Mia has been staying since the Jax Jordan scandal broke.

He didn't like that the general public knew where she was. That couldn't be safe. And yet, this article had been published five days ago, and other than fielding calls from media and fans it hadn't been an issue.

They'd had a marked increase in reservations though. That was good.

What wasn't good was that the thought of business had come second to his concern for Mia. Still, that didn't stop him from doing another search. This time he just Googled Mia's name. Holy cow, there were a lot of articles and photos of her. He started with *Us Weekly*, smirking as he remembered his mistake.

There were older articles about Mia, and he found himself skimming those, along with the photos. Lots of stills from *Into the Deep*. Photos from events: Mia at the Oscars with that guy from *Arrow*; on the arm of a guy who'd played in some Nicholas Sparks movie, according to the caption; at a movie premier with her ex-fiancé, Wesley Hughes.

He looked closely at that one. It wasn't hard to see what she saw in him. His golden-blond hair made him look like a quintessential California surfer dude. He wondered if Mia still loved him.

He poked around more sites, finding many photos of Mia and Wesley, eventually landing on a message board. It was filled with lewd comments that made him want to hunt the creeps down, one by one, and lay them flat. For his own sanity he left the page and continued reading about Mia on the celebrity sites.

He heard a sound at his door and whipped around.

Molly leaned against the doorframe, arms crossed, brow quirked. "Stalking our guest, brother dear?"

He scowled and closed out the internet, his face heating. "You shouldn't sneak up on people like that."

"I came down for tea and saw your light on. You have the morning shift, you know."

He closed the laptop. "I'm well aware."

"So . . . learn anything new? She's nice, don't you think?"

He gave her a look.

"What? She is nice. It's kind of surprising the way she fits in around here. And I think she likes you."

The bubble of hope that expanded inside him was pathetic. Just pathetic. "Butt out, Molly."

She came into the room and plopped down on his bed with her mug of tea.

"Or come in and make yourself comfortable."

"So defensive. One might think I've hit a sore spot."

"There's nothing going on between Mia and me. We're playing roles for the media, that's all."

She blinked, all innocence. "And all that rolling around on the floor I interrupted yesterday?"

He'd known that was going to come back

to haunt him. He opened his mouth to defend himself.

"Not that I'm complaining, mind you. You could do worse than Mia Emerson, you know."

He rolled his eyes. "Life isn't a fairy tale, Molly. She's a celebrity. And she's going back to LA in a matter of days."

"Sounds as if you've thought this through."

He gave her a dark look.

"All right, all right. If you don't want to talk about it, fine. Far be it from me to force an issue. I just wanted to say, in case it matters, I think she's interested in you too. We had a nice little talk out back today." She stood and turned for the door. "But if you don't want to hear what she said I totally respect that."

He knew when he was being toyed with. Even so he couldn't help himself. "All right. Fine. What'd she say?"

Molly turned, took a slow sip of her tea. "Oh, you want to talk about it now, do you?"

He gave a low growl.

Molly chuckled. "You're so easy, Levi. All right, I'll be nice. She said you're amazing. She said you're movie star handsome, and she said that you're 'very special.' "

His pulse fluttered as heat rushed through him. "Is that all?"

Her brows popped up. "Isn't that enough?"

Actually, it was. Those were some nice

compliments in there. Good kisser would've been nice, but he'd take what he could get.

Molly shook her head and headed toward the door. "Good night, Levi."

"Night," he said. Then because she'd pretty much made his night he added, "Thanks, Molly."

She gave him a knowing smile. "You're welcome, brother dear."

thirty-one

Mia pulled a handful of books from the shelves and added them to the stack on the floor. She and Levi had already looked behind every wall hanging in the inn, and now they were in the library, clearing the shelves. The scent of lemon wood polish mingled with the musty smell of old books.

She glanced at Levi, who was working on an adjacent shelf. "I always thought it would be cool to find one of those secret library walls."

"Well, I hate to be a dream crusher. But this is a corner room, bordered by a hallway and lobby, so I don't think it's going to happen today."

"I'd settle for a secret safe containing that necklace."

"Wouldn't we all."

They were running out of places to look. He'd mentioned a crawl space under the house, but neither of them could imagine Dorothy putting the Carolina Breeze in that damp, dark space.

Mia pulled a stack of Lee Child books from the next shelf. "Somebody likes the Jack Reacher series. There must be twenty of them here."

"Those were my dad's. He liked to read as much as Molly."

He hadn't talked much about his parents. It

must be a painful subject. "What was he like, your dad?"

"He was an attorney here in town. He really liked helping people, though that's not something he ever would've admitted to. He was a congenial guy, but he was quiet about it. He had this great dry sense of humor—I didn't really appreciate that until I was in my late teens. I guess most of it went over my head before then. He sure loved my mom though. I used to moan and groan about the way they were always touching each other. But man . . . That's pretty great to be so in love after all those years."

"He sounds terrific. I can't imagine what it would be like to even *have* a dad. I mean, some of my friends did, of course, but—" She shook her head.

"You were five when he took off?"

It warmed her that he'd remembered. "Yeah. That's pretty young, huh?"

"What happened between your parents? Did your mom ever say?"

"She said he couldn't deal with the realities of the business. He was jealous of the men she was with on-screen and jealous of the attention she got in public."

Levi paused in his task. "And you never heard from him again?"

Mia shrugged. "Nope."

She didn't want to talk about her dad

anymore. Maybe she'd come to grips with the abandonment, but it still wasn't a pleasant topic.

"What about your mom?" Mia asked. "What was she like?"

"She was pretty great too. She was more free-spirited than Dad. She was the outgoing one—everyone liked her. We couldn't go anywhere without her running into someone she had to chat with."

"Sounds like Molly."

"Yeah, Molly takes after her a lot. And I guess Grace got our dad's dry sense of humor."

"What did you get?"

He paused, a thoughtful look on his face. "They were very different, my mom and dad. I guess I got my mom's conscience and my dad's pragmatism—and his height."

They'd both moved toward the bookshelf corner, bringing them closer together.

She gave him a look from the corner of her eyes. "I think you got your dad's looks too. I saw the photo hanging in the lobby. He was very handsome." Almost as handsome as Levi, with that dark hair and those sky-blue eyes.

Levi turned those eyes on her now, his lips quirking. His arm brushed hers as he pulled books from the shelf.

His touch made a strange energy hum through her. Made her mouth go dry.

"So . . . you think I'm handsome, huh?" Levi said, his tone teasing.

Men. Hadn't she already told him as much? Mia pursed her lips and went back to work, all nonchalant. "You're okay, I guess."

Levi sat back on his heels, giving her a sly grin. "Just okay?"

The scent of his cologne was yummy. She drew in a deep breath of it. Her hands were suddenly shaky under his perusal, and she was glad for the task at hand. He made her nervous. Made her stomach swarm with butterflies.

Levi watched Mia unshelving books and tried to remind himself of all the photos he'd seen online last night. Mia, with all those famous men on glamorous dates. Mia, smiling at her celebrity ex-fiancé.

But Molly's words kept popping into his mind instead. *Movie star handsome. Amazing. Very special.*

Mia Emerson had said all those things about *him*. It was enough to make a man a little heady. And with her here, sitting close enough to smell her hair, he couldn't resist thinking about it.

Nor could he resist teasing her, just a little. "So you don't think I'm . . . I don't know . . . movie star handsome?"

Mia's gaze darted to Levi. She searched his

eyes for a long moment, those moss-green eyes fixed on his.

"And I'm sure you don't think I'm *amazing* or anything," Levi continued, watching her closely. "Definitely not at all *special*."

Mia's eyes flickered with realization. Her lips twisted. "Molly."

Levi couldn't stop his smug grin. "Don't be mad at her. She meant well."

He hoped Mia couldn't see how hard his heart was pounding beneath his shirt. It had been a bold move, making her own those words. He hoped he didn't regret it.

Maybe Mia had only been giving Molly lip service. Knowing his sister, she'd probably put Mia on the spot. Shame he hadn't thought of that till now. He opened his mouth to tell her he'd just been teasing, but she spoke first.

"I'm not mad at Molly." Mia tilted her head up at him. She was so close, just a breath away. Something in her eyes shifted as they locked onto his. "I would've told you myself if you'd just asked."

His pulse sped. His chest tightened. She was looking at him like . . .

"Would you now?" His eyes fell to her lips. They'd parted—an invitation? He leaned forward slowly, giving her a chance to back out.

His heart beat up into his throat as their lips met. He brushed them softly, tentatively.

His breath caught at her immediate response. At the way she pressed her hand to his neck. There was no photographer this time. No camera to perform for. It was just Mia and him, alone with their thoughts. With their wishes and wants.

And right now he wanted her more than he could say. He went back for seconds because, suddenly, he needed her kiss more than he needed his next breath.

Her hand moved up on his neck, warm and urgent, making desire course through him. Her fingers delved into the hair at his nape, sending a jolt of pleasure through him. He pulled her to him, both of them rising to their knees in a mutual need for closeness.

Levi put everything he felt for her into the kiss. Feelings he couldn't quite cop to just yet. Words he couldn't yet formulate. All of it was there in the way he touched her, the way he kissed her. He couldn't help himself. He could no sooner have stopped it than he could've stopped a ripple on the lake's surface.

Somewhere in the distance the phone rang. Off duty. Not his problem.

He ran his hands over her back as he took the kiss deeper. Her response made blood rush to his head until he could hear his own heartbeat pulsing in his ears.

The image of those online photos flashed

unbidden through his mind like a slideshow. So many men. Famous men. Mia could have anyone she wanted. Why would she want him?

And what was this to her anyway? A diversion? Her life was somewhere else. And his was here in Bluebell for the foreseeable future. Was he getting in too deep? Was he setting himself up for heartbreak?

Reluctantly, he pulled away. The half-lidded look on her face about did him in. Her lips looked bee-stung, ripe and tempting.

His palms were damp. His blood raced through his veins, carrying chemicals that urged him to "fight or flight," and he wanted to do neither.

"What's wrong?" That vulnerable look was back in her eyes.

He hated that he'd put it there. He didn't want to see her guard go back up. He wanted to kiss her eyelids and work his way back down to that delicious mouth.

But that wasn't logic talking. Even if she actually wanted him for more than a stolen kiss, what kind of future could they have?

He was still framing her face, and his fingers twitched reflexively. "I probably shouldn't have done that."

"Why not?" she asked.

Unable to stop himself, he brushed a thumb across her cheek. So soft. "Sometimes I forget who you are, Mia."

She turned her face into his palm, nuzzling the tender flesh.

Have mercy.

"What do you mean?"

Despite how she was responding to him, he was a fool to think she'd ever choose him. She was so far out of his league it was laughable.

He shook his head. "You're Mia Emerson. What could you want with an average guy like me?"

Her brows charged together. She grabbed the hands that were on her face and held them with both of hers. "Levi . . . you're not an average anything. You don't see yourself the way I do."

He gave her a droll look. "I went online and looked you up, Mia. Okay? I admit it. I knew you were engaged to Wesley Hughes, but I didn't know you'd dated so many other celebrities. I'm just a regular guy here. How can I measure up to that?"

"They're just regular guys too, Levi. Don't be blinded by all the hype. I go out with other celebrities because it makes sense to date men in the industry, that's all. They understand the craziness that goes with my life." Her chin came up. "And sometimes a girl just needs a date for the Oscars, you know."

He gave a dry chuckle at the absurdity of that sentence. They were from different worlds.

He supposed that was her way of saying the relationships had been casual.

"Levi, you're an incredible man. I've been watching you around here. You're loyal and hardworking and steady . . ."

He gave a wry smile. "That honestly sounds kind of boring."

She was shaking her head. "No. A girl like me—a girl who didn't have so much of that growing up—values those things an awful lot."

He regarded her for a long moment. "Fair enough. Can I ask what happened between you and Wesley?"

"You didn't read about it online? There are hundreds of articles."

"I want to hear the truth, and I want to hear it from you."

She gave him a long, steady look. Then she sighed and sank to the ground amid the piles of books.

His body groaned at the distance she'd put between them, but he was to blame for that, after all. He made room amidst the book piles and sank onto the floor beside her.

"We met at a mutual friend's New Year's Eve party, and he asked me out. We dated a while, had a lot in common. My career was on the verge of exploding. His hadn't quite taken off yet. But he was tenacious, and he seemed patient enough to wait for his big break. He didn't seem jealous of my success—something I'm really sensitive to because of my parents' relationship.

"Anyway, we fell in love, and when he eventually asked me to marry him I said yes. We started planning the wedding—and the honeymoon—" She gave him a dour look. "Then I heard about this role I thought he'd be great for. I knew the producer and got him an audition. He got the part and soon after that—very soon—he dumped me."

"Do you think . . . ?"

"He used me? Oh yeah. I mean, he never owned up to it. He gave me other reasons. We 'weren't a good fit.' But I couldn't help but notice that insight only came along after I'd gotten him the role of his career."

Levi clenched his jaw. He wanted to pound the guy. No wonder Mia was so guarded. "I'm sorry. It must've hurt to be used that way by someone who was supposed to love you."

She gave him a wan smile. "Sadly, it's just part of the business."

"Don't let him off the hook that easily. Using people is wrong. Using their feelings against them is even worse. He asked you to marry him. That means something where I come from."

She placed her hand over his, and he realized he'd balled it into a fist. "We're from two different worlds, I'm afraid."

Clearly, they were on the same page. "Another reason that kiss was probably a mistake."

She squeezed his hand, then leaned onto her arm, bringing her closer. "That doesn't mean we can't enjoy the time we have, though, does it? I mean, I understand your reservations. I have some too." Then she looked up to him with those wide, luminous eyes of hers. "There's only one problem."

He swallowed hard, his upper body swaying closer of its own accord. "What's that?"

Her hungry eyes were intent on him. Tension hovered in the space between them. "I can't stop thinking about you."

His breath caught in his chest. His lungs forgot how to function. He was completely lost, and moreover he didn't want to be found. He was only human, after all. He leaned in and pressed his lips to hers.

She responded in kind.

It was only when Levi heard feet tromping down the hall sometime later that he finally pulled away.

thirty-two

Mia draped her clothes on the chaise in her room and slipped into her pajamas. What a day. She hadn't found the necklace, but she'd found something so much better.

She sent Brooke a quick text.

> I'm falling for Levi. He kissed me today for real.

She dropped into bed unable to prevent the dreamy sigh. She and Levi had spent most of the day together, sorting through the library. They'd taken a break and gone to dinner at the Country Skillet. There'd been a couple of locals who'd approached, asking for photos with her, but they'd been respectful.

Mia had been impressed with how Levi handled the interruptions. Some men got sulky when fans approached, and others were jealous of the attention. Levi just seemed adorably flustered. He later joked about being her chauffeur and escort. But when they'd gotten home a while ago, she'd made sure he knew he meant more to her than that.

She gave another breathy sigh at the thought of those kisses. His touch did something to her that no other man's, including Wesley's, had ever done. There was just a . . . rightness about it. She'd known she'd wanted more from Levi, but until his lips had settled on hers today she hadn't realized how much her feelings had grown.

The way he'd kissed her . . . his lips so passionate, his touch so reverent . . . as if he treasured her. He made her feel cherished.

Women often thought she was lucky to have been kissed on-screen by so many handsome leading men. But a kiss meant nothing when there were no real feelings behind it. Those scenes were so choreographed. Step closer. Right hand to waist. Tilt head to left. Don't block the camera. Shift. Embrace. And cut. It was all so mechanical. She pretended to be ardent. She pretended to be moved.

With Levi there'd been no pretending. When his lips consumed hers, she forgot the rest of the world even existed. Had to remind herself to breathe.

Fear leached into her thoughts at the depth of her feelings for him. He'd shared his concerns earlier, and they were valid. Even the one about his being a regular guy—but not for the reasons he thought.

A text came in from Brooke.

I thought that photo looked like the real thing!

Mia propped up on her pillows.

He's so sweet. So steady and strong.
And boy, can that man kiss.
How much longer are you staying?
Not sure. Filming doesn't start till mid-
July. Might hang around here until then.
Is it serious then?
Sure feels like it. I should be thinking
in temporary terms, but I don't even
want to think about leaving.
How would something permanent
even work? The long distance?
I don't know. He's pretty tied up here
with his inn for now, but he plans to
move back to Denver once the business
is stable.
That's still a long way from LA.
I know. But maybe he'd consider
moving to LA. Or maybe we could do
the long-distance thing. I get time off
between projects, and I could spend
it here. Or even in Denver if he moves
back there.
And not to be a Debbie Downer,
but you've always been committed to
dating men in the industry. Have you
changed your mind?

This one gave Mia pause. Her mom had been
crystal clear on the reasons why her marriage
hadn't worked out.

Mia wasn't sure how to reconcile that with the way she felt about Levi. Truthfully, she didn't want to think about it right now. She'd rather just remember the way it had felt to have his lips on hers, to have his hands pressing into the small of her back.

Another text came in from Brooke.

> Sorry. Probably shouldn't have said that.
> You're fine. Don't know how I feel about that. All I know is that right now I just can't seem to help myself.
> No problem. And can I just say . . . you have great taste.

A knock sounded at her door. Mia shot Brooke a quick text to close out the conversation and went to the door, hoping it was Levi. When she pulled it open her heart was thumping against her ribs in anticipation.

But it was Grace. She was dressed casually in jeans and a T-shirt that read *Sorry I'm late. I didn't want to come.* Her blond hair was pulled back in a ponytail, and she wore a sheepish look on her face.

"Hi, Grace."

The girl took in Mia's pajamas. "Oh, sorry to disturb you. It's too late. Never mind, it can wait till morning."

Mia grabbed her arm. "Wait. I was just piddling around on my phone. Come on in."

Grace waffled a moment before following Mia into her room. Unlike Molly, her little sister had maintained a professional distance with Mia when they weren't playing cards or eating together. This was the first time she'd been in Mia's room, other than to clean it.

Mia sat on the bed and gestured toward the chaise. "Have a seat. You'll have to move my clothes. I'm not very tidy—but I guess you've noticed that."

"We've seen much worse, believe me."

"I can only imagine."

Grace worried her lip.

Mia suddenly wondered if Grace was concerned for her brother, given the budding relationship between him and Mia. She couldn't imagine what else had brought Grace to her room unless she had aspirations of being an actress or something. Mia had mentored several younger girls, and Grace certainly had the looks for it. But there was a lot more to acting than good looks.

"What can I do for you, Grace?"

The girl met Mia's gaze. "I know this is completely inappropriate, and Levi would have my head if he knew I was involving you, but I was kind of wanting an unbiased opinion about something."

"Sure. Go for it."

"Okay . . . In some of the reading I've done about you I noticed you went straight into acting out of high school."

"Well, I actually did quite a bit of acting all the way through high school. I started very young with bit parts and commercials and such."

"Right, well, what I mean is, you didn't go to college, right? You don't have some kind of degree?"

"No, I didn't go to college. I pretty much had my heart set on an acting career, and I was getting regular parts by the time I graduated. Did you do any theater in high school?"

"What? No . . ."

"All right . . . Well, there are acting schools and even theater degrees where you could learn the ropes, and you could build your résumé by—"

"Oh no." Grace made a face. "I don't want to be an actor. I mean, no offense, but drama isn't really my thing."

"Oh!" Now she was completely confused. Mia chuckled. "Sorry, I guess I misunderstood."

Grace put her fingertips to her temple. "I haven't been very clear. It's just . . . There's lots of pressure on me to go to college."

Mia was starting to see where this was headed. "Ah, I see."

"My parents always told us we needed a college education. I mean, it was drilled into us from the time we were like three, you know? And I get it.

Everyone's going to college these days, and that makes the job market even more competitive."

"But . . ."

"I recently applied to three colleges, only because Levi *insisted*. I haven't heard back yet, but I'm going to soon, and the truth is . . . I don't want to go to any of them."

"What do you want to do?"

Grace drew in a breath. "I want to start an outfitting company here in Bluebell."

The way the words tumbled out made Mia wonder if she'd ever said them aloud.

"I've always loved the outdoors: boating, camping, hiking, climbing, you name it. I could rent equipment to tourists and even be a tour guide—there's nothing like that here now. I could even run it right out of the inn. And while I'm building my business I could keep working here."

"Sounds like you've given this a lot of thought."

"I have, but I know Levi. He's not going to be on board with this. He's going to say it's too risky. He's going to insist on a Plan B."

Mia fought a smile. That did sound just like Levi.

"I really think I can do this, and isn't it up to me? It's my future, my life."

"Are you sure some college classes wouldn't help prepare you for this?"

"I already know how to build a business website, and I've been helping run the inn. I'd start small—bicycle and boat rentals—and Levi could guide me through the financial aspects. I have a plan, and I think I can do it."

She certainly seemed adamant. And she'd been very proficient around the inn. She did her job and seemed pretty mature for her age.

"Well, when I was nineteen I'd already gotten my first role in a drama series. I got a studio apartment with a girlfriend and moved out, and I made it on my own just fine. I'm not saying things work out that way for everyone—there are plenty of wannabes in Hollywood who work as baristas and servers for years before they get a break. And some never do. But in the end, you have to be comfortable with your decision."

Grace's shoulders slumped. "But Levi . . . He's so stubborn about this. You have no idea."

"Have you told him everything you just told me?"

Her eyes flittered off Mia's. "Not in so many words—okay, maybe not at all."

Mia gave her an encouraging smile. "Maybe you should. Maybe you're not giving him enough credit. He loves you and wants the best for you."

Grace quirked a brow. "Too bad we don't agree on what that is."

Mia held the girl's gaze for a long moment. "Give him a chance. He might just surprise you."

thirty-three

Mia took Levi's hand and stepped from the boat onto the wooden dock. They'd had a lovely morning on the lake. The sun was beating down from overhead, having burned off the morning fog. The air was thick with the smell of pine and cut grass.

Levi had taken her around the lake, showing her all the spots she'd missed on their last outing: Summit Ridge, the state park, Stone Gap Bridge.

Two weeks had passed since she'd sprained her ankle. The bruising hadn't quite faded, but it was no longer swollen. And after seeing everything she'd missed, she was eager to get back to hiking—with Levi along this time.

She followed him up the dock. He was due at the front desk, but she hadn't yet told him she planned to stay. There was a part of her that feared he might not be as happy as she hoped. But she was running out of time.

She tugged him to a stop before they reached the grassy bank.

He looked over his shoulder at her; then, seeming to sense her gravity, he turned to her and took her other hand, a frown tugging at his brows. "What's wrong? What is it?"

Water kissed the shoreline, making a soft

rippling sound. Behind her, the boat rubbed against its bumper.

She looked up at him. "I was wondering . . . I know I said I was just staying a couple weeks, but I was thinking of staying a while longer, here at the inn. That is, if you still have room for me and you wouldn't mind."

His eyes lit a fraction of a second before the corners of his lips turned up. "We do have room. And I'd like that a lot."

Relief washed through her. "Desperate to fill up those rooms, huh?"

Those crinkles came out to play. "You have no idea. How long can you stay?"

"Well . . . I don't have to be on set until July twenty-second. And I'm just not ready to go back yet. The folks here are great. They treat me like I'm one of them." There was a lot more to it than that, but she didn't want to scare him too badly. "It's kind of nice."

His lips twitched. "It's the townsfolk you don't want to leave, huh?"

She gave him a saucy look. "And the inn."

"Anything else?"

"Well . . ." She frowned thoughtfully. "Let's see, there's Molly and Grace and Della. They're pretty great too."

He smirked. "That it?"

She blinked her wide eyes. "Am I forgetting something?"

He stepped closer, his eyes trained on hers, growing more intent.

A shiver of anticipation passed through her as she fell into his enigmatic gaze.

"Maybe I can help you remember . . ." he said, his voice as thick as honey.

And then his lips were on hers. She instantly forgot everything but the warmth of his pliant lips, the softness of his reverent touch, the strength of his muscled chest pressed against her heart.

"Can't get enough of you," he whispered against her mouth a long, delicious moment later.

"Don't stop trying."

His lips curved against hers. His arms tightened around her waist, pulling her closer. She hadn't known he was exactly what she needed until he was here, in her arms, in her life. She didn't know how she'd live without him when she left. But she didn't want to think about it just now. Maybe they'd find a way . . .

Somewhere in the distance a throat cleared loudly. "Um . . . hello?"

Grace.

"Go away," Levi grumbled against Mia's mouth.

"It's not enough I have to see this in my Facebook feed," Grace muttered. "Listen, I don't mean to interrupt, but Molly has to leave, and she sent me after you. So there. I've done my duty. I'm leaving now."

Mia pulled away, unable to tear her gaze from the half-lidded look on Levi's face. She brushed her thumb across his cheek. "You have work."

"What's that?"

She fought a smile. "Molly's waiting for you."

"Molly who?"

She chuckled as he gave her one last kiss, one last sexy smile, and headed up the sloped yard.

Levi didn't even try to fight the goofy grin as he slipped inside the inn's back door. He'd had a great time with Mia this morning. She was fun to talk to. Smart, sweet, a little saucy. She kept him on his toes in the best kind of way.

And her kisses. He wasn't kidding when he'd said he couldn't get enough.

He was passing the library on his way to the lobby when Molly's voice, carrying from the front desk, pulled him from his thoughts.

"And last year a famous author stayed here, but I didn't know who he was. Nathaniel Quinn, you've heard of him? He was incognito at the time and writes under a pseudonym, but his real name is Adam Bradford, and now he's actually my boyfriend, believe it or not. Anyway, you don't want to hear about all that."

Good grief. She was in full runaway train mode with some poor guest. He was just in time.

As he approached the front desk he saw why Molly was so flustered. Wesley Hughes stood there in a pair of stylish jeans and a black button-down that hugged his muscular frame. Mia's ex-fiancé was shorter than Levi expected—a few inches shorter than him. His golden-blond hair had been cut short at the sides, the top left longer and flopping over his forehead.

Levi clenched his jaw at the man's casual and confident demeanor. After what he'd done to Mia, Levi wanted to slug the guy on sight.

"Oh, hey, Levi," Molly said. "This is Wes—"

"I know who he is." He turned a dark look on Wesley. "You're a little late for the honeymoon."

"Levi," Molly said, aghast.

"And we're all full up just now," Levi continued. "So if you're looking for a place to stay you'll have to look elsewhere."

"Levi."

Wesley's eyes snapped and his jaw knotted. "I'm not looking for a room. I just need to speak with Mia Emerson. I believe she's a guest here."

"We don't give out that kind of information."

"Um, yeah." Molly stepped around the desk. "Perhaps you could just give her a ring."

"He already did that—and took it right back." Levi received a withering look from Molly.

"Look." Wesley appealed to Molly this time. "The thing is, I can't exactly call her . . ."

"Block your number, did she?"

Wesley's gaze clashed with Levi's. "You have a problem with me, buddy?"

Levi took a step closer. "Yeah, as a matter of fact, I do."

Then Molly was there between them. "Oookay . . . Let's do this, guys. I'll give Mia a ring—a *call*—and see if she's up for company, how's that?" She was already on her phone.

Levi glowered at Wesley.

Wesley glared right back, sizing him up.

"Hey, Mia, it's Molly." She gave a nervous chuckle. "Um, you have a visitor here to see you. It's Wesley Hughes."

Levi held back a growl. He hoped she sent him on his way. Dirt bag.

"Well, that's up to you," Molly said. "Yep . . . Uh-huh. I know . . . You sure? . . . All right, will do." Molly hung up, then gave Wesley a thin smile. "She's out back. You can go down that hall and through the door."

Wesley held Levi's gaze as he headed down the hall.

Levi wanted to wipe that smug look off his face. He started to follow.

Molly stepped in front of him. "Oh no, you don't. Let them talk. What has gotten into you?"

"He's a tool. I don't want to leave Mia alone with him." He watched the guy exit the back door.

"It's broad daylight. What can he do?" Molly squeezed his arm, drawing his attention. "Hey. Mia's a big girl. She can take care of herself."

thirty-four

Mia's heart was assaulting her rib cage, and her palms were suddenly sweaty. She sat upright on the Adirondack chair as the back door opened. She didn't turn even as she heard the swish of feet through the grass.

She hadn't had time to process that her ex-fiancé was here, in North Carolina. At their honeymoon destination.

Wesley stopped at the corner of her chair, a safe distance away.

"You're a little too late to carry me across the threshold." It was only then that Mia looked at him.

He was still as handsome as ever, but her heart didn't flutter as it once had at the sight of him. He'd had a haircut since she'd last seen him—the last time she'd Googled him—and he wasn't exactly dressed for summer at the lake.

Wes gave a rueful smile. "Save it. Your boyfriend beat you to the punch."

That realization gave her a ping of satisfaction. "Well, what did you expect? A welcome party?"

The words sounded a little bitter, but if Mia were honest, there was no real animosity rooting them. She'd come a long way in the last few weeks, she realized. And that was a good feeling.

"Can I sit down?"

"Suit yourself. What brings you all the way out here?"

He perched on the edge of the chair next to hers. "I was on set in Ashville for a few days. I saw you were here at this inn—or at least, had been—and thought I'd try and catch you."

That wasn't really what she'd meant. Their breakup had been pretty sudden. And other than a brief conversation, during which she'd thrown her engagement ring at his chest, they hadn't communicated.

She wondered briefly if he wanted her back. But no, he'd never wanted her to begin with. He already had everything he'd ever wanted: leading roles, steady income, and fame.

"You came on our honeymoon alone?" His voice was filled with bemusement.

"I needed to get away, for obvious reasons. And you know I've always wanted to come here."

"Right, your family. It's a nice place. Maybe a little quiet."

"I happen to like it that way." And so had her grandparents.

"You look well, Mia."

"Thank you. Aren't you going to ask me about Jax?"

Somebody was feeling defensive.

"I don't need to ask. You'd never go after a married man—I've said as much to the press."

Not that she needed his validation, but it was rewarding to hear him say it. "Why are you here then, Wes? I think we said everything that needs saying."

Wes chuckled as he ran a hand through his hair. "Actually, *you* said everything you wanted to say. I kind of just stood there and took it."

"Oh, is that how you remember it?"

Wes raised his hands. "I didn't come here to fight, Mia. You threw out a lot of accusations, and you didn't give me a chance to explain. I'd like that chance now if you're willing to listen."

He always had known how to defuse a situation. Except that night he'd broken up with her. She'd been pretty much undefusable.

Well, what could it hurt to hear him out? He'd come all this way, after all. She hitched a shoulder. "All right. Have at it."

He set his elbows on his knees, staring out over the lake. "I keep remembering those things you said to me. That I was just using you to advance my career. And the longer I sat on those accusations the more I felt I had to talk to you. That's not true at all, Mia. I mean, I'm truly grateful for what you did for me, but that's not why I was with you. The feelings I had for you were real. I was in love with you. That's the only reason I was with you, and when you called that into question the night we broke up—"

"The night *you* broke up. Call it what it was—there's no press here."

He conceded with a nod. "All right, the night *I* broke up. It wasn't an easy decision, Mia. I still had feelings for you, but I felt . . . that things weren't going anywhere."

She gaped at him. "What do you mean 'not going anywhere'? We were engaged and planning a wedding, Wes."

"Those are external things. I mean internally. We enjoyed each other's company, we had a lot in common, and we were in love, but . . ."

She waited for him to finish. He was obviously struggling to get it out. "But?"

He looked at her, holding her gaze for a long moment. "I always felt like you were . . . holding back or something."

Her chest tightened. "Holding back what?"

"I don't know. Like you'd let me get so close, but no closer. I don't mean to put the blame on you—"

"Well, that's how it feels."

"This isn't about blame, Mia. I'm just trying to tell you I wanted to feel more intimacy with you, with the woman who was going to be my wife. I thought surely once we were engaged things would change. And it scared me to death, thinking I might care about someone who didn't care as much about me. I kept trying to draw you out, but it was like there was a wall I couldn't get through."

"That's not true," she said. But his words hit a soft, achy target deep inside.

"I'm just telling you how I felt, and I felt that you held me at arm's length. Some of that may have been me. Who knows? Maybe I didn't make you feel secure enough or something."

She wanted to jump on that last part and refute everything else. But she knew in her core there was some truth to what he said. "Why didn't you just tell me that?"

He gave her a wan smile. "I should have. Instead, I tried to get you to open up to me. I'd ask you questions about your childhood, about your father. You never wanted to talk about any of it. You brushed me off, changed the subject. Made a joke. You never let things get too serious. Never let me get as close as I wanted to be—or at least that's how it felt."

He gave a harsh laugh. "I sound like a girl right now. I know. But I wanted more of you, and I despaired of ever getting it. I eventually decided I just wasn't the one for you. If I were, you wouldn't be holding out, you know? So I made the decision to break it off. It wasn't easy for me though, Mia. I want you to know that."

Her eyes burned, and she tried to place the feeling washing over her. Regret, maybe. But not regret that they hadn't become husband and wife.

The warm way he looked at her was familiar and satisfying. But Mia didn't feel drawn to him like she used to. Even now, realizing their breakup might not have been his fault at all, it didn't bring back those loving feelings. What she'd felt for him was gone.

Maybe it was the recent presence of Levi in her life, or perhaps it was just the realization that she'd never truly felt at home with Wes. She still cared about him, but she didn't love him anymore. It was a freeing thought. A freeing feeling.

In truth, she already felt closer to Levi than she ever had to Wes, something she hadn't been aware of until this moment. How had that happened so quickly? Was it because she was so far removed from her normal life, with more time to think and process? How had she let him in so far, and more importantly, how could she make sure she didn't make the same mistake with Levi that she'd made with Wes?

Wes set his hand over hers and squeezed it. "I just couldn't let you go on thinking I'd used you. That I didn't love you. Because I did, Mia. I just realized I wasn't the man for you, and so I let you go."

Technically Levi was working the front desk. But their guests were out enjoying the sunny day, so his job really only amounted to answering phones. And he could hear them just as well from the back of the inn.

He parted the gauzy white curtains in the library, catching sight of Mia and Wes on the Adirondack chairs. He glared at the back of Wesley's head. What gave him the right to just barge in on Mia like this? She'd come here to get away from everything.

What could the man possibly want that he couldn't have accomplished with a phone call? No need to drop in on her out of nowhere.

Levi wished he could see Mia's face. Maybe then he'd have some clue how she felt about Wesley's sudden appearance. And yes, how she felt about Wesley, period. Last they'd spoken on the subject she hadn't felt too warmly toward him. But men like Wesley could be charming, and she'd fallen for him once before, hadn't she?

"You're spying on them?" Molly leaned on the doorframe, arms crossed, disapproval on her face.

Levi went back to his surveillance. "Weren't you supposed to be going somewhere?"

"I canceled my plans. No way am I leaving you here with Wesley after what just went down in the lobby."

"Didn't have to do that."

"Yes, I did. Look at you."

All Levi could look at was Mia and Wesley. Just then the man reached across the space and put his hand over Mia's.

You've got to be kidding me. Levi's grip tightened on the drapes.

"Come away from the window before you tear the sheers."

His heart was beating hard. His chest squeezed painfully. Molly was right. A play-by-play was only going to drive him crazy.

He let go of the material and turned to his sister. An ache spread from the epicenter of his heart. "What if he wants her back, Molly?"

Her eyes softened. "Honey, you have to trust what you've built with her."

"You mean over the two and a half weeks we've known each other? She was with him almost two years. They were engaged to be married."

"But they broke up. There must've been a good reason."

He wasn't about to divulge Mia's personal business, but that was something to hold onto. Still, he kept remembering the way Wesley had taken Mia's hand just now. That didn't seem like the action of a man who'd used her for selfish purposes. Nor did his traveling all this way to see her. He'd already gotten what he'd wanted from her. Why was he here?

He didn't want to talk about this anymore. Didn't even want to think about it. "I should get back to the front desk."

Molly followed him down the hall. "I noticed

reservations are still going pretty strong since you increased the rates."

"It's only been a week and a half, but yeah, I noticed the same thing."

"That means an 8 percent increase in profit if it continues."

"That would go a long way toward making the inn profitable."

"And we have another wedding party coming later in the summer, so that's good."

"It looks promising," he said.

They talked for a while about what the profit margins would mean as far as selling the inn went. That Molly was willing to talk numbers was a testament to her love for him.

A while later, when they heard a car start up out front, Mia peeked out the window. "He's leaving." She looked at Levi. "Why don't I cover the desk awhile? Go on out and check on Mia."

thirty-five

Levi spotted Mia down on the dock, sitting on the bench. He made his way down the sloped lawn, his mouth going as dry as Lone Creek Falls in August. He thought she might come inside once Wesley left, but she obviously needed time to think. He hoped that wasn't a bad sign.

The wooden dock shimmied as he made his way down it. She must've felt the movement, but she didn't turn.

"Can I join you?" he asked once he reached her.

She smiled warmly at him. "Of course."

He lowered himself into the seat, keeping a respectful distance. He wanted to take her hand. But did he even have the right to touch her anymore? He hadn't known how strong his feelings were until Wesley showed up in their lobby. Now he thought he might burst for fear of losing her. How had this happened so quickly? He wasn't impulsive like Molly. He wasn't a romantic. He sure didn't believe in love at first sight.

Yet even though he'd known Mia fewer than three weeks, he couldn't deny what he was feeling. His pulse throbbed at the realization.

He was in love with the woman.

It didn't matter that he'd only known her a

matter of days. It didn't matter that she lived clear across the country. It didn't even matter that she was a famous celebrity.

All that mattered was that his heart was full of this undeniable, inescapable feeling he'd never before experienced. And he didn't know what to do about it.

"So . . ." Mia cut a look at him. "I guess you know that was Wesley."

"I'm aware." He stared at her profile, his gaze all but burning a laser into her skin. *Tell me he doesn't matter to you. Tell me you don't have feelings for him. Tell me it's me you want.*

"He was working in Asheville and decided to come see me. He wanted to clear up a few things about our breakup."

"Okay . . ."

She gave him a long, unreadable look. "I feel a little silly. It turns out I was wrong about him using me. I guess he really did have feelings for me."

Levi gritted his teeth. He guessed Wesley wasn't finished with his games. "He wants you back. He's trying to charm you back into his arms."

"What? No, Levi. That's not it."

"Don't be naïve, Mia. I mean, it's fine if you don't want to continue with this, you and me. But don't buy into this guy's lies."

Mia's eyes warmed as they roved over his

face. "*Is* it fine if I don't want to continue with this?"

His heart squeezed hard. That was a lie, and unlike Wesley, he wasn't going to play games with Mia. Even if he wound up humiliated by his admission.

Levi's shoulders sank, even as his eyes held hers. "No. It's not fine at all. Not with me. But if that's what you want . . ."

What? He'd understand? He'd be okay? He'd support her decision? None of that was true either. He sighed.

She skimmed her fingers along his cheek, her touch leaving a trail of fire. All she had to do was touch him, and his whole body hummed. He feared he'd never find that with someone else.

"It's not what I want," she said. "Wes didn't come here to resume our relationship. And even if he did . . . I'm not interested in him. I'm interested in you, Levi. Only you."

Relief filled all the spaces around his heart. Her admission made him feel like he could levitate right off the bench. Words scrambled in his brain and clogged in his throat.

Her eyes lighted mischievously as she brushed his cheek. "Now's when you tell me you're interested too."

His laugh escaped on a breath. He took her hand and set a gentle kiss on her fingers. "*Interested* doesn't begin to cover it." He didn't want to scare her off with *I love you,* even though his head was screaming with the words. It was too soon for that. But it wasn't too soon for the kiss he placed on her lips.

A few lingering moments later Mia pulled away, a hand pressed lightly to his chest. "I think I might have a little growing to do. I seem to have a little problem opening up. I may be a little guarded. A little reluctant to let someone else in."

"Why do you think that is? The business you're in? Your mom? Your dad?"

"Maybe all of the above. Mostly my dad's leaving, I think. Even now, with you, it's so scary. My heart's beating so hard just admitting this to you."

"We all have issues and problems, Mia." He held her hand tightly against his chest. "And you don't have to be worried about anything you tell me. You can trust me with your thoughts and feelings. I'll try my best to be a safe place to fall."

Her eyes filled with tears. "I'm afraid I'm going to push you away like I did Wes."

"If I feel that happening, I'll tell you. We'll talk about it. This is a process, a journey. Neither of us is perfect, Mia."

"You're so good to me, Levi. So patient."

"You deserve all that and more," he said. Then he lifted her chin and set a soft kiss to her lips.

thirty-six

Mia awakened to a text buzzing on her phone. She stretched, too cozy to get up just yet. Buttery sunlight filtered through the drapes, warming the room with a golden light. Familiar morning noises sounded in other parts of the inn: floorboards creaking, suitcases rolling by, air conditioning kicking on. According to the mantel clock it was after ten.

A smile curled her lips as she thought back to the evening before. Back to Levi and the sweet confession of his feelings. Back to his promising kisses. He'd had to return to work after their talk, but they'd spent the evening together last night. He'd made her dinner, and they'd eaten alone in the dining room. She'd never had a man cook for her before.

Who would know that her ex-fiancé's appearance would actually be good for her relationship with Levi? It had forced them to declare their feelings and brought them closer together.

She frowned as she remembered what Wes had told her. She'd never meant to hold back. It hadn't been a conscious decision but an automatic defense mechanism. She supposed a girl didn't get abandoned by her father without certain ramifications.

It hadn't been pleasant to hear. It was much

easier to blame their failed relationship on Wes. She'd have to be more aware of that tendency going forward so she didn't drag baggage into her relationships. Into her relationship with Levi. It would be scary, but the alternative—failed relationships—was even more terrifying.

She thought again of Levi and his patience with her yesterday. She'd originally thought he'd be a short-term thing, but that had changed for her. Her feelings had deepened, and she was no longer willing to just let him go.

She hoped he felt the same about her.

She knew he was committed here for a while, but she could visit him between projects. Maybe he could even fly out to see her sometimes. Other actors made it work.

Although, more often than not, they didn't.

Her mother's warnings cropped up in her mind. Maybe Levi wasn't in the film industry, but he'd proven himself supportive and understanding of her career. She was pretty sure he had the makings to survive in her crazy world. They'd be the exception to the rule. She gave a nod as if to solidify the thought.

Resolved, she rolled over and grabbed her phone from the nightstand. There were a few texts from Brooke.

Wesley is there? Why didn't you tell me?

There are pics all over the internet!
What's going on?

Oh no. There was a text from Nolan, too, informing her that photos of her and Wes were making the rounds. In fact, he'd sent her one of them.

In the photo Wes was leaning toward her in the backyard, his hand covering hers. They seemed intent on each other, sharing an intimate moment. Based on the perspective, the photographer had been on the lake and must've used a telephoto lens to capture the close-up shot—an illegal action. But reporters continuously got away with such things.

She stared at the photo, knowing what it implied. This wasn't good. She called Nolan, and he picked up immediately.

"I never knew North Carolina could be the hotbed of so much gossip."

"It's not what it looked like. Wes was in the neighborhood and just came to talk. We resolved some things. It was just . . . closure, that's all." She was almost afraid to ask the next question. "What are the tabloids saying?"

"That your relationship with the innkeeper was nothing more than a ploy to make you look innocent in the Jax scandal. You're trending on social media again, and not in a good way. Whatever you do, don't get online and start reading."

Mia's heart sank at the thought of what people were thinking and saying about her. "Nolan, the thing is . . . Levi and I really are together now. It developed quickly, but it's real. We have feelings for each other."

"Well, that's good, Mia, but unfortunately perception is reality in this business. And right now the public perceives that you faked the relationship to cover your own skin."

Mia cupped her forehead, thinking of the production company. "How much damage do you think is done?"

"I want to get right on this," Nolan said. "I've already started writing a press release. Basic story is this: you and Wesley parted as friends and since he was working in Asheville—a fact that can be proven—he dropped in for a visit. You and Levi are in a relationship, and you extended your stay in Bluebell to spend more time together. How do you like that spin?"

Mia gave a rueful laugh. "Well, it's the truth, so it's great. Do you think it'll work?"

"Will Wesley back this up? If we ask him for a statement?"

"Yes, of course. As I said, it's the truth." Apparently that mattered to her more than most people. She winced a little as she remembered that she had actually faked her "relationship" with Levi for a while.

She was worried for her role in *Lesser Days*.

She appeared to be walking the line of that morality clause in her contract, even though the worst thing she'd done was fake a relationship.

"Have you talked to Maura recently?" she asked. "Does the studio still want me onboard for the movie?"

"They do, but I'm not going to lie, kiddo. Maura's very concerned. The studio isn't digging all this negative publicity. We really need to get on top of this. I'll get a quote from Wesley and get this release out for public consumption. Then we'll just have to see how it plays out."

Mia snuggled closer to Levi on the living room couch. It was a rare night at home with no guests, and they'd decided to watch a movie: *First Man*.

Molly was at Adam's house, and Grace was out with a friend. The movie had been running a while, but Mia was having trouble keeping up with the plot.

Nolan had gotten out the press release around noon. She'd told Levi what was happening, and he'd offered to do whatever she needed to help clear this up. Maybe they should've been seen out together tonight, but she was afraid to do anything that would fan the flames.

She knew she must look like an erratic mess to the general public. Obsessed with Jax one moment, dating a random innkeeper the next, and then having a rendezvous with her ex-fiancé in the inn's backyard! She hoped her fans stuck by her. It was bad enough that the studio might not.

She didn't know what she'd do if that happened.

"I can hear the wheels turning from here," Levi whispered against her temple. He paused the movie, and Claire Foy froze on the screen.

"Sorry. Guess I'm a little distracted."

He pulled her closer. "Talk to me. Are you worried about the press release?"

The realization hit her suddenly . . . This was the type of question she would've brushed off with Wes. She would've put on a brave face and said she was sure it would work out fine. But she was trying to build something with Levi. She wanted more with him than she'd had with Wes. She wanted depth and intimacy and possibly a happily-ever-after.

Did he want that too?

Mia looked up at him, into those steady blue eyes. He wanted to know her, all of her. And if she wanted this to work she had to let go of her fears.

"Mia? You all right?"

"Yeah, I'm just . . . You're right, Levi. I'm worried the press release won't be enough. I'm worried I'll lose my part in *Lesser Days*."

He squeezed her shoulder. "Is that really a possibility? What about your contract?"

"There's a morality clause in it. Most studios aren't so stringent, but this particular one is.

They have a wholesome image, and they're very protective of their brand."

He frowned. "But you didn't do anything wrong."

Her heart squeezed at the way he came to her defense. "There's wording in the clause that includes public perception of immoral behavior. It's about my reputation or image, so I don't actually have to be guilty of wrongdoing. I just have to be perceived as having done wrong by the public."

"That's awful. How could your agent have let that clause stand?"

"I think it's boilerplate stuff, and they never invoke it. But after this fiasco, you can bet I'm going to push for different wording on my next contract."

A call buzzed in on her phone. She checked the screen and saw Nolan's name. Her pulse sped. "Do you mind?"

"Go ahead."

"It's not good, Mia," Nolan said by way of greeting. "Emma was interviewed on the *Entertainment Tonight* site. She says you're so obsessed with Jax that you're trying to make him jealous."

Mia's heart plummeted. "What?"

"She doesn't state it quite so blatantly, but that's the basic narrative. And of course she sounds as if she feels sorry for you and only wants you to get help."

"Jax is the one who needs help. What a narcissist. He sure pulled the wool over her eyes."

"You know that, and I know that, but the public has been fed two explanations for your photos with Wesley today: yours and Emma's. And her story is more salacious."

"Plus, she's perceived as the victim here." Mia leaned forward, elbow on knee, feeling Levi's gaze drilling into her. "Unbelievable."

"I'm sorry to bother you with this. I know it's late there, but I didn't want you to be blindsided in the morning."

"What are we going to do?"

"We'll just have to see how it plays out. Hopefully the moral support is on your side."

But two days later, Mia discovered that was not the case. The inn was bustling with guests on Saturday when Nolan called. The producer was sympathetic to her situation, but the studio had decided to invoke the morality clause in her contract. They were officially seeking her replacement.

Mia got off the phone and sank onto her bed, unable to breathe. *Why is this happening, God?* A sob caught in her throat for only a moment before it spilled out. The feelings inside roiled, stirring up something far deeper than she'd expected. She buried her face in a pillow and let it all go.

She'd never been fired from a job. And of all jobs to lose, this one! She'd taken the part in *Into the Deep* because it was a great script, and she'd known the movie would further her career.

But Fiona was her dream role. When Mia had read the script she'd felt like she knew Fiona. Like she *was* Fiona. She'd wanted to tell this woman's story. And now someone else would get it.

She sobbed harder. Her chest was so tight it ached, all of it seeming somehow out of proportion with the actual event. She could hardly think past the visceral reaction. What was wrong with her? She had been through a lot these last few months. Had she just reached her limit?

It was so unlike her to just lose it. She couldn't remember the last time she'd cried like this—she'd been a child. Maybe something else was going on. Maybe this loss had triggered something, like a past loss. Like a previous event in which she'd been replaced. The thought held weight, made her sobs come harder. She could hardly breathe through the pain.

It wasn't just that she'd lost this role. It was that she'd been rejected again. That she was being replaced. Another person had judged her and found her lacking. It made all the old wounds fresh again. So fresh. She ached from the depths of her core.

And of course the news of being let go

would immediately go public, bringing further humiliation. It would also make her look even guiltier. The realization only made her weep more.

She was also out of work. She'd need to scrounge for another role, and quick. Sometimes the public's attention span seemed eternal, but in other ways it could be very short.

She couldn't focus on that right now. Instead she let herself have a good long cry.

It was a long time later when she collected herself enough to text Nolan and ask if anything interesting had come across his desk lately. His answer made her spirits sink even lower. She set down the phone and fell back onto the bed.

thirty-seven

Mia walked hand in hand with Levi on the way back down Lone Creek Trail, loving the feel of his sturdy hand in hers. She'd worn her ball cap since it was the Fourth of July weekend and the path would be crowded with tourists. The inn was booked full for the holiday, and Levi only had a few hours to spare.

The past couple weeks they'd spent a lot of time together. They'd gone shopping again in Asheville, hiked a few times, and on days when the inn was quiet, they'd played cards or games with his sisters. Mia loved Levi's family. Grace and Molly were becoming like the sisters she'd never had.

And Levi . . . He was becoming so much more. A lot had happened to her in the past month. Losing the role had been the final emotional straw, and Levi had been such a rock for her. She was so used to putting on a brave face. What a relief to have someone she could really talk to. It was hard for her to put herself out there, but Levi had a way of making her feel safe.

He helped her over a fallen log. "Have you had a chance to look at the new scripts your agent sent?"

Mia was still a little heartbroken about losing

the role of Fiona. "They're pretty good. Solid plots with compelling characters."

He gave her a wan smile. "You don't sound very excited."

"They'll probably be commercially successful with the right actors. But yeah. They don't exactly grab me by the heart. On the other hand, I need to keep working. I'll talk it over with Nolan."

"You must trust him a great deal."

"He's been on my team from the beginning. He knows what he's doing."

Levi was quiet a minute. "It's just . . ."

"What?"

They reached the trailhead and started walking toward the car. "I don't know. You had so much passion when you talked about Fiona. I'd hate to see you settle, that's all."

"That's really sweet. But I have to put Fiona behind me. They can't all be passion projects. Look at you and your inn. This isn't what you want to do long term, but it's a responsibility you've taken on, knowing you'll get back to what you love later. I've taken a lot of roles just because I thought they'd be good for my career."

Levi opened the car door for her but paused to place a kiss on her lips. "I'm sure you'll do what's best." His gazed at her steadily, his eyes saying so much as they roved her face.

Something in his eyes shifted. His lips parted,

and Mia got the idea he was about to tell her he loved her. The last few days he'd been saying it with his eyes, with his touch.

Her heart palpitated in her chest. She forgot how to breathe.

Then he tipped her face up and set a kiss on her nose. "We'd better get back."

Levi wondered if he should've let the moment pass. A declaration of love had been on his lips, but was it the right time? He was sweaty from the hike, and they'd been standing in a parking lot. Mia deserved better. Maybe he'd plan something special next week when the inn wasn't so busy. Now that she wasn't due on set in a couple weeks, they'd have more time together.

On the way back to the inn they grabbed a quick meal at a drive-through and Levi found a shady picnic table in Pawley Park where they could settle with their food.

Levi said grace. Then they tucked in. As he watched her gaze out over the lake his mind flashed back to a scene in *Into the Deep*. She'd been spellbinding in that role.

"What?" she asked when she caught him staring.

"Nothing, I just . . . I watched your movie— *Into the Deep*. I Netflixed it a while back." He scanned her features. "You're really good. I was impressed."

She returned his smile. "Thank you. That means a lot to me."

"What's it like, being a Christian in Hollywood? It must be hard."

"Sometimes. I'm careful about the parts I take, the people I hang with." Her eyes fell to her salad. "If I'm honest, my faith life hasn't been that great lately. I mean, I go to church and all, but . . . the depth of it has been lacking."

He liked her honesty. "Why do you think that is?"

"I've been doing a lot of thinking about that. I think things kind of got derailed when Wes broke up with me."

"How so?"

She shrugged as she chewed a bite. "Maybe it was a trigger of sorts—the whole abandonment thing. Even though my dad left when I was young, it had a big impact on me."

"Of course it did. What do you remember about him?"

Mia stared off through the trees, a wistful smile forming on her face. "I remember him pushing me on a swing set. I remember helping him in the kitchen—I think we were making pancakes. I have a fuzzy memory of being on his shoulders at a parade or something." Her smile fell away. "Then one day my parents were arguing in their bedroom, and I didn't want to hear them so I went out to the porch. It was raining. Dad came barreling out of the house with a suitcase, and he just . . . got in his car and left. Didn't see me. I watched his car disappear down the road. I waited a long time for him to come back, but he never did. The smell of rain still reminds me of that day."

His heart squeezed for her. "I'm so sorry. That's a big loss in a little girl's life."

She was quiet for a minute, working on her salad. Then she said, "I hired a PI to find him when I was eighteen. I've always kind of longed for family. For real roots like other people had. Grandparents and history. My mom always kind of scoffed at that. But she had those things, and she chose to give them up. I think that's why I went looking for my dad. That and answers. I wanted him to look me in the eyes and tell me why he left. Why he just abandoned me."

His heart squeezed. "And did you find him?"

"Yes." She took a sip of water. "He was living in Las Vegas at the time. I drove all the way to his house."

Levi waited through the long pause, giving her time to tell a story that was obviously difficult.

"He lived in a regular middle-class neighborhood. Nothing special. There was a small SUV in the drive. I sat in front of his house for a long time trying to get up the nerve to go to the door. After a while a woman came out and then my

314

father, followed by two little kids, a boy and a girl." Her eyes teared up. "A little family. I felt . . . so replaced. The girl was about the age I was when he left. I wondered if he pushed *her* on the swing now, made pancakes with her and lifted her up onto his shoulders."

Levi wanted to wrap her in a hug. "Oh, Mia."

She pushed the salad bowl aside and met his gaze with a look so vulnerable his heart nearly cracked in two. "Sometimes I wonder if it was . . . you know. Me. If I was the reason he left."

Levi reached out and thumbed away the tear that rolled down her cheek. "It wasn't you. Kids often blame themselves, but it's never their fault. You were only five, Mia. If you weren't the center of his world, the fault lies with him."

"I know you must be right. But sometimes the truth is hard to believe."

Lord, heal her heart. "Well, now I know how I can pray for you."

She cleared her throat and gave a nervous chuckle. "Well, that turned serious in a hurry, didn't it?"

He squeezed her hand, amazed by her bravery. "I've never told anyone all that before."

"I'm honored then. Thank you."

"Tell me something you haven't told anyone."

The first thing that came to Levi's mind was the inn's financial condition. The weight of it had been like cement blocks sitting on his shoulders.

"I haven't been forthcoming with my sisters about our financial situation."

She tilted her head, her eyes searching his face.

"It's not good. We're in debt, and my credit cards are maxed out. Things are starting to turn around, but we have a long way to go to get ourselves out of the hole."

"Oh, Levi. I've noticed you seem stressed out sometimes. Is that why you have so many headaches?"

"Probably."

"Levi . . ." Mia's eyes sharpened as she leaned forward. "Let me help you. I can give you whatever you—"

"No, Mia." That was the last thing Levi wanted. "That's nice of you to offer, really nice. But that's not why I told you."

"I know that. But a temporary loan might be all you need to—"

"Thank you." He squeezed her hand. "Really, I appreciate it. But no. We need to do this on our own. And as I said, things are turning around. Reservations are up, and the rate increase has helped." He tried for levity. "Your stay has brought us some much-needed attention. Consider that your contribution to the cause."

She gave him a long, steady look. "If you change your mind . . ."

"Thanks. I appreciate the offer."

"We should keep looking for that necklace.

Imagine what that would do for your financial situation."

"I don't know where else we'd look." It had been all but forgotten lately because they'd been so lost in each other. Levi had never experienced this all-consuming love. No wonder Molly had been AWOL so much when she was falling for Adam. Levi hadn't been prepared for this depth of feeling.

Mia made him deliriously happy. There. He'd said it. He wasn't sure exactly what made them work so well. On the one hand, they were very different, led such dissimilar lives. On the other hand, they were both realists, they shared a faith, they were resilient in the face of trials, and they worked well as a team.

When they finished eating they headed back to the inn. On the way home, as they passed the marina, Levi glanced at Mia. She'd really opened up to him today. And he'd opened up to her. That gave him hope for a future with her.

When they reached the inn he took a parking slot in front. He had to work the front desk soon. Molly and Grace were still here, but judging by the empty spaces, most of the guests were gone. The sun hadn't set yet, but everyone liked to save a good spot for the fireworks.

Levi wished he'd thought ahead. A boat on the darkened lake with the fireworks blooming overhead would've been the perfect time and place to tell Mia he loved her. But one of the guests had their boat for the night, and chances of borrowing another one at this late date were slim to none.

He assisted Mia out of the car and held her hand as they walked up the porch steps. He grabbed yesterday's mail from the box and opened the door for her.

Molly was at the front desk on the phone, taking a reservation.

"I'll grab our bag," Mia said.

"I'll bring the chairs later so you don't have to carry them."

"Sounds good." At the turn in the stairs she sought out his gaze and winked at him. Maybe he'd tell her tonight anyway. He could think of worse settings to declare his love than a beach on the Fourth of July.

"Somebody's completely smitten," Molly whispered with a haughty grin.

Levi tore his eyes from where Mia had disappeared, wiping what was probably a dopey look from his face. "Anything I need caught up on?"

Molly gave him a look that said *I know you're changing the subject, and I'm letting you get away with it.* "Our guests are out enjoying the festivities for the moment. Reservations are looking good for the next few weeks. In fact, every weekend is booked through the rest of the summer, and our weekday reservations have picked up. I have to hand it to you, Levi. Your marketing plan seems to be working, and the rate increase hasn't harmed us at all."

Levi gave a smug grin. "Go ahead and say it."

"I don't want to."

"Say it."

"Fine. *You were right.*"

"About . . . ?"

"Everything. You were right about everything. Happy?"

His lips twitched. "Actually, yes, I am."

"Everything's on schedule for the wedding party to arrive next week. I've ordered flowers for the bride's room and talked to Miss Della about the extra pastry selection they requested."

Levi slipped behind the desk. "Great."

"Oh, and I replaced the Keurig in room three."

He sorted through the mail. "Thanks."

Mia came down the stairs, the beach bag on her shoulder, looking like a patriotic angel straight from heaven in her red, white, and blue. After stopping to chat a moment she said good-bye, waggling her fingers at Levi before she slipped out.

Grace tramped down the stairs next, dressed in a pair of white shorts and a blue T-shirt, her blond hair in a high ponytail. As she and Molly talked about their evening plans, Levi's eyes caught on a large white envelope in the stack of yesterday's mail.

"Grace . . ." A grin tugged his lips as he held it up triumphantly. "Look what came in the mail."

"What is it?"

"It's from UNC at Charlotte." He was so excited for her. "And it's thick, so that means it's good news. You got in, Grace."

"Well . . ." She shifted. "We don't know that yet."

"Open it and find out," Molly said.

Grace took the envelope and slid a finger under the flap. She seemed to be working in slow motion. Finally she slid out the sheaf of papers and began reading.

A moment later she looked up. "I got in."

Molly whooped.

"Yes." Levi held his fist out to Grace.

She met his fist bump with all the enthusiasm of an inmate headed to death row. He studied her face. Her frown lines, her unsmiling mouth, her slumped shoulders.

Dread coiled in Levi's gut. "What's wrong? Isn't this what you wanted?"

"Are you hoping for one of the other schools?" Molly asked. "Don't worry. I'm sure you'll get in both. Their acceptance rates are higher than UNC."

Grace looked between her siblings, a heavy sigh finally escaping. "That's not it. I haven't been entirely up front with you guys. It's just that . . . I don't want to go to college."

Levi blinked. This couldn't be happening. Sure, she'd dragged her feet on the applications, but she was just a kid. Teenagers were known to procrastinate.

"Grace . . ." he said intently. "You have to go to college."

Her eyes sharpened on him, and her chin thrust forward. "No, Levi. Actually, I don't. Not everyone has to go to college, you know."

"Everyone gets a degree these days, Grace!"

"That's right, and they come home and get hired as baristas because all the good jobs are taken."

"She's got a point," Molly said.

Levi shot Molly a dark look. "You're not helping. Grace, this is ridiculous. What are you going to do with your life? You said you wanted to study business."

"Because I didn't know what I wanted to do. But now I have a plan." Her gaze went between the two of them, finally stopping on Levi. "I want to open an outfitters business, and I already know everything I need to know."

"Grace, we're already struggling to run one business!"

"This would be my venture, not yours."

"Fifty percent of businesses fail in the first five years." A statistic that kept him up at night. "Even if that's what you choose to do eventually, a degree will give you credibility, and you need a backup plan just in case—"

"No, I don't. I can start small and run it right out of the inn. I don't want to be saddled with college loans like all my friends."

"We'll be able to pay them off when we sell this place."

"Or I can put the money into my business instead."

Levi palmed his neck. A headache throbbed at the back of his skull. "If you don't want to go far from home, you can go to the Asheville campus. You can still come home every weekend. You could even live here if you wanted to."

"He's not even listening to me," Grace said to Molly, then gave Levi a withering look. "That's not what this is about."

Levi leaned forward, his palms digging into the counter. His head dropped between his shoulders. His heart was beating too fast, and he could feel his blood pressure shooting up.

He didn't want to do it, but she was giving him no choice. He raised his head, drilling her with a look and taking great care to keep his voice steady and calm. "You know Mom and Dad wanted you to go to college, Grace."

Her eyes went glossy. "That's not fair. Stop guilt-tripping me."

"It's the truth."

Grace glared at him, tears clinging to her lashes. "I told Mia you wouldn't listen!" She whirled around and stormed out of the house.

He winced as the door slammed shut.

Mia knew about this? Levi's head was spinning. He felt a little dizzy.

"Let's talk to her later after she settles down," Molly said.

"She's obviously felt this way a long time. But she has to go to college. We're on the same page here, right?" He realized his tone left little choice, but he didn't care. He knew he was right.

"Why don't we talk about this later? Nothing has to be decided tonight, and I'm due at Adam's."

"Yeah." He ran his hand over his face. "You're right."

"But Levi . . ." Molly squeezed his arm and held his gaze for a long moment. "Next time you might consider doing a little less talking and a lot more listening."

thirty-eight

What a night. Molly was ready for some quiet time with Adam. She sat beside him in the pontoon boat as he guided it quietly through the choppy water. The sun had set and darkness crept across the sky. Already a few stars twinkled on the cloudless palette.

Boats crowded the lake, all headed toward the main basin, which would offer the best views of the fireworks. The boats' navigation lights reflected off the water, and the quiet strains of a country tune carried from a nearby radio. A mild breeze drifted across the lake, already carrying the flinty smell of fireworks.

Molly shifted on her seat. Even though she'd just come from a family squabble, that wasn't what was usurping her thoughts. Things had felt different between Adam and her since three weeks ago when he hadn't proposed. Conversation didn't flow like it used to. A barrier seemed to have been erected between them. Worse, she'd started to doubt him.

A week ago she'd thought back to that call he'd received from Tiffany, and it occurred to her that the screen might not have said Tiffany & Co. at all. It may have just said Tiffany. Maybe she'd only presumed it to be the jewelers because she'd had proposal on the brain. Maybe Tiffany was really the name of some woman.

The thought had gutted her.

She didn't want to think Adam could be talking to another woman, or worse, seeing another woman.

And yes, yes, she knew. Adam was not the cheating type. He wasn't some playboy. But her ex-boyfriend Dominic had done a job on her. Shaken her trust in men. She thought she'd gotten past that, but here she was in doubting mode again. And there was that distance between them that hadn't been there before. How could she explain that?

She wiped her sweaty palms down her shorts. The thought of losing Adam was unthinkable. It would be so much worse than losing Dominic. She loved Adam with all her heart. She wanted to spend the rest of her life with him. She couldn't imagine a future with anyone else.

"You've been quiet." Adam shot her a sideways glance, his face unreadable in the shadowy light.

"I know. Sorry. There was a big blowup between Levi and Grace before I left the house. She told him she doesn't want to go to college, and things got pretty heated. I can see both sides. But the bottom line is, it's Grace's life, and Levi needs to back off. But you know Levi. He can be pretty single-minded."

"He cares about both of you."

"Of course he does. But he has a tendency to be a little bossy, and that just makes Grace buck up. They both need to cool off before they talk about this again. I'll work on Levi in the meantime, see if I can soften him up a little." She gave him a wry grin. "A middle child's work is never done."

Her attempt at levity went unrecognized. Adam fell quiet again. That had been the way of things lately. What was going on? Her eyes burned. She was grateful for the darkness and glad they'd reached a good spot to anchor down.

Adam shut off the engine, leaving the nav lights on, and dropped the anchor.

Distant laughter and music carried from the boats around them. Seeing the fireworks on the lake had always been a highlight for Molly. And she'd looked forward to sharing it with Adam. But now it was all ruined by . . . whatever this was between them.

He turned on the captain seat to face her. "That isn't what I meant, Molly."

She blinked at him. "What do you mean?"

"I mean . . ." he began in a voice that was low and measured. "You've been quiet lately. It seems like you've got something on your mind, but every time I ask what's wrong, you say you're fine. But you're not fine, Molly. Something's wrong, and I need to know what it is. Please."

He sounded so sad and confused. Just like she was. Maybe Mia had been right. Maybe Molly should just tell him. Just get it out on the table. Whatever was happening between them couldn't be worse than all this suspicion and speculation.

Her pulse increased until she feared her heart would pound right out of her chest. "I thought you were going to propose," she blurted.

A beat of silence. "What?"

And then the words tumbled out of her like water down Lone Creek Falls. "Before we went to the Crow's Nest I heard that you'd made the reservations—quiet table by the window—and it's a special occasion type place, and we hadn't been there before, you know? And then a few days later we were at your house, and you were in the kitchen, and your phone was sitting out on the coffee table, and a call came in. The screen said Tiffany & Co., so I thought you must be planning to propose, because *Tiffany!*

"And so that night I got all dressed up, and dinner came and went, and you drove me home and left me on the porch—proposal-less! And I was so disappointed because I thought I must've done something to change your mind."

"Oh, Molly."

"And after that things just seemed weird between us. And then I thought, did the phone actually say Tiffany & Co. or did it maybe just say Tiffany? Maybe I just jumped to conclusions because I was so excited about you asking me to marry you. But then you didn't.

Are you seeing someone else, Adam? Because if you are, I have to know, 'cause I'm just about to go batty!"

"Molly." Adam slid over into her seat, placing his arm around her. "Why didn't you tell me all this? Of course I'm not seeing somebody else. I love you and only you."

She let his words sink in deep. Allowed her lungs to draw another breath. "Then why did—"

He placed his fingers over her lips, looking at her as if he really did mean what he'd just said. "My turn. I *was* planning to propose that night, Molly. And I don't know what the screen said, but I do know that call was from the jewelry store, and I did buy your ring there. I don't even know anyone named Tiffany, and I would never cheat on you, ever."

"I'm sorry." She let his words settle all the way into her heart. Okay, so there was no one else. She believed him. But . . .

"Then why didn't you propose that night? Did you change your mind?" An ache bloomed in her chest at the thought. She'd never had a single doubt about him since they'd starting dating last fall. Not until this proposal debacle.

"That's my fault. I jumped the gun a little. I bought the ring back in May when I was in New York visiting my publisher. And since your father wasn't here to give his blessing I planned to ask Levi instead. But I kept putting it off because . . .

328

well, you know I'm just not good at that kind of thing."

Dread squirmed inside.

"By the time I finally got up the nerve to ask him, I already had the ring and already made the dinner reservation. But Levi thought it might be better to wait a little while, so I decided to put it off a bit."

"Hold up . . ." She ran his words back through her head, bristling as her gaze focused more intently on Adam. "*Levi?* Levi thought it might be better to *wait?*"

thirty-nine

Levi had stepped outside for only twenty minutes. Thirty at most.

He was twitchy after his argument with Grace and needed something productive to do. There was no reason to guard the front desk. All the guests were out for the festivities, and the No Vacancy sign was on. The three shrubs out front hadn't been trimmed in a few weeks, and he could knock that out quickly and burn off his excess energy in one fell swoop.

He turned on the exterior lights and fetched the hedge trimmer from the shed. The physical job didn't keep his mind from spinning while he worked though. Or keep the headache at the base of his skull from throbbing. It only provided a valid explanation for his tense shoulder muscles and his racing heart.

Where had he gone wrong with Grace? How was he going to change her mind about college? Because he had to. His parents would have found a way to do just that, and since they weren't here it was his job.

He finished the shrubs too quickly, raked up the trimmings, and dumped them in the compost pile in the backyard. He stored the rake in the shed and entered the inn through the back door, his mind still on Grace.

It was the sound of trickling water that snapped his thoughts to the present. Had someone returned for a shower? He turned the corner to the lobby and stopped, staring in disbelief.

A steady drizzle of water trickled like a waterfall under the railing of the second flight.

He charged up the stairs two at a time. His shoes slipped on the wet wood. He stopped at the top, gaping. The hallway was covered in water.

But where was it coming from? He forced himself to slow down and try and see how the water was moving. The suite. Had Mia left the water running?

He needed the key. He flew back downstairs and grabbed it. Then he ran back upstairs and down the hall. His hands shook as he keyed open the door.

The water was deeper in here. It swirled beside one of the interior walls where water rushed from beneath the baseboard. His stomach filled with lead.

A pipe had burst. He had to turn off the water supply.

He dashed back through the water, taking the stairs at a reckless pace. Once on the main floor he ran around to access the basement steps. Thank God he knew where the valve was from when he'd worked with the plumber on their renovation.

He charged to the opposite wall, located the

valve, and grabbed it, twisting. It was stuck. He turned harder. Finally it gave. The round wheel squeaked as he turned it, but gradually the water flow slowed, then stopped.

He dropped his head to his arm, breathing fast. This was a disaster. He had to think.

Turn off the electricity. But he'd waded through water . . . better to call an electrician. They'd be closed for the holiday, but he had Ed Barrick's number in his phone.

He shouldn't go back into the flooded area until the electricity was off. But he needed to move his guests' belongings to higher ground.

Levi headed back upstairs, his eyes taking in the puddles once he reached the lobby. He'd grab towels from upstairs. He headed back up.

The water was a couple inches deep in the suite. Mia's things were in drawers except for a pair of sandals. He moved them onto the chaise, then went to check the other rooms.

He spent a good thirty minutes moving suitcases and shoes. Then he grabbed towels and mopped up the puddles in the lobby. He left a tub from the kitchen under the railing to catch the dripping water.

How had this happened so quickly?

His mind raced with all that needed to be done *now*. He had to get the water up. They had a Shop-Vac in the shed. He could call Erik and ask him to bring his over too.

But no. First he had to call Ed. He went outside. This was a complete disaster. The whole upstairs had flooded except for his sisters' room. It would take weeks to repair. They'd have to shut down the inn.

He couldn't think about that now. He found Ed's number in his contacts. Standing on the darkened lawn he tapped the name and sighed audibly when Ed picked up. Levi told him what had happened, and Ed promised to be right over.

"Stay out of the house," he said. "And call your insurance company."

After hanging up Levi did as he suggested. They weren't open, of course, but he left a message. He turned and stared at the inn, the porch lights still aglow. Some of the shock had worn off and reality was setting in, making his gut twist.

Water produced mold, and mold was damaging and potentially toxic. All soft surfaces were at risk. The drywall was soaking up water even now. It would all have to be cut out, new drywall taped into place, mudded, and painted.

The entire second story might need to be refloored. All the wood trim replaced. All the other hard surfaces would have to be treated. It was going to take weeks, possibly months, depending on how much help he could find around here during the busy summer.

And the money . . . He didn't even want to

think about the money. He had insurance of course. But that wouldn't cover the lost business, because he'd canceled the interruption insurance in January to save a few bucks.

He closed his eyes. Kneaded the muscles at the back of his neck where a full-fledged headache was brewing.

He was unaware he had company until he heard Molly's voice.

"How could you."

He turned around, his thoughts still a jumbled mess. "What? What are you doing here?"

He registered the look on his sister's face. Even in the shadows he could see the tense, angry set of her shoulders. The straight line of her brows.

"What gives you the right to tell Adam not to propose to me?" Her voice boomed across the space between them.

Levi blinked, now fully onboard with the subject at hand. "Molly, this isn't a good time. The house has been—"

"No, Levi! We're going to talk about this. Why did you tell Adam that?"

"I—I didn't exactly . . . I just—I thought it was a little too fast, that's all. So I suggested—"

"Fast? You think it was *too fast?* You, who fell head over heels with Mia Emerson in two weeks flat?"

His face warmed. "There's a difference between developing feelings and committing to a—"

"And even if it was too fast, Levi, it's none of your business! You had no right to tell Adam to hold off. Do you have any idea what you did? All the problems you created?"

"That wasn't my inten—"

"I knew he was going to propose that night, and when he didn't, I thought something was wrong. I thought he'd changed his mind! I've been miserable for weeks, thinking I was losing him or that there was someone else. But no. No! It was just my intrusive, bossy brother trying to control my life again!"

Oh boy. "Listen, Molly, I'm sorry. I was just trying to—"

"No, Levi! No. Do not write this off as you trying to do what's best for me. You're not my dad. And you're not Grace's dad either. You're our brother, and that gives you zero right to interfere with our lives. We're adults! We're perfectly capable of knowing what's best for us, and if you disagree with our plans, so what? That's your problem, not ours. I'm so done with this, Levi. *Done!*"

She charged toward the house and up the porch steps.

Remembering the water, Levi snapped to attention. "Molly, no! Don't go in there."

"Stop telling me what to do!"

But when she reached the inn's threshold she stopped of her own free will.

• • •

Mia checked her phone. It was almost time for the fireworks to start. She'd expected Levi half an hour ago. She'd texted him ten minutes ago, but he hadn't yet replied.

She tapped his name, placing the call. Maybe he'd gotten busy taking reservations or a guest had needed his help. Still, it was unlike him not to respond.

Finally he picked up after several rings. "I'm so sorry, Mia. We've had a—a mishap here at the inn. The upstairs is flooded, and I won't be able to—"

"Flooded!"

His sigh sounded soul deep. "A burst pipe. Long story. Listen, I'm up to my ankles in water, and I have to get this dried out. I'm sorry to cancel on you."

Mia was already packing up their things. "I'm coming home. I'll be right there."

forty

Levi shelved his hands on his hips. The mantel clock said it was nearly four o'clock in the morning. His shoulders felt as if they weighed a thousand pounds. Each.

He surveyed the suite. The rug had been taken up, exposing the damp floor, the boards already warping near the wall where the pipe had burst. A water line rimmed the wide baseboard.

The closet door was flung open. The space had been full of stuff, all of it removed to the porch with the rugs. The windows were open, and every fan they could find was running. A dehumidifier hummed in the corner.

Molly had worked on finding emergency lodging for their guests—not easy on the holiday weekend, but she'd somehow pulled it off. She'd then called all their guests and told them they'd have to evacuate the inn immediately. They'd comped their stays to help soothe ruffled feathers.

Once Molly finished that task, she'd worked on finding alternative lodging for the wedding party the following week—another difficult task. She'd have to call the bride with the bad news in the morning. Once she'd done all she could she joined the cleanup, but Levi could feel the cold waves of anger radiating off her. Grace wasn't much better.

At Ed's recommendation, they'd documented the damage with their cell phones for the insurance company before cleanup.

Now that the floors were drying up, Levi sneaked down to his room and dug up the insurance policy. He hoped he'd remembered wrong about the interruption insurance.

But no. He had canceled the policy. At least the flood damage would be covered.

He made his way from his room, swallowing hard. He was officially in over his head. He didn't know how he was going to get them over this hurdle. And the worse thing about it all was that it was his fault. Not only had he canceled the interruption insurance, he'd also neglected to update the pipes, something the plumber had suggested during renovations. But Levi had been so focused on staying on time and on budget that he'd declined.

The girls were on the porch now sorting out what was salvageable and what was headed for the dump. Sodden rugs were draped over the railings. He could see Mia through the living room window, removing items from a cardboard box. She'd come home and jumped right into the fray.

He thought back over the last twelve hours, beginning with his argument with Grace. He was failing at everything. He was failing Grace. He was failing Molly. And worst of all, he was failing his parents. He and sisters were on the very edge of losing their legacy.

And it was all his fault.

Take care of your sisters.

His dad's words echoed in his ears, settled in the back of his neck, tightening the corded muscles.

Inhale. Exhale. Inhale. Exhale.

A wave of dizziness washed over him. His vision blackened at the edges, and he grabbed hold of the mantel. His heart was beating too fast, he realized. And maybe he was a little short of breath. But it had been a busy night and it was late. He was exhausted. They all were.

He blinked, his vision gradually returning to normal. If today had taught him nothing else, it had taught him this: he had to make some changes. He'd alienated his sisters, and he had to fix that. He'd allowed himself to become distracted, and chaos had erupted. He couldn't keep up this pace and hold them all together.

Mia's melodic laughter tinkled through the open window like a magical wind chime. His gaze followed the sound even as his heart sank like a leaden weight.

There were certain responsibilities he couldn't shed. His sisters. This inn.

But Mia was new to his life. Clearly he wasn't

capable of maintaining a romantic relationship on top of his other responsibilities.

Her words from that day in the library came back. *That doesn't mean we can't enjoy the time we have.* They'd repeated themselves to him before. *The time we have.* She'd always looked at their relationship as a short-term thing. A summer romance. Somehow he'd forgotten that these past couple weeks. Allowed himself to believe it could be more.

She'd never said anything to make him think she might've changed her mind. She had to go back to LA eventually, and then the relationship would die a natural death. He'd just need to end it a little sooner.

He watched her through the window, admiring the joy on her face despite the difficult night. He ached inside at the thought of giving her up. Molly was right. He'd fallen for her in two short weeks. And now barely five weeks after meeting her, he was head over heels. It wasn't logical, but it was true.

Levi had been planning to tell her tonight that he loved her. And he realized now that could never happen.

Mia threw the sodden cardboard box into the trash pile and listened as Grace told the story of her worst day in high school. She had Molly and Mia in stitches with her dry delivery.

Mia glanced at the window, catching Levi staring at her with an intense expression. He grasped the mantel with one hand, his shoulders sagging as if they held the weight of the world.

She searched his face. But before she could decipher his expression something shifted in his eyes, and his lips lifted in an unconvincing smile.

"Be right back," Mia said as she came to her feet, her body aching from sitting so long. They'd decided she would stay in the girls' room rent-free. She didn't like freeloading off them, but she understood the legality of the situation.

When she reached the living room, Levi was pulling off the rubber boots Erik had brought over. He set them on the fireplace hearth.

He turned and gave her a placid smile. "We should probably head to bed. The rest can wait for morning."

She walked closer, studying him. He looked so weary. "Are you all right, Levi?"

His gaze skittered around the inn, avoiding her gaze. "I'll be fine. This is a little overwhelming, that's all."

She could only imagine, considering what he'd confided earlier about the inn's financial condition. "Of course it is. I'm so sorry this happened. How long do you think the repairs will take?"

"I don't know. Weeks. Months. Depends how

busy the tradespeople are. And being summer, I imagine they're pretty tied up already."

She wanted to wrap him in a big hug. He seemed like he needed one badly. But he also seemed unreceptive, which was unlike him.

She set her hand on his arm instead. "One thing at a time. It'll all work out."

His lips pinched together. "I should tell the girls to get some sleep."

She tightened her grip on his arm. "Wait."

He paused, meeting her gaze with eyes that looked very different from the ones that had gazed back at her this afternoon. These eyes were cooler. Sadder. Detached.

Her chest squeezed tight, even as her heart punished her ribs. "Is there something else, Levi? I mean, I know this is a lot. But . . . are we all right? You seem . . . It seems like there's a canyon between us suddenly, and I'm not sure why."

He flinched, then quickly offered her a benign smile. "I'm just tired. It's after four o'clock. We're all beat. Let's get some sleep."

"It's more than that." The words were out before she had a chance to contemplate them. It was late—a terrible time to discuss important things. And yet she sensed this was important. And the way her heart was ready to rocket out of her chest she knew she wouldn't be able to sleep.

"Please." She squeezed his arm. "Tell me what it is."

"Mia . . ."

"Please, Levi. I'm already worried, and . . . just tell me."

Levi shifted, his gaze skittered away before returning to hers. "I've just got so much on my plate right now. I have too many responsibilities, too many people counting on me. And I'm letting them all down."

He was so hard on himself.

"You're doing better than you think."

"Reality would suggest otherwise. Mia . . . tonight's made me realize that I need to make some tough decisions. I don't have room in my life for a relationship right now, no matter how much I might . . ." He gave her a pained look. "I've really enjoyed getting to know you—more than you might realize."

Mia's heart twisted. She resisted the urge to clutch at her chest. "This is awfully sudden."

"I'm sorry, but I just need to focus on my duties right now. I wish that weren't the case. I hope you believe that."

"You're just tired." Her voice was a raspy whisper she hardly recognized. "You'll feel differently in the morning."

His eyes went soft, and for one hopeful minute she thought he was going to take back everything he'd said.

"I wish that were true, Mia. But I have a lot of responsibilities right now. Things I put my life in

343

Denver on hold for—important things. And I've let all that slide lately because I was too busy—"

"Entertaining me?" Mia removed her hand from his arm, her body going rigid.

It was becoming real now, and all her defenses were rising to the surface. So much for trusting. So much for letting her guard down. Stupid!

He opened his mouth, then closed it again. His hand enveloped hers. "I've enjoyed every moment we've spent together. I don't regret getting to know you, Mia. It's been . . . I'll never forget you."

She pulled her hand away, her eyes burning, her throat swelling. "It's fine. Of course it's fine. I'll be out of your hair in the morning." She turned to go.

"You don't have to go, Mia," Levi called.

Oh, she thought as she took the stairs one last time. *But I do.*

forty-one

Levi sopped up the excess water around the suite's hearth with a towel. He hoped the efforts would help minimize damage to the original fireplace. It had been constructed with stone from the mountains surrounding Bluebell Lake. He could already see some loose grout between the lower stones, but that was repairable.

He'd encouraged his sisters to go to bed a while ago. Thanks to their bedroom's location on the other side of the stairwell, theirs had been the only one upstairs untouched by water. Earlier he'd heard the floors creaking with their movements, but all was quiet now.

As tired as he was, he hadn't let himself stop. There were three women in the house, and they were all mad at him for different reasons. That took a special kind of talent.

He worked on things that could've waited till morning. He pulled the baseboard from the walls, drying them with towels. He hoped they could be salvaged with a little TLC.

And now he worked on the fireplace. He moved around the hearth, hunching over it, blotting the lower stones. His body worked at the task while his head spun with thoughts of Mia. Of the look that had come over her face when he'd explained his situation.

Disbelief. Raw hurt and vulnerability.

That was the image he couldn't erase from his memory. He hadn't known how much pain it would cause him to hurt her. He'd considered recanting for just a moment. But then he thought of his sisters. His parents. *His deathbed promise to his father.* A sacred promise he'd sooner die than break.

But that look on her face. He closed his eyes for a long second, gritting his teeth, wishing it away. But when he opened them again it was still there. He was just failing all the way around, wasn't he?

Along with everything else he'd lost, he'd had to give up the only woman he'd ever loved to take care of sisters who apparently *didn't even want his help.*

An angry cloud of billowing steam built up inside, making his face heat. His body broke out into a sweat. He smacked a stone with his palm. His flesh stung, and he welcomed the pain.

He'd displaced the stone. Great. He frowned at it. Now he'd broken the fireplace. He pushed the piece back into place, but it was looser than he'd anticipated. Probably needed more grouting. He pulled it out and set it on the hearth, surprised by its shallow depth. He glanced back at the space left by the rock's displacement, his eyes sharpening on the cavity.

There was something tucked back in there. A wad of trash. Or fabric. Frowning, he reached in and pulled it out. It was cheesecloth, he thought, though why anyone would stuff it back there, he couldn't imagine. Dust and grit floated down as he unfolded the material.

Then he noticed its weight. Its bulk. There was something solid inside. His heart jittered. His clumsy fingers reached the end of the fabric, and his breath caught at the prize nestled inside.

Hanging from a delicate gold chain was a stunning blue jewel. He stared at the necklace for a full minute.

The blue diamond.

The gem was still dazzling, having been covered and protected from the elements. Dorothy Livingston had indeed hidden her precious necklace in a safe spot. No one had found it in all these years—even those who'd been looking for it. It had been resting here all along, untouched.

A smile broke loose, and he leaped to his feet. He couldn't wait to tell—

Mia.

His smile fell. She was in bed, fast asleep. And she was angry with him—not that he could blame her.

He stared down at the exquisite piece of

jewelry, suddenly remembering its value. He was no expert, but it had to be a carat or two. How ironic that the disaster that had fallen on the inn tonight had also exposed the very thing that could save it.

The money would be more than enough to tide them over until they could house guests again. They could even offer a full-fledged restaurant, like Molly wanted, and raise their salaries past minimum wage level. Best of all, he wouldn't have to worry about losing his parents' legacy. They'd already been on an upward trajectory all summer, with his marketing and the publicity, courtesy of Mia's presence.

Mia.

He looked through the doorway to the hall that led to the room where she was bedded down. He remembered everything she'd divulged to him today. Remembered the longing on her face, the loneliness, as she talked about her family. Her father. She'd come here searching for her roots.

Then his eyes fell to the necklace, taking in its design. The style reflected a bygone era. It was old. It was an heirloom.

Mia's heirloom.

forty-two

Mia woke as a ray of light broke through the slit in the drapes. She closed her eyes against the brightness, last night rushing back. It had taken forever to get to sleep, and a soul-deep weariness lingered even now.

But it wasn't really lack of sleep causing her body to feel weighted to the bed. No, she'd suffered worse nights.

It was Levi's sudden rejection.

Even now, in the hope of a new morning, she was devastated. Her eyes felt swollen from the quiet tears she'd cried. She wanted to leave, go home, even if it meant facing the public scrutiny and scandal she'd left behind. That would be easy compared to being near the man who'd ravaged her heart.

She should never have let herself get involved with Levi. What had she been thinking? She lived in California, and he lived in the wilds of North Carolina. It was never going to work. Had always been destined for failure. And yet she'd gone and made herself vulnerable. She'd gone and fallen in love with him.

The breakup with Wes seemed like child's play in comparison. And it was her own darn fault. She'd allowed herself to open up to Levi in a way she never had with Wes. She'd taken the risk, allowed him to know her—the real her.

And he'd dumped her. As if their relationship was disposable. As if *she* were disposable. And once again, for the umpteenth time, she felt unwanted and unworthy. As if she weren't enough. As if she were undeserving of love.

Oh, she understood why she felt this way. After all, if her own father, her flesh and blood, could abandon her, who would ever stay? But that head knowledge didn't quite translate to her heart. The heavy feeling inside weighted her lungs, making her breaths cumbersome.

She needed to get out of here.

On the other twin bed Molly still slept. Grace snored lightly from a pallet on the floor.

Mia grabbed her phone and began checking flights. A last-minute flight on a holiday weekend was expensive, but she couldn't stay here another day. She selected a flight for the evening and purchased the ticket.

The bed squeaked quietly as she left it. She went into the bathroom, dressed, and gargled with mouthwash. There was no water for a shower, so she swept her hair back into a ponytail and slid on a ball cap.

She began packing up her things. Levi, Molly, and Grace had insisted that Dorothy's journal rightfully belonged to her, so she tucked it into her carry-on bag. She'd reread it when she got home. It gave her a little comfort to know she'd always have a little piece of her grandparents.

She was just zipping her bag when Molly began stirring. Just as well. Mia wanted to say good-bye.

"Where you going?" Molly asked, her voice scratchy.

"I think it's time I go home and face my mess."

"But what about . . . what about Levi?"

Mia gave her a wan smile. "We broke up last night."

Molly gasped. "What? Are you okay?"

"I'll be fine." But judging by the tears swelling her throat she wondered if that were true. She thought of Levi. Of all his burdens and the flood on top of it all.

A wave of concern washed over her, crushing in its force. "Look out after your brother, okay? He's got a lot on his plate."

Molly looked a little sheepish. "Right. I will."

"What time is it?" Grace grumbled. "And why are people talking?"

"Mia's leaving," Molly said. "You need to say good-bye."

Grace squinted open an eye. "Seriously? You're leaving now?"

"The rumor is true," Mia said lightly. "And I want you both to know how much I appreciate your hospitality. It's been . . ." She swallowed back the tears. "You've been great. I hope you'll keep in touch."

Molly came forward for a hug. "I don't want you to leave. You've become a good friend."

"Here come the waterworks." Grace stood, tugging down her cow-print pajamas.

Mia leaned back to glimpse Molly's face and saw that Grace was right. "I'll miss you."

"Me too," Molly said. "Don't be a stranger."

Grace gave Mia a swift hug, minus the tears. "You're not what I expected."

A chuckle gurgled from Mia's constricted throat. That was a compliment in Grace-speak. "You're pretty great too."

"Bye, guys," Mia said as Grace disengaged from the hug.

Then she grabbed her things and left the room before she embarrassed herself. She breathed in. Breathed out. It was hard saying good-bye to her new friends. They didn't feel like new friends. They felt like sisters of her heart.

And the hardest part was still ahead. One wimpy part of her hoped to sneak out without seeing Levi. He might still be in bed, after all.

But that wasn't right. If she were going to get any closure at all it would have to be now. And despite the deep wound he'd inflicted, she knew he hadn't wanted to end things. He just felt like he couldn't manage a relationship with her on top of everything else he had going on.

352

Despite the hurt, she had to respect that. He saw his limitations and wanted to prioritize his life.

She just wasn't a priority.

A vise tightened around her heart, squeezing until an ache bloomed in her chest. She closed her eyes against the pain as she worked her way down the stairs.

She could get through this with her dignity intact. Without causing additional harm to either of them. And she didn't want to hurt Levi. Especially when she remembered the weary look on his face last night. The way he'd seemed to age ten years in one day. This wasn't easy for him either.

She stopped at the bottom of the stairs, listening. Normally, Della would be making noises in the kitchen. Often Mia could hear clanking silverware and the chatter of guests enjoying breakfast in the dining room. And always she could smell the delicious aroma of baking muffins.

Not today though.

Then she honed in on the muted sound of Levi's voice and caught sight of him on the porch. He was pacing, talking on the phone.

She exited the front door, her bags in tow, blinking against the beam of sunlight that hit her face.

Levi turned, his eyes catching on her, phone still held to his ear.

She suddenly felt exposed, the morning light no doubt highlighting her tired, bloodshot eyes. But a quick scan of Levi's face showed she wasn't the only one who hadn't slept well.

"Okay. Thanks. See you then." Levi tapped a button and looked back at her, at her bags, his face falling. "You don't have to go, Mia."

She gave him a sad smile. "Yes, I do."

He seemed to weigh her words. A shadow flickered in his jaw. Then he gave a small nod. "You need that floatplane?"

"I scheduled a flight out of Charlotte."

"A ride to the airport then?"

She couldn't tell whether it was hope or dread on his face. Maybe both. She was feeling the same way herself. "I have a car coming."

"Right." Disappointment flickered in his eyes.

That shouldn't make her feel better, but it did. "What are you going to do? About the inn?"

He lifted a heavy shoulder. "It's officially closed until the repairs are complete. The insurance adjuster will come tomorrow. I'm sure it'll work out fine."

But she knew being shut down in the middle of peak season was going to be devastating for a business that was already struggling. "How long do you think the repairs will take?"

"I'll have a better idea of that in the next few days. Hopefully we can get right on it."

Molly had told her all that would need to be

done. There was at least a month's work here if not more.

"Levi . . . please, why don't you just let me help—"

"Have you told Nolan you're going home yet?"

She sighed. He didn't want her money. Or her, for that matter. It took all her skills to maintain eye contact and pretend like this wasn't killing her.

"He thinks it's a good idea at this point. I'm sure it'll be just fine," she said, repeating his words and hearing the same futile hope in them.

"And your next project?"

She shrugged. "We'll see. I guess it'll all work out the way it was meant to."

The way it was meant to. This wasn't the way she'd thought it would work out at all. She'd been planning a future with Levi. A future he obviously didn't want as badly as she did. She supposed one never got used to rejection.

She swallowed against the lump in her throat and checked her phone, a necessary distraction. "My car's here."

"Wait," he said as she started moving toward the door. "There's something I want you to have." He walked past her, through the door, and to the check-in desk.

Leaving her bags, she followed him.

He reached under the desk then extended a white tissue–wrapped bundle the size of her fist.

A horn tooted outside.

"Thanks." She took it and placed it in her purse. "And thank you for your . . ." She struggled for a way to describe all the things he'd done for her. Everything he'd meant to her.

"You're welcome." He stepped closer, his eyes warming. "Mia, I'm really sorry that . . ." He was the one at a loss now.

She saw the struggle in his eyes, the hurt. And knew she had to let him off the hook. "It's okay, Levi."

He reached out to her, and that was all it took.

She flung herself into his arms, buried her face in the nook between his neck and shoulder, and inhaled him. Memorized the spicy scent of him. The gentle scrape of his jaw against her forehead. The needy feel of his hands at the small of her back. She was grateful, so grateful, for this last contact. In a few minutes she'd only have memories to keep her heart warm.

She swallowed back tears, her throat aching with them, her eyes closing against them. She wished she could stay here forever, in his arms, in his home, in his heart. But maybe she'd never really been in his heart to begin with. He'd already left her, after all. Now it was time for her to leave him.

She should've done it first. Then maybe it wouldn't hurt so much.

The horn honked again.

Mia gathered her fortitude to say a final good-bye and reluctantly pulled away. A smile in place. Not a trace of tears. All her barriers up, all those years of training allowing her to pretend, once again, that she was fine. She was just fine.

forty-three

Levi was not fine. Mia was gone, and she'd taken his heart with her. He'd never in a million years dreamed he was capable of such a Molly-like thought, but there it was.

For the past hour, while the plumber worked to restore water on the main level, he'd sorted through soggy items on the porch. The mundane task gave him plenty of time to review their good-bye. So brief. So heartbreaking. But Mia had seemed just fine as she'd shouldered her purse and walked out his door for the last time. Maybe that's what was most heartbreaking of all.

He was getting nowhere but down with that line of thinking. He had to put Mia aside and focus on the problems at hand. That was why he'd broken things off with her, after all.

He threw the last soggy towel into the pile of items to be washed and looked through the window. His sisters would be up and moving around by now. It was time for a family meeting.

Levi was seated across from his sisters in the inn's library. The house had taken on a musty smell that he hoped would soon dissipate. This whole thing seemed like a nightmare. And it wasn't over. Not by a long shot.

Molly returned his gaze, her eyes not quite as stormy as last night, but not exactly oozing warmth either.

Grace's arms were folded across her chest, regarding him with a familiar *Well . . . ?* look.

"Shouldn't we be doing something upstairs?" Molly asked.

"It's still drying out," Levi said. "There'll be plenty to do later. Right now I think we need to have a heart-to-heart about the business. Among other things."

"We just had the Huddle of Horror." Leave it to Grace to be firing on all cylinders, despite so little sleep.

"We're not going over financials today."

"Thank God," Grace said.

"The flood changes things. A lot of things, and . . . I haven't exactly been honest with you about our financial situation."

Molly's eyes sharpened on him. "What do you mean you haven't been honest?"

"Things aren't as . . . stable with the inn . . . as I've led you to believe."

"But we see the spreadsheet every month," Grace said. "Even I can read the bottom line."

Levi's face heated. Only now did he realize how wrong his actions had been. It was time to face up to his misdeeds.

"I manipulated the numbers. Things weren't going well, and I didn't want to worry you unnecessarily."

Molly gave him a withering look. "You've got to be kidding me."

"How bad is it? And how long has this been going on?"

May as well lay it all out there. "Pretty much from the beginning. I've got two credit cards—in my name—at their limit. It just kind of spiraled out of control. At first I just used one to keep us in the black on paper. I thought I'd be able to pay the balance off after our first season. But we needed that money to get us through the winter. Then I realized we were going to have to step up the marketing. But that costs money, so I opened another credit card, and now it's maxed too."

"Levi!" Molly said.

"The good news is that the plan's working. Our reservations are up, and the rate increase is already paying off. We're in a much better position than we were at this point last year. But then the flood . . ."

Molly leaned forward. "I can't believe you've been hiding all this from us, Levi. We're supposed to be partners, and you're making unilateral decisions. This inn doesn't belong to just you."

"I know that—"

"Apparently you *don't*."

360

"This is a universal issue with you," Grace chimed in. "You think you run everything around here, including our lives. You've gone way past big brother and straight to control freak."

"It's not like that."

"Then what's it like, Levi?" Molly said. "Because that's exactly what it seems like from this side of the desk. You're trying to dictate Grace's future. You interfered with what should've been one of the happiest moments of my life. And now you're telling us that the inn—the inn that belongs equally to the three of us—has been in financial danger all along, and you've hidden that from us for over a year!"

Levi palmed the back of his neck. Tried to slow his breathing. It was time for complete honesty, and this part wasn't going to make them happy either. There was something else he'd kept from them.

Before he could lose his nerve, he spit it out. "There's one more thing I wasn't honest about."

Grace tilted her head at him.

Molly speared him with a look.

"It's about Dad . . . his last words to me." He paused for a moment to let them adjust to the change in subject. "He did say he loved us. He wanted you to know that. But that wasn't all he said. He told me—" Levi swallowed against the emotion bulging his throat.

His heart was thudding in his chest the way

it always did when he remembered those last seconds with his dad.

"He made me promise to take care of you."

A lengthy silence settled over them like a heavy wool cape.

"Maybe you weren't aware of it," Levi said, "but he always used to say that to me. Mom too, but Dad especially. 'Take care of your sisters.' First day of school, when I'd babysit, when you'd go anywhere with me. 'Take care of your sisters.' From the time you were born it's been my job as your big brother."

"But Levi," Molly said, "we're adults now. We can take care of ourselves. That's not your job anymore."

Levi's eyes stung. "I promised him, Molly. It was his last request, and that's what I've been trying to do. I've been trying to hold all this together. The inn, you, Grace. And I've failed in every single area."

"I don't think Dad meant for you to run our lives, Levi," Molly said. "And you haven't failed. This inn is a joint effort. Relationships are a joint effort. Your only failure was failing to see that. We need to work together in all of this. You have to stop being a Lone Ranger and realize this is a group effort."

"No wonder you're stressed out all the time," Grace said. "It was one of the best things about having Mia here. She got you out of your funk. Reminded you how to have fun."

A wave of pain washed over him. He felt the loss afresh.

"And while we're on that subject," Molly said, "why'd you go and break up with her? She was good for you."

Levi gaped at her. "Look around you, Molly. This place, our family, is falling apart around our ears. Losing this inn . . ." His throat closed up. His palms grew damp. "It feels like I'm losing Mom and Dad all over again."

Molly squeezed his hand. "We haven't lost the inn, Levi. We're going to get through this."

"The bottom line is, I can't handle the load I've got. And Mia isn't going to be another casualty of my life."

"You can't handle the load," Molly said, "because you're trying to run three lives plus a business! Let us run our own lives, and we'll work together on the inn. The damage can be repaired—that's what insurance is for."

"It doesn't cover the weeks or months we'll be without guests."

"How much is on your credit cards?" Grace asked.

He winced, and the back of his neck broke out into a sweat. "Twenty-five grand."

Molly gasped.

Saying it out loud was like a punch to the solar plexus. He felt the shame of it. He had a business degree, for crying out loud. He was blowing it in his own area of expertise. And admitting it to his sisters was almost worse than admitting it to himself.

The girls sat silent for a long moment, staring somberly at him.

"I'm sorry I did this. I'm sorry I didn't trust you with the truth."

Levi had realized one more thing while sitting under his sisters' blazing eyes. He'd made yet another unilateral decision very recently. He'd given away something that actually belonged to all three of them. Might as well get it all out in the open.

"There's something else I need to tell you . . ."

Grace threw her hands up.

"Last night—or rather, early this morning—I found Dorothy's necklace. The blue diamond."

Molly gasped. "Where'd you find it?"

He told them the whole story, then waited while they absorbed the information. Molly was mostly excited about the historical discovery. Grace soon became excited about the financial windfall.

"Hold up," Levi said, bracing for more anger. "Before you get too excited I have to tell you . . . I gave the necklace to Mia before she left. I realize now I should've talked it over with you—unfortunately that thought came a little late."

His sisters were shooting daggers at him.

"I know I acted in haste. But it was a family heirloom for her, and she's had precious little from her family. The necklace rightfully belongs to her—I still believe that—and I didn't feel right about keeping it."

Grace crossed her arms.

Molly scowled.

"I'm sorry," Levi said. "If I were you I'd probably be angry too. I know we could really use the money right now, and maybe I should've thought with my head and not my heart, but—"

"We're not mad that you gave her the necklace," Molly said.

"We're mad that you bypassed our input—*again*," Grace said.

Levi gaped at the two of them. Okay, he definitely hadn't given his sisters enough credit. He hadn't even thought about getting their input on the necklace before he handed it over to Mia.

"I might have a problem," he said.

"Might?" Molly asked.

"Fine. All right. I have a problem. I'm sorry I left you out of the process—again. I'll do better. I promise."

Molly and Grace looked at each other for a long moment, some of the wind leaving their sails.

"I forgive you," Molly said. "You were right to give the necklace to Mia. It was her grandmother's, after all. If it were my heirloom, it would mean an awful lot to me."

Grace shrugged. "Yeah, I get it. Not that the money wouldn't have been nice."

He shook his head in wonder. "Thanks, guys. That's generous of you."

Levi sank back in his chair, the load of guilt making him feel lighter even while the task in front of them weighed heavily on his mind.

"Now that all that's cleared up," he said, "we've got a real mess upstairs."

"And now that we know what we're up against," Molly said, "we need a plan. I suggest we call in the forces and get it done quickly."

"The whole town came together to help us get this place off the ground," Grace said.

"She's right," Molly said. "We've got a caring community who'll want to help us. We have to let them."

Grace nailed Levi with a look. "And you have to let us lead our own lives."

"She's right," Molly said. "Advice is welcome, mandates are not. Even Dad didn't order us around, Levi, and he wouldn't expect you to either. You have to trust us to make good decisions and let us fail when we don't—just like good parents do. Anything else is overreaching."

Levi weighed her words. It was hard to let go of this. Maybe he really was a control freak. But he knew Molly was right. He couldn't imagine their father *demanding* Grace go to college. Or withholding his blessing from Adam. Both their parents had guided him and given advice, less and less often as he'd gotten older.

"He's not agreeing." Grace arched a brow at Molly.

"I'm thinking. I know what you're saying makes sense. And I'm sorry." He looked at Grace. "I'm sorry for trying to railroad you into college. It's just that starting your own business is harder than you might imagine. Most start-ups fail within—"

He stopped at Grace's dark look. He was doing it again. "I'll try and be supportive of whatever you choose," he grated out.

Grace gave him a placating smile. "That's all I'm asking."

"And you." Levi gave Molly a sheepish look. "I really blew it with Adam. I shouldn't have interfered, and I'm sorry. I'll try and keep my nose out of your business."

Molly gave him a strained smile. "Fair enough."

"That doesn't mean I won't mess up again," he warned.

"Oh, we know," Grace said.

"Don't worry," Molly said with a saucy tilt of her chin. "We'll be sure and set you straight."

forty-four

Mia turned off airplane mode as soon as her flight landed at LAX. Her phone buzzed with multiple notifications. Texts and calls from Brooke, Nolan, and Lettie.

Great. What now?

She couldn't take more bad news. She ignored the notifications, making her way toward baggage claim instead. A college-age girl lingering around one of the gates homed in on her face. Mia looked away, tugging her cap lower.

She'd been in survival mode since she'd left the inn. Left Levi. Busying herself with activity: notifying Lettie of her impending arrival, reading the script Nolan had sent, catching up on email between flights. Somehow she'd managed a nap on the second flight.

She didn't brave another look at her phone until she reached baggage claim. And even then she took a moment to prepare herself for the worst. But how much worse could it be? She'd already lost her reputation and the biggest role of her life.

Oh, and Levi.

She listened to Nolan's voicemail first. "Hey, kiddo. I know you're probably in the air right now, but I wanted to let you know the latest. It's good news this time, Mia. It was just released that Emma was behind those photos of you and Jax. She hired a PI some time ago to catch him in compromising situations. It seems she's the one having an affair and wants a divorce. She wanted the fans in her corner before she filed for separation. The source of the comments is reputable—one of Emma's friends—so I think this one's gonna stick. Good news for us."

It was over. Mia's shoulders sank in relief even as guilt pinched hard. A marriage, a family, was wrecked. What a terrible thing for Emma to do to her husband and unborn child. Not to mention Mia. Emma's "America's sweetheart" reputation was going to be in shreds after this.

Head still spinning, Mia clicked over to Brooke's voicemail. It said much the same thing as Nolan's, with the addition that there was now speculation over whether or not the baby Emma was carrying was even Jax's.

Oh boy. What a publicity nightmare for Emma. But she'd brought it on herself.

As the news sank in, Mia took a moment to breathe a prayer of gratitude. The truth had come out, just as she'd prayed. *Thank You, God. Thank You.* She could hardly think beyond that, such was her relief. Just like that, her reputation had been restored.

Her phone rang. Nolan.

She slipped away from the crowd. "Hey, I just got your voicemail. I can hardly believe it."

"You can believe it. The friend who gave up Emma even gave her name. She said she couldn't stand by anymore and let Emma do this to innocent people."

"I guess that friendship is over."

"Fair guess. And I have even better news for you. Maura just called. The studio would like to extend their apologies for acting prematurely— and they'd like to re-offer you the part of Fiona. They understand if you've moved on, but they haven't been able to find anyone who holds a candle to you. They're willing to up their offer."

Mia's mouth dropped at the figure Nolan casually rattled off. She would've jumped at the chance with no increase in salary.

"I can go back to them with a higher number," Nolan said when she didn't respond immediately.

"That's more than I expected. Much more."

"They don't have to know that. At least make them squirm a little."

Mia chuckled. "I'm just glad to get the role back."

"You do your job, and I'll do mine," he said, his tone wry. "This is a happy day, Mia. Let's celebrate over dinner once you're settled."

Mia was walking in her back door by the time she remembered the little package Levi had handed her. She'd been on the phone with Brooke the entire ride home. When she arrived she had the driver crawl through the swarm of reporters at her curb. She could hear them shouting through her window.

"Mia, what do you want to say to your fans?"

"What do you think of Emma's actions?"

"Do you feel vindicated, Mia?"

"Mia, how do you feel about Jax Jordan?"

Shaking away the questions, she pulled her suitcase to the base of the stairs and dropped her carry-on bag beside it. The house smelled of artificial pine. She knew the difference now, she realized, after taking in the authentic scent of mountain pine for five weeks.

She walked across the expanse of the living room, her heels clicking on the ceramic tile—the only noise in the house. A cold and sterile sound. Her eyes swept the living space. The black Italian leather living room suite, special ordered. The white luxurious rug spanning the space. Those were the only soft things in the room. Everything else was glass and metal and concrete, the architecture bearing a sort of stark beauty.

She grabbed her bags and headed up the glass steps. She suddenly missed the charm of squeaky wooden floors, cozy furnishings with a hodgepodge of knickknacks, and the ever-present sound of people moving about.

Once in her room she dropped her bags and reached into her purse. The small package had sunk to the bottom, but she found it with little trouble. She pulled it out, her heart suddenly beating too fast. This, whatever it was, was her last contact with Levi. There was already an ache where her heart rested.

She held the package in her palm, feeling its weight, wondering what it might be. Some trinket she'd pointed out in a shop, probably. A souvenir. A memento of a place and person she'd never see again. Or maybe it was the engraved watch they'd found in the attic—possibly her grandmother's.

She wasn't ready to face it, this last connection between them. She opened a dresser drawer and placed the package beneath the folds of silky lingerie where she wouldn't have to see it until she was ready.

forty-five

Levi stepped up on the ladder again and went to work around the gutter at the rear of the house. He checked his watch. He was losing light as the sun set across the lake and running out of time. At least the heat was waning with the end of the day.

Repairs to the inn had been in full swing for a week. The plumber had repaired the pipes, replacing all the old ones to prevent a reoccurrence. He was a relative of Della's and was doing the work at cost. Della bribed him daily with baked goods to rush the job.

Donald Walters, one of his dad's old friends, owned the local hardware store. He'd donated the necessary drywall, and friends from church were volunteering their time to put it up. They'd have to hire a professional to tape and mud it, but Levi already had a guy lined up. From there, they'd paint and put the trim back up: Levi, Molly, Grace, Adam, and anyone else who was willing to pitch in. It was all hands on deck.

Thankfully the wood floor had survived, only requiring the replacement of a few boards. Altogether Levi thought they could have the job done in two more weeks. They were still out a lot of revenue, but hopefully they'd finish the season strong.

He had a new hook to help with marketing—it had come in the form of a brief note Mia had left in his sisters' bedroom. The words were now embedded in his heart.

> From the cozy bedrooms to the warm hospitality and delicious breakfasts, my stay at the Bluebell Inn exceeded my expectations. Enter a world where every detail is considered, every need anticipated. Both in town and on the lake, the inn is the perfect point from which to explore the beautiful Blue Ridge Mountains and the area's many natural attractions. The Bluebell Inn is a destination of its own. I can't think of any place I'd rather be.

That last sentence made his breath hitch every time. He couldn't think of any place where he'd rather Mia be either. As busy as he'd been, the last week had dragged. He thought of her a thousand times a day. Sometimes the memories made him smile, and other times he wondered if he'd need to carve his heart out of his chest to stop the ache.

He'd thought he'd hear from her—because of the necklace if for no other reason. He'd thought that gesture would've meant something to her. But maybe it didn't. Or maybe she simply couldn't bring herself to make contact with him again.

He'd been tempted a hundred times to reach out to her. But after what he'd gone through with his sisters he was trying to stay in his own lane. And whenever he got down about her lack of communication he remembered her generous endorsement.

Grace had already placed it front and center on their website and added it to the review pages on numerous travel sites. He had bigger plans for the quote once he had a little space on his credit card.

He continued working along the gutter, making good progress. He'd been at this for almost three hours, but he was almost finished. Just one last . . .

His phone buzzed with a text and he checked the screen. Just in time.

Molly set down her brush and glanced at Grace in the mirror. "What is this event anyway? And since when do you hobnob at the Biltmore?"

Grace had begged Molly to go along tonight and had dragged her through shops all afternoon, searching for the perfect dress.

"I told you it's an appetizer fund-raiser thing. Sarah got tickets and thought it would be a good way to network for my website business. But she can't go with me, and I can't go alone."

Molly scanned her sister's long, lithe form. "You look good in a dress. You should wear them more often."

"Not happening. But I like yours too."

Grace had all but insisted Molly get the floral sundress when she saw it on display. She had to admit it totally suited her, and it clung and flowed in all the right places.

Molly checked her watch. "Are you sure it doesn't start till nine thirty? Isn't that kind of late?"

Grace looked up from her phone. "It started at nine but, you know, fashionably late and all. Ready?"

Molly pushed away from the mirror and slipped into her heels. "Let's drive Levi's car. I don't want a breakdown on one of those switchbacks."

"Don't forget your purse."

"Oh. Right." Molly led the way downstairs. She didn't get dressed up often, but she felt pretty swanky in her new dress, with her curled hair flowing around her shoulders. She only wished Adam could see her, but he was out of town.

She turned at the bottom of the steps, holding out her phone. "Take a picture. I want Adam to see my new dress."

Grace rolled her eyes but accommodated. She

was just reaching for the doorknob when Levi came down the hall.

"You guys look nice."

"Thanks," they said.

"Can I get your help out back before you go, Molly?"

"We're on our way out."

"I see that, but it'll just take a minute."

"Will it dirty up my dress?"

Levi smirked. "Not even a little."

Molly shrugged. "Fine. I'll be right out," she told Grace.

She set her dainty purse on the check-in desk and followed Levi down the hall. She couldn't imagine what he was working on outside in the dark, but he was always puttering around with something. Especially since Mia left. He was working himself to the bone over this inn.

But she had to admit he'd kept his promise where she and Grace were concerned. Whenever Grace brought up her new business he was supportive. He even offered business and marketing advice. And even though Levi hardly sat still these days, he seemed a little less tightly strung. And that benefited all of them.

Levi opened the back door for her, and Molly stepped down onto the back patio.

Suddenly there was light. White twinkle lights. Everywhere.

And standing in the center of the beautifully lit

patio was Adam, handsome in a black suit. His lips curved in a sheepish smile.

A wave of gooseflesh pebbled her arms. Her breath caught. She placed a hand to her heart, sure it had swollen to twice its normal size.

A shuffle sounded behind her. She tore her eyes from Adam and caught Levi's gaze, holding it for a poignant moment. Then he gave her a knowing grin and slipped back inside.

She faced Adam again. He looked so precious, standing there, all uncertain and shy. And she felt blessed beyond words to be loved by him. She walked forward, closer, closer.

She could hardly catch her breath. "Oh, Adam."

"You look so beautiful. And I'm trying very hard not to spew random facts, but the urge is strong."

The laugh gurgled from her tight throat. "I'm actually speechless. You better go quick before the moment ends."

He took her at her word, sinking onto the mossy pavers, one knee down, and took her hands. His were shaking, but so were hers. And she couldn't tear her gaze from the love shining in his eyes.

"Molly Elaine Bennett, I knew there was something special about you from the moment I stepped through your door. In a matter of seconds you had me neck deep in a project."

She breathed a laugh at the memory.

"And it didn't take much longer until I was

completely over my head. Even though I write about love and soul mates, I'd never experienced any of it . . . until you.

"Every day you surprise me, you confound me, you amaze me, and I don't even know how I was satisfied with the colorless life I had before you brightened it. There's no one else in this world I want to be with, Molly. I want to see your face first thing every morning. I want to share every moment of the day with you, good and bad. And when I fall asleep at night, it's you I want in my arms."

He dropped her hands and withdrew a box from his pocket, lifting its lid to reveal a beautiful marquise diamond that sparkled under the lights.

"Molly . . . will you make me the happiest man alive? Will you marry me?"

"Yes." Molly stared into his eyes, mesmerized by his words. Someone sniffled. Maybe her. "Yes, yes, yes. Now get up here and kiss me."

"Um . . ." He looked so sweetly uncertain. "I'm supposed to put the ring on now."

Laughter gurgled from her again. "Right. Yes, of course. Go ahead."

He took the ring from its velvet nest and slid it on, his fingers a little clumsy.

Molly's eyes fastened on the diamond, glinting under the twinkle lights. "Oh, Adam, it's beautiful. It's perfect. I love it."

He rose to his feet, framing her face, thumbing

away her tears. "You're beautiful and perfect. Perfect for me."

Her heart rolled over in her chest. "I love you, Adam."

His eyes were wet. "I love you too, Molly. So much."

And as his lips met hers, softly, sweetly, reverently, Molly felt more alive, more blessed than she ever dreamed possible.

forty-six

I quit." Mia shoved the cheesecake closer to Brooke. "It's all yours."

"Don't have to tell me twice." Brooke dug her fork into the creamy slice of heaven, dragging the bite through the raspberry swirls that decorated the plate.

Somewhere on the coffee shop's patio a chair grated across the cement. Cars rumbled by, the traffic slow on the Sunday afternoon. In the distance a siren wailed. As was their tradition when they weren't on set, she and Brooke had stopped for lunch after church.

She'd been home for two weeks now. Thankfully the hullabaloo surrounding the scandal had died down on her end, allowing her to get back to her routine: working out, church, outings with her "little sister." She'd been working hard on the *Lesser Days* script, and on Wednesday she was heading overseas to begin filming.

She'd also gotten back to a Bible study she used to attend. It was time to get serious about her faith again. She was learning to let down her walls with people, but she needed to let God in too. Him, most of all.

"You've been quiet since you've been home," Brooke said.

"I've had a lot to think about."

"If I didn't know better I'd think you left your heart in North Carolina."

Mia took a sip of her water, then gave her friend a wan smile. "I'm afraid you might be right."

Brooke blinked. "Wow. Did not expect that."

"Well, you've been tiptoeing around it for two weeks."

"True, but . . ." She leaned into the table, wincing as she placed her hand over Mia's. "Gosh, Mia. I'm so sorry. You finally fell hard for a guy and he just . . ."

"Rejected me?"

"That's harsh. You said he has a lot going on right now. Maybe the timing's just not right. Maybe later . . ."

She couldn't let herself think like that. It had been doomed from the start, hadn't it? They were too different, like her mom and dad had been. Mia had to move on. But she'd told herself that a thousand times since she'd been home. Her heart seemed to have ideas of its own.

"I just need to focus on my work right now. It'll be easier once I'm in Ireland." At least that's what she told herself.

"That's probably a good idea. Stay busy. It'll get better with time."

"Problem is, this role . . . Fiona."

"I thought it was your dream role."

"It is. But it's also dredging up a lot of stuff

from my past. I mean, that's partly why I wanted it so badly—I relate to her. But yeesh. I went to bed last night crying over my dad's abandonment, Brooke. I mean, that was years ago. What is wrong with me?"

"Nothing's wrong with you. That's a deep wound, honey. The kind that could take a lifetime to resolve. Do you think maybe the breakup triggered some of this? You had a bit of a setback when you and Wes broke up, remember?"

"Yeah, you're right. But I just wish . . ." What? That the breakup had never happened? That she'd never met Levi at all? No. She wouldn't trade one moment with him. Even if it had ended in heartache.

"What, honey?"

Mia met her friend's gaze head on. "You know what I really wish? I wish I'd finally be *someone's* priority. I wasn't my dad's, and I wasn't my mom's. I just want someone to look at me and say, 'Mia, you are worth my time and attention. You're *worthy* of it.' " Mia's throat closed up. Her eyes burned. She blinked the tears away.

"Oh, honey. I don't mean to get preachy on you right here, but you know Someone's already said that." Brooke squeezed her hand. "And anyway, what am I, chopped liver?"

A laugh burbled out Mia's throat. Brooke was right. God loved her. He'd never abandon her.

She sat still a moment, breathing, just letting that soak in. Why was she always looking for something more? She acted as though *God* wasn't enough for *her.* The realization made her heart clench.

Oh, God, I'm sorry. If I made You feel the way I sometimes do, I'm so sorry.

Mia took in the compassion in Brooke's eyes and was grateful for a friend who'd tell her the truth in love. "You're a good friend. I really appreciate you. And you're absolutely right. I don't know why I keep forgetting that."

"Don't worry, I'll keep reminding you." Brooke leaned back and placed her napkin on her plate. "I just wish there were some way of finally getting closure about your dad. Or your mom for that matter."

"I never even went through her things after she died. Remember, I was on set in Vancouver when it happened? Your mom settled the estate for me. Sold the furniture. Mom wasn't very sentimental. Her personal life pretty much boiled down to three cardboard boxes. How sad is that?"

"What was in them, the boxes?"

"I don't know. They're still in my spare room closet under a pile of blankets." She recoiled at the thought of them. But maybe that was just habit. When her mom had died she'd been too hurt to face the memories. But maybe it was finally time.

"Maybe it's time," Brooke said, echoing her thought.

Mia considered the idea, her head nodding, almost of its own volition. "Maybe it is."

No time like the present, Mia thought as she entered her house and shrugged her purse from her shoulder. She should get this done while she had the nerve. Brooke had offered to go through the boxes with her, but this was something Mia needed to do alone.

She made her way upstairs and toward the bedroom farthest from her own. No coincidence, she realized. Her legs trembled as she entered the room. Her hands shook as she opened the closet's French doors. She pulled away all the blankets until she found the three boxes. The flaps were folded in, and Lettie had written *Personal Items* in a black marker.

Let's do this. Mia dragged out the boxes and sat on the carpeted floor. She opened the flaps of the first box. It was filled with cosmetics, perfumes, and products—so many products.

She breathed in the scent of her mother, closing her eyes. Memories flooded her. Her mom teaching her to apply mascara when she was in the sixth grade. A shopping spree that ended with a dress Mia had been eyeing for weeks. Running lines for her first big role in a children's program. Maybe they weren't typical mother-daughter moments. But they were hers. And they were good ones.

Feeling wistful, she pushed the box aside and tugged the second one close. It was large, but not as heavy as she'd expected. When she opened it she saw why. It was filled with clothes and shoes. She sorted through them, finding as expected that most of them were haute couture. Others were just obscenely expensive labels. Some of them—items probably purchased on a manic shopping spree—still had price tags dangling from the labels.

Mia wasn't sure whether it was relief or disappointment that made her sigh as she pushed the big box aside and pulled the last one closer. Was this all that was left of her mother? A bunch of expensive material items? What had she hoped to find?

She pushed away the large box. At least she could donate the clothes. She knew of a reputable dealer who sold celebrity items to auctions. And a couple charities that would make good use of the money.

But still that hollow feeling was already swelling inside. The one that made her feel unvalued, unloved, unworthy. She reminded herself of the truth Brooke had just spoken. Mia was worthy in God's eyes. He loved her. He wanted her. He'd never leave her. She wasn't replaceable in her own life or in God's story.

That was the truth, and that was enough to sustain her.

She'd believed a lie for too long. It had caused her to hold back, and that was self-sabotage. If she was going to get her life together—and she was—she had to believe she was worthy of love, even if people left her. Even if everyone left her.

It sure was easier to think the notion than it was to believe it was true.

But one step at a time. If she reminded herself often enough, she'd come to believe it. Just as she'd once come to believe the lie.

The last box was smaller than the others and disappointing in its slight weight. Taking a deep breath, she pulled back the flaps. An old black Bible rested on top. Mia opened it and read the inscription. *To Katherine. Love, Mama and Daddy.* It was dated May 30, 1978.

Her mother would've been . . . eighteen at the time. Maybe it had been her graduation gift. Mia frowned. Her mother had left home shortly after her graduation. Had she brought the Bible with her? She must've, since her parents had written her off after she'd left.

Mia set aside the Bible, revealing a shoe box beneath it. She pulled out the box, which was filled with envelopes. Unopened letters, she realized as she withdrew a handful.

Her eyes homed in on the return address of the first one, written in a familiar script. The sender was Dorothy Livingston. Sucking in her breath, Mia flipped through the entire handful—ten or twelve letters, all from her grandmother.

A sudden coldness swept over Mia. Her mom had lied to her. Her parents hadn't written her off. Dorothy had obviously made an effort to stay in contact. And Mia's mom hadn't even cared enough to open the letters.

Mia began sorting through all the envelopes in the box. When she was about halfway through, she found an envelope with different handwriting, the scrawl darker, more masculine. She pulled it out. The sender's name was Everett James.

Mia's father.

Mia blinked at the envelope as her heart flopped around her chest like a fish. The letter wasn't addressed to her mom, but to Mia.

She turned the envelope over. Still sealed. She hastily went back to the box and continued sorting. She found more letters from her dad. Postcards too. She pulled them all out, a crazy mixture of excitement and wonder flooding through her.

Anger breathed just beneath the surface. Her dad had tried to keep in contact with her, and her mom had hidden that from her. How different might her life have been if she'd only known?

Mia put aside her feelings toward her mom and focused on the letters from her dad. She pulled out the tenth one, the twelfth one, and kept going.

He cared about me. He loved me.

The envelopes blurred as she sorted through them, but even through her tears she easily recognized the masculine scrawl. She got all the way through the box and counted the letters. Twenty-eight. There were twenty-eight letters from her father. She clutched them to her chest, her heart leaping with joy.

forty-seven

On Monday night Brooke came over to hang out. She'd brought Chinese food, and they chowed down before settling in the living room to watch their favorite Netflix movie. Brooke was heading out of town tomorrow morning, so it was their last night together before Mia went to Ireland.

Mia shifted on the sofa. The movie had been going for a while, but her mind was on other things. Her father, her grandparents, her mother, Levi. All of it was tangled up in her head like last year's Christmas lights.

The image on the screen froze, and Mia's eyes darted to Brooke, who was pointing the remote at the TV but looking at Mia.

"What's wrong?" Mia asked.

"That was your favorite part, and you didn't even laugh. You want to watch something else?"

"No." Mia played with the tassel on a pillow. "It's not the movie. I'm just distracted. Sorry."

"What's going on?"

She gave Brooke a long look. "I went through those boxes of my mom's."

"I was wondering. Did you find something upsetting?"

"You could say that. There were letters from my dad in there—unopened letters."

"Mia." Brooke shot upright in her seat. "Your dad wrote you? When?"

"Apparently he wrote me a lot when I was a kid—twenty-eight letters in all. He loved me, Brooke. His letters . . . They just made my heart melt. And all this time I thought he walked out the door and never looked back. My mother let me think that. Why would she do that?"

Brooke winced. "I don't know. But at least you have the letters now. Did he say why he never came back to see you? Why he didn't try to get visitation rights?"

"He didn't mention anything like that. He asked about my life, even though he must've known, after a while, that I wasn't going to write back. He must've thought I didn't care about him. That I didn't want him in my life. That I still don't want him in my life."

"Well, it's not too late, is it? You can always write him or even go see him."

"I don't even know where he's living now. He moves around a lot with his job, remember?"

"So hire a PI again. By the time you get back from Ireland you might have an answer."

Mia had been weighing that thought since she'd finished reading the letters last night. She'd been a soggy mess, lying in bed amongst a graveyard of crumpled tissues. But she was thinking clearly now, and she knew Brooke was right. She had to do whatever was necessary to find him. She had

391

to let him know she hadn't received his letters.

"I'm going to do it." She looked at Brooke, her heart in her eyes. "My dad cares about me, Brooke."

Her friend reached over and took her hand. "How could he not?"

After Brooke left, Mia located the PI she'd used before. It was after hours, so she left a voicemail. Then she settled in her bed and began reading through her grandmother's letters. They made her heart hurt.

Dorothy may not have written about her daughter in her journal, but in these letters she'd poured out her heart. Her grandparents had obviously grieved their daughter's absence. The relationship sounded nothing like the way her mother had portrayed it. But then, her mother hadn't been very stable.

Why had Mia taken her word on so many important things? How many other things had she lied about?

She shifted in her bed, her eyes clinging to the words her grandmother had written.

Lake season is upon us, and your father and I are busy with guests. The dogwoods have bloomed, and the weeping willows you loved so much are dipping their fingers into the water. The mountains are green with life, and the lake ripples with activity.

Mia's eyes stung as she thought of Bluebell. Of the inn. Of Levi. What was he doing right now? She wanted to tell him about the letters from her father. She wanted to tell him she was going to find him and held out hope for a relationship with him.

Levi would be so happy for her. He'd hold her in his arms, stroking her back until she felt worthy of a father's love.

Mia hugged a pillow to her aching chest. She missed Levi so much. Especially when the busyness of the day was done, when the moon rose high in the sky. Some nights she thought she'd die of missing him. She'd picked up her phone a dozen times only to make herself put it back down. If he wanted to talk to her he'd call.

There was only one final connection between them. The package. She hadn't seen it since she'd buried it under her clothes—the same way she'd buried her mom's boxes in the closet. Was she going to wait seven years to face his parting gift?

No. She was done with hiding from things that might hurt. She was going to live bravely, pain or no.

She slipped from bed and walked to her bureau. The drawer glided open easily, and her fingers sifted through the silk to find the package at the bottom. Once she had it in hand, she closed the drawer and sank onto her bed.

Steeling herself, she began undoing the generous strips of Scotch tape. She smiled wistfully, envisioning Levi wrapping the gift, his thick fingers clumsy with the delicate task. She unfolded the layers of tissue, and when she got to the center she gaped at the prize nestled there.

A necklace. Her eyes fastened on the sparkling blue stone. The Carolina Breeze. She blinked in disbelief.

He'd found it.

When?

Where?

And why had he given it to her? It belonged to him. She thought of the mess the flood had created. Of all the money Levi was losing while the business was down. He was so stressed. That inn meant everything to him and his sisters.

And all he had to do to save it was sell this necklace. She looked down at the jewel, still sparkling with life even after all these years. But he'd given it to her instead.

Her heart caught at the thought. She clutched her fist to her chest. He'd never even told her he loved her. But hadn't he shown her in a hundred different ways? He'd taken care of her when she'd fallen. He'd supported her through the scandal. He'd listened patiently as she'd shared her deepest wounds.

This necklace was just one more piece of evidence—and a very convincing one.

Maybe he did have too much on his plate right now. But couldn't she partner with him, share some of the load? Long-distance relationships weren't easy, but she had significant time off between projects. Surely there was a way to work through these challenges if they loved each other enough.

But Levi couldn't know how she felt because she'd never told him. Despite her efforts to open up and allow herself to be vulnerable, she'd held back this one thing.

She palmed her forehead. How had she forgotten to tell Levi the most important thing of all?

forty-eight

Levi ran the roller over the base coat of paint in the upstairs hallway. The drywall was now up, taped, mudded, and sanded. The last few days an army of friends/painters had come and gone at the inn, putting in what time they could.

They had guests arriving this weekend—a full house. Two more days of painting and almost a full day to air out the house. He thought they just might make it.

The insurance check had been deposited, and they even had a bit left over, since they'd employed so many volunteers. They'd use the extra money to pay down his credit cards. It would leave enough wiggle room for small emergencies.

Next on the agenda was phase two of his marketing plan. They couldn't afford to implement it this year, but hopefully they'd make enough during the rest of the season to kick it off next spring. That was wishful thinking, since they also had to make it through winter. He'd share his concerns at the next Moan and Groan because he'd promised himself—and his sisters—that he wasn't going to carry this burden alone anymore.

He had to admit, sharing the load had relieved

a lot of stress. Funny how that worked. And even though he'd told his sisters many times that they were headaches, the truth was they were actually helping to alleviate them. He was keeping that information to himself though.

The girls had been all atwitter since Molly's engagement a little over a week ago. She and Adam were more inseparable than ever. Even though Levi still ached for Mia, it did his heart good to see love going right for his sister. The wedding was going to be next summer sometime, and Grace was already whining about the dress she'd have to wear as maid of honor.

Speaking of Grace, she was making progress on her business. She'd had business cards printed and was designing her own website in her spare time—though there hadn't been much of that. She'd promised to keep her hours at the inn and focus on her business on the side for the time being. She needed time and money to buy equipment.

Now that the flood damage was almost repaired and his sisters' lives were, well, his sisters', Levi realized he might've acted in haste where Mia was concerned. Hours spent wielding a paintbrush and roller had given him too much time to think about her.

The memories were his constant companion, both a blessing and a curse. He missed those big green eyes staring up at him with affection.

He missed the gentle curve of her waist, just the right size for his hands. He missed everything about her, all the time. He hadn't known it would be this hard.

And, in retrospect, he even felt a little jilted. Maybe he'd been the one to end things, but she hadn't exactly fought him on it. And she hadn't contacted him once—even about the necklace. It was all he needed to confirm her feelings were just as he'd suspected. He'd only been a stopgap. A romance to while away the summer.

She was Mia Emerson, after all. She could have any man she wanted.

He scratched his nose, the paint fumes filling his nostrils even though all the windows were open. The sucking sounds of rollers carried from the other rooms along with the idle chatter of Adam and Molly, Grace and her friend Sarah.

The door in the lobby downstairs opened, and footsteps sounded below. Fresh air flowed up the stairwell. Since no one called up and they weren't expecting more painters tonight, Levi climbed down from the ladder.

"Be right with you," he called.

He set his roller in the pan. Even with their No Vacancy sign lit, people still stopped in to inquire now and then. He made his way down the steps. With his paint-splotched shirt and jeans he didn't look much like an innkeeper, but that couldn't be helped.

As he rounded the turn, he caught sight of the lower half of a woman, standing near the door. "Sorry to say, we're closed for renovations at the—"

He caught sight of her face. His feet stuttered along with his tongue. He blinked. Wondered if the paint fumes were messing with his mind. Because he could swear Mia Emerson was standing in his lobby, clutching her purse with both hands. Staring back at him with those beautiful green eyes.

"Mia."

Her smile wobbled uncertainly. "Surprise."

He thought he could trust his feet to function again, so he descended the remaining stairs. "What are you doing here? Aren't you supposed to be in Ireland?" Then his face heated because he only knew she'd gotten the role back from stalking her online.

"I'm kind of headed that way now." Noises came from overhead, and her eyes followed the sounds. "Hope I'm not interrupting anything."

"Not at all. I was just . . ." He looked at his clothes. "Painting. Obviously."

"How's the inn coming along?"

"We're almost finished. We'll be open this weekend, in fact. Our neighbors descended on us and . . ." He shrugged. "They're getting the job done."

What was she doing here? And why were they

talking about mundane things like renovations when all he wanted to do was sweep her into his arms?

"Wow, that's so great. Good old Bluebell."

There were a hundred things Levi wanted to tell her about. Molly's engagement, Grace's business, every monotonous restoration detail. He wanted to ask her about her upcoming role and if she was excited about Ireland and if the paparazzi were still hounding her.

But most of all he wanted to tell her he'd missed her more than he'd ever dreamed possible. And he wanted to know . . . Did she miss him too?

Even in his paint-spattered clothes Levi was the most beautiful man Mia had ever seen. Her heart tugged at the sight of him. At the streak of beige paint on his nose and the speckles scattered throughout his dark hair. She loved that he was a hard worker. That he was steady and dependable. Traits that might be overlooked as boring, but to a girl from a chaotic childhood, they were everything.

She shifted her purse to her shoulder, fingers twitching in the awkward silence. He was wondering why she was here. She could see the question in the tilt of his head, the pinch of his brows.

She was starting to wonder too. Maybe she should've just handled this via mail. But it was more than the envelope in her purse that had brought her here.

"I—I have something for you." Mia took a brave step closer, her legs trembling. "But first there's something I want to say."

He stuffed his hands into his pockets, regarding her with those patient blue eyes. "All right."

"Things were kind of crazy when I left with the flood and all. And I was caught off guard when you ended things."

He started to speak.

But she held up a hand, needing to get this out. "A lot has happened in the past two weeks. Life-changing stuff. It's made me realize that there are some things that went unsaid when I was here. Or maybe I just wasn't brave enough to say them.

"Opening up is something I have to work at, Levi. And I thought I was making good headway while I was here. But last night I realized I'd left out the most important thing of all." She found his eyes, locked onto them, relieved to find warmth there in the blue depths.

Tension crackled between them, and her heart jimmied in her chest.

"I love you, Levi," she said in a throaty whisper. "I knew it even before I left, but I never had the—"

Suddenly he was there, his lips on hers. His hands framing her face, his body flush against hers. Heat and warmth and heaven.

She surrendered to his touch, her heart breathing a sigh of relief. She'd been so afraid . . .

But he was kissing her like she was all he'd ever wanted. Like he'd never let her go again. She lapped it up, every brush of his lips, every sexy sigh. And she couldn't seem to stop the curve of her lips.

She felt his responding smile just before he pulled away, their breaths falling heavily between them.

His eyes, filled with so many wonderful things, pierced hers. "I love you too, Mia. Probably goes without saying."

"A girl can never hear that too many times."

"I love you." He rubbed her nose with his. "I've missed you so much. I've been beating myself up for acting so rashly that night. I never should've let you go. But I thought I didn't think you saw me as a permanent fixture in your life."

"Let's not ever break up again," she said lightly. "I don't think my heart can take it."

He regarded her steadily, his thumb brushing her cheek. "You're it for me, Mia. There's no one else."

His words hit a soft target deep inside. "I feel the same, Levi. But we do have some challenges ahead, especially geographically."

"We'll manage them as they come," he said. "It won't be forever."

"I'll be in Ireland for a couple months, but we

can keep in touch. And I usually have long breaks between projects."

"You could come here . . ."

Her smile broadened. She might've been beaming. "I *could* come here."

"See . . ." Levi gave her a sleepy-eyed smile. "Look at us, handling the challenges."

"Look at us." Her eyes fell to his mouth, and her lips soon followed. This kiss was slower, but her heartbeat was not.

He commandeered the kiss, pulling her closer, making her remember all the delicious ways he liked to please her. His uncanny ability to make her forget the outside world. Except the outside world was one of the things she'd come to talk to him about.

Reluctantly she eased away. Just until their breaths mingled in the space between them. She played with the soft hair at the back of his neck. "I know you have a lot on your plate, Levi. But I want to share those burdens just the way you shared mine. I want to make your life easier, not more difficult."

His lips twitched. "Funny thing, that. Seems I may have been overreaching where my sisters were concerned. I got fired from my position as leader of their lives. And as you know, I was overstepping with the inn too. We're working it out. There's plenty of room for you in my life, Mia. I'm sorry I ever made you feel like there wasn't."

She did love a man who could admit when he was wrong. "Good for you, Levi. I'm proud of you."

When she lowered her hand to his arm, her purse dropped to her elbow. Something rattled. The envelope.

"Oh. I have something for you." She gave him a mock accusing look. "Sometimes you make me forget to breathe."

The beginnings of a smug smile formed on his lips. "Anytime you want."

She held him off. "Later. This is important. I wanted to thank you for the necklace. I never expected that, Levi, all those hours we were searching for it."

He waved her off. "I want you to have it. It belongs to you."

"Where'd you find it? I thought we'd looked everywhere."

He chuckled. "It was behind a stone in the fireplace—the one in your suite."

Mia huffed. "Are you kidding me? We turned that room upside down."

"I guess sometimes you don't find what you're looking for until you stop searching for it. The stone was wedged in there pretty good—I accidently dislodged it. But the important thing is, it's now with its rightful owner. I hope . . ." He paused, his eyes shifting in a way that set butterflies loose in her stomach. "I hope it gives you comfort. Gives you a little of those roots you've always longed for."

"I have roots I didn't even know about, Levi. But I'll save that for later. First there's this . . ." She pulled the thin white envelope from her purse and handed it to him.

He looked at her questioningly. "What is it?"

"Open it."

He drew away from her enough to slip his finger under the flap, giving her another searching look as he did so. When he pulled out the piece of paper, his eyes widened. His lips parted.

Right before they slammed together again.

"I want you to have it," she said. "For the inn."

"Mia." He gave her a pained look. "What did you do?"

"I sold the necklace. The check is from the auctioneer who purchased it. I want you to use the money for the inn. To preserve your parents' legacy."

"But I wanted you to have it."

"I don't need a necklace, Levi. I don't even need roots anymore. I don't think that's what I've ever needed. I just needed to know I'm loved, and I know that now. It makes my heart happy to do this for you and your family. Please, take it."

He wavered, obviously torn, his eyes steady on hers.

"I know you don't really need the money. You're good at what you do, and I have every faith you'll make this place an amazing success with or without it."

She placed her hand on his neck where his pulse thrummed. "But the necklace rightfully belongs to you and your sisters. And the fact that you'd give it up for me . . . You don't know what that meant to me, Levi."

He shook his head. "I didn't even have to think twice."

Her eyes roved over his features, a smile curling her lips. He had a beautiful face, no doubt about it. But his heart was even more beautiful.

She lowered her hand until her palm rested over it. "And that's just one of the many reasons I love you, Levi Bennett."

Epilogue

A smile tugged Mia's lips as the floatplane swooped to the left, granting her first aerial view of Bluebell Lake, nestled in the mountains. She leaned closer to the window. The lake was clear of traffic on this September weekday, the bright sunlight glinting off the water like a million diamonds.

Skeeter's voice sounded in her headphones. "Now there's a pretty sight if I ever saw one."

"It's beautiful." Her eyes swept the familiar bays and peninsulas, following the shoreline to the edge of town in the distance where the Bluebell Inn hunkered on a rise. Her heart tugged at the sight.

Skeeter aligned himself from the opposite side of the lake, losing altitude as he approached. The inn vanished from her line of vision.

She could hardly believe she was about to see Levi. She'd missed him so much the past two months. They'd weathered their time apart well, Skyping, texting, and talking on the phone. He'd kept her up on the goings-on at the inn. With the proceeds from the necklace they'd been able to pay off his credit cards and had enough left over to implement an extensive marketing plan.

The plane sank lower and lower, her stomach

dipping with the motion. Finally the plane touched down, more smoothly than she would've expected. They began gliding across the water.

"Well done," she said into her microphone.

"We'll be there in a jiffy."

They floated past the larger lake homes, then the smaller ones that stair-stepped up the mountain. Mia took in the beautiful views, feeling everything inside her settle. She could almost smell the woodsy pine and fresh air. Home.

Her heart fluttered in her chest as they drew nearer. The plane's nose was aimed straight for the bay, blocking her view of the inn. But Levi was probably waiting for her. She'd texted him with their ETA.

The engine went silent, but the plane continued drifting forward. They took a sharp right turn, finally bringing the inn's dock into view.

Levi stood at the end, waiting. His hands were tucked into his jeans pockets, and a black T-shirt stretched across his chest.

Her heart clutched at the sight of him. She knew the moment he caught sight of her in the window. He broke out into a wide grin, and she couldn't stop the smile that formed in response. She couldn't wait to get her arms around him.

When the plane glided close Levi reached for the bar under the wing and pulled them in to the dock.

She took off her headphones as Skeeter said, "Go on out. I'll grab your bags."

Levi opened her door and grabbed her hand, helping her onto the float, then safely onto the pier.

She had only a moment to take in his beautiful face before he pulled her close. She wrapped her arms around him and nestled her nose into the space between his neck and shoulder, breathing in the familiar scent of him.

"I missed you," he whispered against her temple.

"I missed you too."

He eased back and cradled her face. His heated gaze roved over her features as if he were trying to memorize them. Then, finally, he leaned in and brushed her lips with a soft kiss before easing away.

It had been two months.

Two. Months.

Mia grabbed his face and brought it back to hers. She kissed him again, her lips lingering over his like she'd dreamed of doing when she was three thousand miles away from him.

Levi slanted his lips over hers and took the kiss deeper.

Better. So much better. She snuggled closer, losing herself in the warmth of his touch, in the safety of his arms, in the passion of his kiss.

"Uh, don't mind me," Skeeter said from

someplace far away. "I'll just be taking off now."

Mia felt Levi's hand leave her back long enough for a wave, and then she was again oblivious to anything but his demanding kiss.

Moments later when he finally drew away, breathless, they were alone. He kissed her forehead. "Have a seat. Let's talk. I want you all to myself for a few minutes."

Mia edged around her bags and sank onto the bench beside him.

Levi tugged her close. "I can't believe you're finally here. You're probably exhausted."

"A little. But at the moment I'm feeling pretty content."

"How were your flights?"

"On time. That's about the best you can hope for. It's so good to be back here."

They sat silently for a long moment. Mia closed her eyes and drank in the feel of his arms around her. The taut muscles of his chest under her head, the heavy thumping of his heart beneath her ear.

He pressed a kiss to the top of her head. "You never said how the phone call with your dad went last night."

When she was partway through filming, the PI she'd hired had located her dad in Louisville. Unable to wait, she called him from Ireland. Those first teary words after she'd identified herself were something that would stick with her for a lifetime.

"It went well. I finally got a chance to ask him all my questions."

"Tell me."

"There's a lot I didn't know. He was an alcoholic when he was married to my mom. Apparently they'd enabled each other. And it took him until a few years after the divorce to get sober. That's when he started writing me."

"How do you feel about all that?"

"Sad. And relieved, I guess, just to have answers."

"Did he say why he didn't try to see you after he was sober?"

"He said he didn't feel worthy to be my father. And that when he never heard back from me he thought I didn't want him in my life anymore. But he kept writing because he wanted me to know he loved me."

"Well, that's something, I guess."

"He was so upset when I told him I never got his letters."

"With your mom?"

"That too. But mainly he was distraught that all through my childhood I thought he didn't care about me. He's been keeping up with my career. He saves all the newspaper and magazine clippings. Isn't that sweet? And he prays for me daily."

"Did you tell him you tracked him down when you were eighteen?"

It put a lump in her throat just thinking about it. "Yeah. He got pretty emotional when I told him about that. About how it made me feel. He still has the same wife, Laurel. Those two children I saw that day are my siblings. Dylan is twelve now, and Jessica is ten."

"Mia, that's huge. You have a family."

Her face broke out into a smile. "I know. He invited me for a visit."

"That's great. I'd love to go with you."

"I'd love to have you along for moral support." Mia took his hand, loving the way it engulfed hers. "Everything good around here? The inn? Your sisters?"

"Business as usual. Better than usual, actually. Revenues are up 24 percent for the year so far, even with the shutdown."

"Levi, that's great."

"I'd love to credit my marketing plan, but I think we both know better."

Word of the Carolina Breeze had spread once it sold at auction to a couple from Texas. Articles appeared in newspapers and magazines, detailing the jewel's rich history, which, of course, centered around the Bluebell Inn. The publicity hadn't exactly hurt the business.

"A couple more solid seasons, and we can think about putting it on the market."

On one hand Mia thought that was kind of sad. On the other hand . . . She leaned back to look at him. "That means you'll be free to pursue other things."

"That's what it means. I've already been scoping out commercial builders in LA." He gave her a long, searching look. "Does that scare you?"

"Scare me? It thrills me to death. But what about that opportunity in Denver? I don't want you to pass up something you love just because of me."

He tilted her face up, gazing into her eyes. "You have no idea the things I'd do 'just because of you.'"

He lowered his head and brushed her lips slowly. Mia placed her hand on the back of his neck, letting her fingers reacquaint themselves with the soft thickness of his hair.

A squeal sounded someplace far away. Quick footsteps swished through grass. Then the pier shimmied beneath them.

Levi sighed against her lips.

"You're here!" Molly called. "How was your flight? How was Ireland? Did the filming go all right? I want to know everything."

Levi disengaged with obvious reluctance to let Mia greet his sisters.

Mia hugged Molly first, then Grace. "You guys look great. I missed you both."

"We missed you too. So the movie—did the filming go well?"

"It was terrific. It's all wrapped and in post-production now." She was proud of her work on *Lesser Days*.

"When does it hit theaters?" Grace asked.

"Not till May." She elbowed Levi, who'd joined them. "I'm taking your brother to the premiere."

Levi gave a barely audible groan.

"Hey," Molly said. "If you don't want to go I'll gladly take your place."

Grace gave a rueful grin. "You and about a million guys I know."

Levi gave a low growl and tightened his arm around Mia. "No one's taking my place."

"Let's go inside," Molly said. "I made your favorite cookies." They headed up the dock, Levi lagging behind, toting Mia's luggage.

As they started up the grassy incline Mia linked arms with Molly. "So when do I get to see this ring I've been hearing so much about?"

Molly squealed, proudly sticking out her hand, waggling her fingers so the sunlight caught on the marquise diamond.

"Oh! It's so gorgeous. Adam has wonderful taste in jewelry."

Molly gazed at her finger adoringly. "I just love it."

"Tell me about the proposal—and don't leave out a single detail."

"Not again," Grace muttered.

Undeterred, Molly dove into the story, bubbling

with excitement as if the proposal had happened two hours ago instead of two months.

Midstory, Mia glanced over her shoulder, catching Levi's gaze locked on her. They shared a long moment, a private smile. Her insides melted at the tender look in his eyes, and Mia knew she'd finally found what she'd been searching for all her life.

For a bonus epilogue, go to
www.DeniseHunterBooks.com/books
-carolina-breeze.html.

Acknowledgments

You don't write thirty-six books without realizing the monumental team effort it takes to get a novel from the page to the shelf! I'm so incredibly blessed to partner with the fabulous team at HarperCollins Christian Fiction, led by publisher Amanda Bostic: Jocelyn Bailey, Matt Bray, Kim Carlton, Paul Fisher, Kerri Potts, Jodi Hughes, Becky Monds, Marcee Wardell, Margaret Kercher, Savannah Summers, and Laura Wheeler. Not to mention all the wonderful sales reps and amazing people in the rights department—special shout-out to Robert Downs!

Thanks especially to my editor Kim Carlton for her incredible insight and inspiration. You help me take the story deeper, and I'm so grateful! Thanks to editor L. B. Norton, who saves me from countless errors and always makes me look so much better than I really am.

Author Colleen Coble is my first reader and sister of my heart. Thank you, friend! This writing journey has been ever so much more fun because of you!

I'm grateful to my agent, Karen Solem, who's able to somehow make sense of the legal garble of contracts and, even more amazing, help me understand it.

The town of Bluebell was inspired by the little town of Lake Lure, North Carolina. Don and Kim Cason, innkeepers of the beautiful historic Esmeralda Inn, were so kind to host my husband and me for a few days and answer all my pesky questions. If you're looking to visit Chimney Rock and Lake Lure, I highly recommend it! Visit https://theesmeralda.com.

Kevin, has it really been thirty-one years? You've supported my dreams in every way possible, and I'm so grateful! To all our kiddos: Chad, Trevor, and Justin and Hannah, who have favored us with a beautiful granddaughter. Now I know what all the fuss is about! Every stage of parenthood has been a grand adventure, and I look forward to all the wonderful memories we have yet to make!

Lastly, thank you, friends, for letting me share this story with you. I wouldn't be doing this without you! Your notes, posts, and reviews keep me going on the days when writing doesn't flow so easily. I appreciate your support more than you know.

I enjoy connecting with friends on my Facebook page, www.facebook.com/authordenisehunter. Please pop over and say hello. Visit my website at the link www.DeniseHunterBooks.com or just drop me a note at deniseahunter@comcast.net. I'd love to hear from you!

Discussion Questions

1. Who is your favorite character and why? Which Bennett sibling did you most relate to?
2. Mia's job is something she loves, but it comes with public scrutiny. Discuss the ups and downs of celebrity life. What would you have done if faced with the scandal Mia found herself embroiled in?
3. Mia's lonely childhood left her yearning for a place to belong. Can you relate? What kind of role has your family, or lack thereof, played in your life?
4. Levi's deathbed promise to his father left him with a responsibility that weighed him down. How did you feel about his role in his sisters' lives and his doggedness to make the inn a success?
5. What do you think Mia's search for Dorothy's necklace might have represented? If you could discover something in your own home, what would you wish to find?
6. Mia's father's abandonment left her with trust issues. Discuss how those played out in her relationships. Have you ever found yourself holding back out of fear?
7. Mia feared she was unworthy of love. Have

you ever felt similarly? Does knowing God will never leave you offer comfort?

8. Have you ever had a "head knowledge" that didn't quite translate to the heart? Discuss.

9. Mia finally broke when she lost the role of Fiona. Discuss why being replaced might have triggered her breakdown.

10. What was your favorite scene and why? What do you think might happen in the next book in the Bluebell Inn series?

About the Author

Denise Hunter is the internationally published bestselling author of more than thirty books, three of which have been adapted into original Hallmark Channel movies. She has won the Holt Medallion Award, the Reader's Choice Award, the Carol Award, and the Foreword Book of the Year Award and is a RITA finalist. When Denise isn't orchestrating love lives on the written page, she enjoys traveling with her family, drinking good coffee, and playing drums. Denise makes her home in Indiana, where she and her husband are currently enjoying an empty nest.

DeniseHunterBooks.com
Facebook: Author Denise Hunter
Twitter: @DeniseAHunter

Books are produced in the United States using U.S.-based materials

Books are printed using a revolutionary new process called THINKtech™ that lowers energy usage by 70% and increases overall quality

Books are durable and flexible because of Smyth-sewing

Paper is sourced using environmentally responsible foresting methods and the paper is acid-free

Center Point Large Print
600 Brooks Road / PO Box 1
Thorndike, ME 04986-0001 USA

(207) 568-3717

US & Canada:
1 800 929-9108
www.centerpointlargeprint.com